WISH YOU WERE HER

JE ROWNEY

LITTLE FOX
PUBLISHING

Other thriller books by this author

I Can't Sleep
The Woman in the Woods
Other People's Lives
The Book Swap
Gaslight
The House Sitter
The Work Retreat
The Other Passenger
Waking Up in Vegas
Xmas Break
Where No One Can Hear You

Find out more about the author and her books at
http://jerowney.com/

If you enjoy reading this book, please remember to leave a review. Reviews help readers find new books and help authors to find new readers.

This is a work of fiction. Names, characters, businesses, events, and incidents are the products of the author's imagination. Any resemblance to actual persons, living or dead, or actual events is purely coincidental. Where the names of actual persons are used in this book, the characters themselves are entirely fictional and are not intended to bear any resemblance to persons with those names.

CHAPTER ONE

I have hit rock bottom so hard, I think I've left a dent.

This motel room is what people politely call *no-frills*, which is a lie. There are frills, they're just the kind that fray and gather dust. The curtains don't meet in the middle, the TV only shows static punctuated by occasional glimpses of game shows, and the mattress is thin enough that I can feel every metal spring, like a row of crooked teeth pressing into my spine.

I've been here for eleven nights. Long enough to know which vending machine snacks are least likely to get stuck before they dispense (Diet Coke and the sour cream Pringles), long enough to stop flinching when the couple in the next room scream at each other at midnight, and long enough for the front desk clerk to stop asking if I'm checking out tomorrow.

I'm not.

Tomorrow, I'll still be here. Pretending I have a plan. Pretending I'm not a walking disaster.

The kettle in the corner blew a fuse on night four. I boil water using the iron now. Fill the mug from the bathroom tap, balance it on a towel, press the iron on top, and wait. I call it desperation tea. Tastes like rust and sadness.

I haven't had a proper shower in days. The water only gets lukewarm if I hold the handle at a weird angle and whisper encouragement. My shampoo ran out three days ago. I've been washing my hair with a bar of motel soap and a prayer. My once-glossy brown waves now hang limp and dull around my face, and the dark circles under my eyes have become a permanent feature. I catch glimpses of myself in the bathroom mirror - pale skin, hollow cheeks, a stranger's haunted eyes staring back - and barely recognise the woman I've become. I am one gust of wind away from being mistaken for a ghost.

My last proper meal was a tuna sandwich I found in the reduced section at the petrol station; 39p and already curling at the edges. I ate it as though it was a gourmet meal. That was the night I officially accepted that I am not *'between things'*. I am in something. And it's bleak.

I am broke. I don't mean *'oops, better not buy that dress'* broke. I mean I have £2.43 in my account and 11p in coins I found under the motel bed. My bank card was declined at the shop when I tried to buy tampons. I walked out with my dignity in one hand and my shame in the other.

This is what people don't tell you about collapse. It doesn't happen all at once. It's not a dramatic crash, it's a quiet crumble. It's little pieces falling away until you're left with nothing but the bones of a life you don't recognise.

I had a husband. I had a job. I had a flat, a car, a calendar full of dinner plans.

Now I have... this. A duffle bag with a broken zip. A phone charger held together with tape.

And I've got memories that cut sharper than the day they were made.

I sold the car to afford the day-to-day cost of this shitty room. You'd be surprised how the offer price sinks to nothing when the showroom smells your desperation. I didn't have the luxury of being able to quibble. It was sleep in the car or sell it.

I pawned my wedding ring weeks ago for a fraction of its worth, although by that point, it was worth nothing to me.

So, what went wrong? Was it my fault? Was any of it my fault?

"You're impossible to please," Daniel said in our final argument, eight months ago. "Always dreaming up businesses, never following through. Always comparing yourself to everyone else."

If that's what got me here, yes, it was my fault.

He wasn't wrong.

When your own husband of four years leaves because you're '*exhausting to be around*', it might be time for introspection.

I had the drive but never the follow-through. I'd had so many *brilliant ideas* over the years. Marketing concepts. App designs. Social communities. Each one began with fervour and fizzled when the real work started. Each abandoned project another small death.

The marketing agency let me go a month after Daniel moved out.

I'd been showing up late when I showed up at all. Depression, you know. With the husband leaving me and feeling like an absolute messy failure, I don't know what they expected. Once Daniel left, things snowballed. Of course my manager didn't say it was because of my mental health. That would be a shitty move and probably wouldn't have sat well with HR.

'*Restructuring*', they called it, but I saw the relief in my manager's eyes.

One less problem for them to deal with. One more for me.

So, then I couldn't afford the mortgage, couldn't afford the car, couldn't afford the life I'd clawed out for myself with Daniel.

He's not even a part of this story. He's just the catalyst. He flicked the first domino that sent my life into a full on collapse.

So, thanks for that.

It was my fault for wanting a husband, a home, a life. It was my fault, sure.

I've thought about leaving this motel. But where would I go? There's nowhere that wouldn't feel just as empty. My family aren't exactly lining up to take me in, not after I skipped my sister's wedding to attend a business retreat that went nowhere. And my friends? They disappeared faster than my bank balance.

Divorce makes people uncomfortable. It's like catching failure. Nobody wants to sit too close in case it's contagious.

I spent three hours today googling '*how to get your life back on track*' and came away with a bullet list of vague nonsense: sleep more, hydrate, forgive. Nobody mentions that if you don't have a home to live in or a pound in your pocket, forgiveness feels like a luxury item.

It's only 6:30pm, but it's already dark outside. I'm under the duvet fully clothed, doom-scrolling. My phone is cracked and my data's throttled. Of course there's no Wi-Fi package included in the mot-hell's basic room, so every video stutters like it's buffering me straight into oblivion. In a few days, my phone will be cut off and I'll have to find a new way to amuse myself.

I scroll past smiling couples, polished women sipping espresso martinis, inspirational quotes on pastel backdrops. I hate them all. I double-tap out of spite, hoping my digital fingerprint of bitterness somehow transfers through the screen.

That's when I see her.

Erin Blake.

Her photo pops up like an optical illusion. She's backlit by golden sunlight, standing by a sea that's aggressively turquoise, with a white bikini that looks like it costs more than my entire wardrobe. Her hair is curled in the effortless way that takes three hours and a team of stylists. She's laughing, chin tilted, looking just over the camera like she's gazing at a better version of me.

The caption reads: "Manifest it, baby. The life you want is already yours 🌊 ✨ 🌴 "

I laugh. It comes out as more of a snort, and I immediately feel the prickle of shame rise in my cheeks.

This is *not* the life I want.

If I manifested this, I deserve every last bed bug.

I used to know her. Used to sit on her floor in our university flat and eat Wotsits while we talked about the future and bitched about everything. And now she's someone who uses emojis unironically and has three million followers hanging on her every manufactured word.

Erin was my best friend once. We met in the first year at uni, bonded over cheap red wine and missed lectures and this stupid belief that we were destined for something more. We had plans. I had ideas. So many ideas that I shared with her over those four years. Business concepts sketched on napkins. Brand strategies mapped out in the margins of lecture notes. Late night brainstorming sessions where I outlined exactly how we'd change the world.

She made it. I didn't. And she never looked back.

Of course she's in a bikini in some tropical heaven running a wellness retreat, while I'm wrapped in a synthetic blanket that smells like old soup.

Of course she's glowing with fake gratitude and curated light, while I can't remember the last time someone looked at me with anything other than pity or impatience.

Of course she still wins.

I tell myself not to engage. Not to get sucked in. Not to zoom in on her teeth to check if they're real or chemically enhanced. But my thumb is already twitching.

Just one closer look. Maybe her roots are showing. Maybe she has a weird elbow. Maybe I'll spot a wrinkle.

Anything to make her less perfect.

I zoom in, and that's when it happens.

My thumb jerks on the stupid, smashed screen. A horrible, clumsy double-tap.

The heart goes red.

I've liked the photo.

My blood turns to ice. My heart begins to race, each beat a hammer against my ribs. I can't seem to draw a full breath.

For a second I stare at it, frozen, like if I don't move, the algorithm won't notice. Like maybe Erin won't notice. Like maybe the universe will take mercy on me just this once and undo it all.

But no.

Of course not.

Because this is my life now. A string of humiliations stacked like dominos, each one tipping me closer to whatever version of hell is reserved for women who peak in group projects and die in motel rooms.

I let the phone slide out of my hand and onto the floor. I close my eyes and try to pretend I'm somewhere else. Someone else. But even my imagination is tired of me.

The phone vibrates against the thin carpet.

My stomach lurches as I reach for it, expecting some automated notification about running out of data or another rejection email from a job application.

Instead, I see her name.

Erin Blake sent you a message.

CHAPTER TWO

My finger hovers over the notification, trembling slightly. I shouldn't open it. Nothing good can come from reconnecting with Erin after everything that happened between us. The woman whose success I've both resented and obsessively followed for years.

But in this moment of absolute rock bottom, curiosity is the only emotion strong enough to cut through the fog of my despair.

I tap the message.

Samantha! Oh my god, is that really you? I was JUST thinking about you the other day! How are you? It's been forever!

Forever. Six years, to be exact. Six years since our friendship imploded. Six years of watching from the shadows as she built an empire while my life gradually fell apart.

I blink at the screen. There's something unsettling about her immediate response. It's crazy, I know, but it's almost as if she's been waiting for me to make contact. As if she's been watching my life spiral downwards.

Movement in the corner of the ceiling catches my eye. A spider, dangling from an invisible thread, slowly descending into the room. It hangs suspended before continuing its inevitable journey downward, spinning helplessly as the air from the rattling motel heating vent pushes it in lazy circles.

I watch, oddly transfixed by its vulnerable position, neither up nor down, just suspended in a dangerous in-between. One strong blast from the vent and it'll be blown against the wall. Or worse, straight into the heating element, where its tiny body will sizzle into nothing.

That's me. Dangling precariously. One wrong move from disaster.

And Erin's message is that unexpected gust, pushing me in a direction I know I shouldn't go.

The spider drops another inch on its silken thread, spinning faster now, its legs scrambling at empty air.

No amount of sunshine is going to help either of us climb back up once we fall.

Another message appears before I can respond.

We have SO much to catch up on. Tell me everything!

Tell her everything? What exactly am I supposed to tell her? That I'm destitute? That my husband left me? That I spend my days staring at water stains on motel ceilings and my nights scrolling through her perfect life?

I type the only response that feels appropriate.

Sorry. Accident.

Send.

Get away while you have the chance.

Three dots appear immediately. She's typing. Of course she is. Erin was always quick to respond, quick to act, quick to take what she wanted.

Don't be silly! I'm so glad you reached out, even accidentally! 🩶 **I've missed you!**

The audacity of her warmth makes my teeth ache.

I shouldn't respond.

I should block her number and go back to my scheduled breakdown.

But something stops me. A small, dangerous thought flickers in the darkest corner of my mind.

What do I have to lose? My dignity? Left that behind when I started bathing with a bar of soap thinner than a credit card. My pride? I think I pawned that along with my wedding ring.

I've been better, I type, fingers trembling slightly. **Life's been... challenging.**

That has to be the understatement of the century.

Three dots again. A quick reply for someone who should be on a beach somewhere, living her best life instead of texting a ghost from her past.

I'm so sorry to hear that, Sam. Do you want to talk about it? Sometimes it helps just to vent.

The gentleness in her question catches me off guard. I expected dismissal or shallow sympathy, not an actual invitation to unload my problems. For a moment, I almost feel the echo of our old friendship... the late nights spent talking through crises, planning our futures, sharing secrets.

It's a long story, I reply finally. **Not exactly light catching up material.**

I have time if you do. Besides, I'm pretty good at listening to long stories these days. Comes with the wellness guru territory.

I stare at her message, weighing my options. What harm could it do to share a sanitised version of my collapse? It's not like my circumstances could get any worse.

My marriage ended, I type, each word feeling like ripping off a plaster. **Lost my job. Lost my flat. Currently residing at the Bates Motel's less reputable cousin.**

I hit send before I can reconsider, watching the message bubble away, taking with it the not-very-tightly guarded secret of how far I've fallen.

Oh, Sam. That's awful. I'm so sorry you're going through all that alone.

Alone.

How did she know? I never said I was alone. Never mentioned that my friends disappeared faster than my bank balance after the divorce. Never told her that my family hasn't returned my calls in months.

Yet somehow, Erin zeroed in on my isolation immediately, like a predator sensing weakness.

But she's right. I am alone. Completely, utterly alone.

God, listen to me. A few days in a motel room with nothing but my spiralling thoughts for company, and suddenly I'm seeing conspiracies everywhere. Of course Erin assumed I was alone. Most people going through divorce and financial collapse don't have a robust support network cheering them on.

Still, I can't shake the feeling that there's something calculated about her response. After what happened between us, I'd be an idiot not to keep my guard up.

Yeah, well. That's life, I reply finally. **Some rise, some fall.**

I wince at how bitter that sounds, how nakedly resentful of her success. But Erin doesn't seem put off.

Where are you staying exactly? Is it safe?

Safe enough, I lie. **The lock works most nights, and the roaches are relatively friendly.**

Sam, that's terrible. Listen, I've got a place in the Cotswolds now. Nicholas and I prefer being away from all that. You could come stay, take some time to reset? Get away from whatever's going on?

London was our shared dream once: the big city where we'd both make our mark. We spent nights in our university flat planning our glamorous London futures, mapping out which neighbourhoods we'd live in once we'd *made it*.

I made it to London, all right. Made it to a grimy bedsit in Finsbury Park, then a shared flat in Hackney with damp walls and zero heating. Then there was the brief interlude of respectability with the flat in Islington that Daniel and I bought, stretching ourselves thin on mortgages and credit. I'd thought I was finally living the London dream.

Until the divorce.

Until I couldn't afford the mortgage alone.

Until I sold at a loss and watched my share disappear into debts and legal fees.

Then came a series of gradually deteriorating accommodations until I landed in this motel on the outskirts, clinging to the city by my fingernails.

Meanwhile, Erin did exactly what we'd planned. She moved to London, became successful, and then promptly left for greener, more exclusive pastures. Classic. Make it big enough in London and the first thing you do is escape it.

I'll be fine, I type reflexively.

No offence, but you don't seem fine. And you know what? That's okay. Nobody's fine all the time. Not even me.

The last part feels like bait. Like she's fishing for me to ask about cracks in her perfect life. I don't bite.

I've got a guest room, she continues. **Peaceful, private, yours as long as you need. No strings.**

No strings. There are always strings.

But as I look around the dismal room, the peeling wallpaper and the mysterious stain on the ceiling that looks disturbingly like a face, I realise something that chills me more than Erin's message: I'm out of options.

I can send a car for you, Erin writes. **Just say the word.**

Those words. The casualness of them. *Send a car.* As if it's nothing. As if summoning a private vehicle to collect someone is as easy as ordering a coffee. For her, it probably is.

I think about the £2.43 in my account. About how I've been rationing tea bags. About the fact that yesterday I walked three miles to a job interview because I couldn't cover the bus fare, only to be told I was *overqualified* for a position stacking shelves.

And Erin Blake can *send a car* without a second thought.

Of course she can.

The offer hangs there, tempting and terrifying all at once. I try to imagine saying yes, try to imagine putting myself back in Erin's orbit after everything that happened.

Is my pride worth sleeping on the street?

I type a response, then delete it. Type again. Delete again.

Are you still there? Erin asks. **I'm serious about the offer. No pressure, but you know I mean it.**

Do I know that? Do I know anything about who Erin Blake is now, with her millions of followers and her perfect husband and her obviously perfect house in the Cotswolds?

The woman I knew at university wasn't capable of this level of generosity. She was ambitious, yes. Charming, absolutely. But generous? Only when it served her purposes.

People change, I suppose. Though rarely for the better.

Why? I ask, unable to contain my suspicion. **Why offer me help after six years of silence?**

The dots appear quickly. Disappear. Appear again. She's revising her answer. Interesting.

Life gets busy, you know? And after everything that happened between us... I guess I thought you wouldn't want to hear from me. But I've never stopped thinking about you, Sam. About the fun we had, the dreams we shared. Sometimes I wonder what would have happened if we'd stayed friends.

If we'd stayed friends. As if our friendship ended naturally, evaporated like morning dew rather than being deliberately destroyed.

I wonder too, I type, surprised by my own honesty. **Maybe I'd be on a tropical island right now instead of this motel.**

I regret the words immediately. They sound petty, jealous. They are petty and jealous.

Oh, Sam. Please let me help. Whatever's going on, you don't deserve that.

I laugh, a dry, humourless sound that echoes in my empty room. Don't I? Don't I deserve exactly this? I had every opportunity Erin had. The same education. The same ideas. Better ones, even. I just lacked her ruthlessness. Her willingness to step on anyone in her way.

I don't need charity, I write.

I wish I'd never clicked on that dumb photo.

I wish I'd never looked through her feed, making myself dizzy with everything she has and everything I very much do not.

It's not charity. It's friendship. Or at least, it could be again. I've made mistakes, Sam. Big ones. Let me try to make things right.

The admission catches me off guard. There's a hint of something that sounds almost like remorse in her message.

What mistakes? I ask, my pulse quickening despite my better judgement.

I know full well what happened, and I'm pretty sure the definition of 'mistakes' doesn't cover it.

17

Another pause. Longer this time.

We grew apart when we should have grown together. I got caught up in my own life and career. And after what happened... well, I should have handled things differently. It happens to everyone, but that doesn't make it right. I miss having someone who knew me before all this. Someone who calls me on my bullshit.

It's not an apology. It's not even close to addressing what happened between us... the betrayal that shattered our friendship and set us on such divergent paths. But it's something, a crack in the perfect facade she presents to the world.

I should call her on her bullshit right now.

I should have done it six years ago.

I shouldn't care.

I shouldn't want more.

But I do.

Things are really bad, Erin, I type, the words feeling like surrender. **I'm out of money. Out of options.**

Then let me help.

My eyes fixate on those words, trying to think of any other option. There's nothing. I don't have any.

But of course, there is one tiny little problem.

I can't get to the Cotswolds, I admit. **I have less than a tenner to my name.**

Quite a lot less, but she doesn't need the exact details of my destitution.

That's not a problem. I'll send a car to collect you, or I can transfer money for the train. Which would you prefer?

The ease with which she offers money makes my skin crawl. How much does she make in a day? A week? Enough to save me from homelessness without even noticing the expense, clearly.

The train is fine, I type, clinging to what little dignity I have left. **But I'll pay you back.**

Don't be silly. Consider it an investment in your fresh start.

An investment. Of course she'd see it that way. Everything is a transaction to Erin. Always has been.

But I currently live at number one Desperation Street and my tenancy is about to expire.

I can be ready tomorrow, I tell her.

I can be ready right now. I have nothing left to take. But that also means I have nothing left to lose.

Perfect! I'll book you a ticket and send the details. First class, of course. Let me know where from. And Sam?

Yes? I type.

I'm really glad you liked my photo. Call it fate, but I think this is exactly what both of us need right now.

Both of us. What could Erin Blake possibly need from me?

What do you mean? I ask.

Oh, nothing specific. Just that sometimes life has a way of bringing people together at

exactly the right moment, you know? Anyway, I need to run, but I'll message you the ticket details. Can't wait to see you tomorrow!

And just like that, she's gone. No explanation for her cryptic comment. No further information about what she expects from me.

I set my phone down on the bedside table and stare at the ceiling. What have I just agreed to? Walking into the lion's den because I'm too tired and hungry to keep running.

Maybe this is exactly what Erin wants. Maybe this has always been her plan: to watch me fail, to wait until I was desperate, and then to swoop in like some benevolent goddess, magnanimous in her success. To rub my face in how far I've fallen while pretending to help me up.

Or maybe she really has changed. Maybe six years and several million pounds later, she's developed a conscience.

I don't believe that for a second.

But it doesn't matter what I believe. What matters is that tomorrow, I'll leave this motel behind. I'll shower in hot water. I'll sleep in a clean bed. I'll eat something that doesn't come from a vending machine.

My phone pings again. It's Erin.

Ticket booked! You'll get off at Moreton-in-Marsh station. Nicholas will pick you up. He's so excited to meet you! I've told him all about our uni days.

All about our uni days. I wonder which version of our history Nicholas has heard. They say there are three sides to every story, don't they? Yours, mine, and the truth. I doubt Erin's version matches either of the other two.

Thank you, I type, the words hollow. **See you tomorrow.**

Can't wait! Get some rest, Sam. Tomorrow is the first day of your new life!

My new life. As what? Erin's charity case? Her restoration project? The before to her after?

I look around the dingy motel room, at my few possessions, at the wrappers from meals I couldn't really afford, at the desperation that has become my constant companion.

Whatever game Erin is playing, whatever she expects from me, it has to be better than this. Nothing could be worse than this slow, miserable decline.

I begin to pack my meagre belongings, folding each item with care, as if treating them with dignity might somehow restore my own.

This is the right decision. The only decision.

This is what I *have* to do.

Tomorrow, I'll board a train to a new life. I'll smile and say thank you and pretend that seeing Erin again doesn't make my blood boil with resentment.

I'll do whatever it takes to get out of this hole.

Even if it means crawling into another one.

CHAPTER THREE

The train journey feels like stepping into someone else's life. First class seats. A table that doesn't stick to my elbows. Two businessmen across from me tap importantly on laptops while I clutch my shabby duffle bag, conspicuously out of place in clothes that I've been wearing for four days straight.

I drink so much of the complimentary coffee that I have to pop to the loo three times on the way. This feels like luxury to someone who picked up the free sugar packets in the petrol station so she could have a little treat after her crappy sandwiches. Me. I mean me.

I spend the entire journey rehearsing what I'll say to Erin when I see her. Something casual but dignified. Something that says, *'Yes, I've fallen on hard times, but I'm still Sam. I still have my pride.'* But every line sounds hollow, even to my own ears.

The truth is, I don't really know who I am anymore.

As the train pulls into Moreton-in-Marsh station, I catch my reflection in the window. My hair is limp despite my best efforts with the motel soap. My eyes are shadowed. My skin is dull. Six years ago, Erin and I were equals, at least on the surface. Now she's a goddess, and I'm... this. A ghost of myself.

The station is quaint in that irritating way that costs a fortune. Hanging baskets overflow with flowers. The platform is spotlessly clean. Even the bilingual

English-Japanese signs seem designed for a tourist brochure rather than to give actual directions.

I scan the small crowd gathered at the platform exit, my stomach knotting. I've never met Nicholas and have no idea what he looks like. He wasn't in our lives at university, and I've never seen him on Erin's social media. It's all about *her*, not her family. She's more personality than personal. Nicholas could be any of the men waiting at the station: the silver-haired businessman checking his watch, the bearded guy in hiking gear, or someone I haven't even noticed yet.

What if he doesn't show? What if this is all some elaborate prank, Erin's final twist of the knife after years of silence? There are probably worse places to be stranded than the English countryside... especially in the Cotswolds, where everything feels quintessentially, stubbornly quaint.

I shift my shoddy duffle bag from one shoulder to the other, trying to look like someone who belongs in this picture-perfect town rather than a charity case awaiting collection.

Then I notice a man standing apart from the scattered passengers, watching me with an expression I can't quite place. Recognition without warmth. As if he's confirming I match a description, nothing more.

Tall, precisely groomed, wearing clothes that whisper money rather than shout it. Dark hair, strong jaw, watchful eyes. The kind of handsome that belongs in luxury watch advertisements.

"Samantha," he says when I approach. Not a question.

"That's me," I reply with false brightness. "You must be Nicholas."

He doesn't smile. Doesn't offer to take my bag. Just nods toward the car park. "This way."

The awkward silence as we walk makes me babble.

"Thanks for picking me up. The train was lovely. I hope it wasn't too much trouble coming to get me."

He glances at me, his expression unchanged. "Erin insisted."

Three syllables that tell me everything I need to know. He didn't want to come. Didn't want me here. But Erin *insisted*, and what Erin wants, Erin gets.

The car is exactly what I expected: a Range Rover so clean it might have been driven straight from the showroom. I hesitate before climbing in, suddenly conscious of my grubbiness against the pristine leather interior.

Before leaving London, I endured my final motel shower. The water ran barely tepid as I used the last of the cheap toiletries. Instead of refreshing me, they left a residue on my skin, as though my circumstances had become too ingrained to be washed away with diluted soap and apathetic water pressure. I felt dirtier coming out than going in.

Still, I clamber aboard and try to feel comfortable amidst the luxury.

"Don't worry about it," Nicholas says, noticing my hesitation. "It's just a car."

The dismissive tone suggests he's used to people being intimidated by his wealth and equally used to dismissing their discomfort.

Nicholas starts the engine, his movements precise and economical. As we pull away from the station, I notice his eyes flick to the rearview mirror, then to me, then back to the road. It's a quick assessment, impossible to read. The wedding band on his left hand gleams as he adjusts the steering wheel, platinum, not gold. I'd expect nothing less.

We drive in silence for several minutes, the English countryside rolling past in picture-perfect waves of green. It's beautiful in a way that feels unreal, like we're moving through the pages of a glossy magazine.

"So," I venture finally, "how long have you and Erin been married?"

"Four years." His eyes don't leave the road.

Four years. So much has happened in that time. Erin built an empire, married this stranger, moved to the countryside. Meanwhile, I've been living an entirely different life. I want to ask how they met, what drew him to her, whether she ever mentioned me when she talked about her past.

They must have married around the same time Daniel and I did. They seem to have done somewhat better with their marriage, and with their lives.

It's jarring to realise how little I know about the person Erin has become, despite her constant online presence. The polished, successful woman with the Range Rover and country house might as well be a stranger wearing my old friend's face.

"And you live out here full time?" I ask. "Not in London?"

"We have a place in London, too. But this is home."

I wait for him to ask something personal, something that shows a genuine interest in who I am beyond my connection to Erin. Instead, he shifts in his seat, his posture stiffening slightly.

"Erin mentioned you were having a difficult time," he says finally, his tone clinical. "She didn't give specifics."

I feel heat rise to my face. "I'm between things at the moment."

I fall back on the old lie.

"That can sometimes happen when you don't choose which way to go," he says.

The comment is so unexpected that I turn to study his profile. There's something in his voice, a brittleness beneath the polish, that catches me off guard. But his expression gives nothing away.

My stomach tightens as the silence stretches, heavier than before. Regret prickles at the edges of my thoughts. I don't fit in. Not with the First Class train journey, not in this expensive car, and I already know, not in Erin's life.

What have I done? Left one bad situation for what might be an even worse one? The memory of my motel room, as grim as it was, suddenly seems almost comforting in its familiarity. At least I understood the rules there. At least the only person making me uncomfortable was myself.

I watch the countryside roll by, each mile taking me further from the life I knew and deeper into whatever strange dynamic exists between Erin and this closed-off man she married. Maybe I should have stayed with the spider dangling above my bed, the water stains on the ceiling that looked like faces. At least those demons were ones I recognised.

Then again, why shouldn't I accept her offer of help? After what Erin did, after everything that happened between us, this isn't charity. It's the bare minimum of what she owes me.

But that tiny voice of pride is drowned out by practical reality. My old room will already be occupied by some other desperate soul, and my £2.43 won't get me back to London, let alone pay for another night anywhere. Besides, part of me wants to see exactly what she's built for herself, what she became after she left me behind.

Finally, we turn off the main road onto a private drive bordered by perfectly maintained hedgerows. The car purrs along the winding gravel path, each curve increasing the tightness in my chest. My palms are damp against the leather seat as we round a final bend.

And then I actually gasp.

Erin and Nicholas's home is not a house, it's an estate. A mansion. The kind of place featured in historical documentaries and luxury real estate specials. The kind of residence that has a name rather than an address.

As the car slows to a stop, I feel myself becoming breathless. I'm not ready for this. Not ready to face the life that could have been mine, the success I should have shared.

But ready or not, here I am.

I have nowhere else to go.

27

CHAPTER FOUR

The first thought that enters my mind is that Erin doesn't just have money, she has the kind of money that reshapes the world to its will. The estate rises before us, honey-coloured Cotswold stone catching the afternoon light, making the whole structure seem to glow with quiet prosperity. Climbing roses frame imposing double doors, while perfectly symmetrical mullioned windows reflect the drifting clouds. The gravel beneath my feet is not *just* gravel, it's been raked into pristine patterns, each stone seemingly placed by hand.

It looks like the kind of place that hosts magazine photoshoots and celebrity weddings.

And it probably does.

My throat tightens as I take it in, the physical manifestation of the plans Erin and I once shared over cheap wine and late night takeaways. It's the kind of place I once dreamed of owning when Erin and I would sit at the cluttered kitchen table, designing our futures, sketching business models on napkins, imagining success we were certain awaited us both.

Only one of us made it.

And in case you hadn't guessed, it's not me.

Nicholas watches my reaction with detached interest, as though measuring the precise depth of my discomfort.

And then I see her, waiting in the doorway like she's posing for an architectural digest spread. Erin.

Six years have only enhanced her beauty: honey-blonde hair falling in perfect waves and skin that glows with the unmistakable radiance of someone who has never worried about paying bills, who has regular facials and drinks the daily recommended amount of water. Her pristine floral dress manages to look both casual and couture, a glimpse of a gold bracelet at her wrist catching the light.

The smile spreading across her face seems genuinely delighted. But there's something in her eyes that doesn't quite match the warmth of her expression.

It's gone so quickly I might have imagined it.

She's helping me. I have to remind myself.

There has been bad blood between us for so long that it has blackened my thoughts.

"Sam!" she calls out, her voice musical with rehearsed delight. "You made it!"

I step forward, suddenly hyperaware of every scuff on my shoes, every wrinkle in my shabby clothes. The contrast between us couldn't be starker if she'd planned it.

She embraces me before I can prepare myself, enveloping me in expensive perfume and effervescent warmth. Her arms are thin but strong around me. When she pulls back, her smile is dazzling, but her eyes are assessing, taking inventory of every flaw and failure written on my face.

I have to stop thinking like this.

I am here.

I have accepted her offer of salvation, and now I have to roll over, kick my legs up in the air and accept the tummy rubs like a good little rescue dog.

"It's so good to see you," she says, squeezing my hands. "You look exactly the same."

The lie is so brazen I almost laugh. I look nothing like I did in university. I'm hollowed out, worn down. She knows it. I know it. Even Nicholas, who never knew me before, can surely tell.

"You look amazing," I say, because it's true and because anything else would sound like jealousy.

I didn't expect those to be the first words I spoke to her after all this time, but everything else can wait.

"Oh, stop," she waves away the compliment with practised modesty. "Come inside! You must be exhausted."

Nicholas retrieves my duffle bag from the trunk, and with it, my entire worldly possessions. Wordlessly, he follows us inside.

The interior of the house is even more. The traditional exterior gives way to surprisingly contemporary spaces. Walls have been removed to create soaring open areas while preserving select original features like the massive fireplace and showcase beams. Antique furniture mingles with designer pieces, each item placed with deliberate precision. Every surface gleams. Every cushion is plumped. It doesn't look lived in; it looks *designed.*

"Your home is beautiful," I say, the inadequacy of the words hanging in the air.

"It's a work in progress," Erin replies with practised humility. "We've only had it a year. The renovation was a nightmare, wasn't it, Nick?"

Nicholas looks up from my pathetic duffle, which he's been examining with something like distaste.

I can't say that I blame him. He and Erin probably have a walk-in wardrobe filled with hard shell Louis Vuitton cases and no doubt use Neverfulls for their trips to Waitrose.

As if Erin does her own grocery shopping.

"Absolute hell," Nicholas agrees flatly. Then, without another word, he hoists my bag and strides from the room, his footsteps fading down the hallway.

For a brief, crazed moment, I imagine him taking it to a furnace out back and incinerating it. Too dirty or too cheap to stay in their home.

My expression must give away my surprise, as Erin smiles sweetly and puts her hand on mine.

It feels unnaturally smooth.

Or maybe mine are unnaturally rough. I wouldn't be surprised.

"He's taking your things to the guest suite," she explains. "He's not much of a talker with new people. You'll get used to him."

The casual assumption that I'll be around long enough to '*get used to*' her husband makes me uneasy. What exactly is she planning?

"How long did you want me to stay?" I ask directly.

Erin's smile doesn't falter.

"As long as you need, silly! There's no rush. I want you to treat this as your own home. Reset. Recharge. Figure out your next steps."

Her kindness feels like a trap, though I can't articulate why.

Deep down, I know.

I know that it's my understandable paranoia.

I trusted Daniel, and I ended up with nothing.

I trusted Erin, and she ended up here.

With everything.

I have to stop thinking like this.

"That's... incredibly generous," I manage.

"What are friends for?" She links her arm through mine. "Let me give you the tour, and then you can shower and rest before dinner. You must be exhausted."

The house is a prime example of subtle luxury. Every room is more perfect than the last. Guest bedrooms that look as though they have never known guests. A kitchen designed by someone who's never cooked. A dining room arranged for photoshoots rather than meals. Nothing out of place. Nothing real.

"And this is your suite," Erin announces finally, throwing open double doors with a flourish to reveal a space so vast it makes me momentarily dizzy.

The bedroom alone dwarfs my entire motel room, with ceilings so high my voice might echo. A four-poster bed dominates one wall, dressed in crisp linens that look cloud-soft and impossibly expensive. Fresh peonies spill from a crystal vase on the nightstand. I wonder if she remembered they are my favourite or if it's a pleasant coincidence.

I get the feeling that with Erin, nothing is accidental.

I hover at the threshold, overwhelmed. The room looks both meticulously prepared and strangely impersonal, like a high-end hotel suite rather than a friend's guest room. Either Erin arranged all this since yesterday's message, or this pristine space has been waiting for someone, anyone, to fill it. Both possibilities feel unsettling in ways I can't express.

"There are toiletries in the bathroom," Erin says. "And I've put some clothes in the wardrobe that should fit you. Nothing fancy, just some basics until you can get your own things."

I stare at her, unable to process this level of presumption. I *have* my own things. They are in the bag that her husband has left on the floor beside the bed here. Not incinerated, but clearly not up to Erin's standards.

"Thank you," I say stiffly. "That's very thoughtful."

I don't want to sound ungrateful, but I don't quite know how I *should* be. The one thing in this room that she hasn't mentioned is the elephant, and I'm not ready to acknowledge it either.

Six years of silence, and now she's gifting me clothes like nothing happened.

Replacing my clothes.

Upgrading me.

"It's nothing," she says, her voice light, dismissive. "Dinner's at seven. Very informal. Just the three of us.

She kisses my cheek, her lips barely grazing my skin, and then she's gone. I'm left alone with the lingering trace of her expensive perfume and the shock of being back in Erin's orbit.

I remain motionless for several minutes, trying to orient myself to this strange new reality. Twenty-four hours ago, I was in a grim motel, contemplating homelessness. Now I'm in a mansion, being treated like a combination of houseguest and restoration project.

How did I get here? The question feels both literal and existential. One Instagram like, one impulsive response to a message, and suddenly I've been swept up in Erin's life again after six years of silence. Six years of carefully maintained distance after everything fell apart between us.

I sink onto the edge of the immaculate bed, the duvet so plush it feels like sitting on a cloud. My fingers trace the expensive thread count of the sheets.

Why did I accept this offer so readily? Pride would suggest turning it down, telling Erin exactly where she could shove her charity. But pride doesn't keep you warm at night when you've got £2.43 in your account and nowhere to sleep. Pride doesn't wash away the smell of a motel room where the previous occupants' lives still linger in the carpet fibres.

And if I'm being honest, there's a certain justice to this. After what happened, after what Erin took from me, doesn't she owe me this much at least? A few weeks of luxury, a temporary lifeline. It's hardly adequate compensation for what I lost. What she cost me.

I push away the thought. Dangerous territory. Better to focus on the present, on survival, on getting through each day until I can figure out my next move. Because this, this perfect room in this perfect house, isn't mine. It's a temporary reprieve, not a solution.

And yet, as I glance around, I can't help but wonder what it would be like to have this life. To be Erin, with her perfect husband and perfect home and perfect career. The life I might have had if things had gone differently between us.

CHAPTER FIVE

I dwell on the past and wallow in self-pity for a few more minutes, but eventually I can no longer resist the call of the shower. The days of motel hygiene only added to the months of gradual erosion: my self-esteem, my standards, my hope. They all washed away long before I checked into that dismal room. I want to feel clean again. I want to feel restored to myself, to the person I was before everything was taken from me.

And I am desperate to wash away the soap scum from my exhausted body.

The ensuite bathroom is a symphony of marble and brushed gold fixtures. A freestanding tub sits beneath a window with a view of perfectly manicured gardens, while the shower enclosure could comfortably fit four people. Heated floors warm my bare feet as I pad across to inspect the array of products lined up with military precision. Expensive brands I've only ever seen in magazines, their labels promising transformation through botanical extracts and scientific-sounding compounds.

I catch sight of my reflection in the oversized mirror above the double vanity. The contrast between my worn-down appearance and the pristine surroundings couldn't be starker. It's like I've wandered into someone else's life by mistake. But then, isn't that exactly what's happened? I've stepped into Erin's world, a place where people like me don't belong. The thought settles uncomfortably as I turn away from my reflection.

I strip off my clothes and step into a shower with more settings than my old car. The water pressure is divine, the temperature perfect. I stand under the spray until my skin pinks, washing away the grime of the motel, of the day's travel, of my old life.

The toiletries all have French names I can't pronounce. I use them liberally, shampooing twice, conditioning, exfoliating, until I feel almost human again. It's going to take more than a hot shower, of course, but it certainly helps.

I step out onto a bathmat so plush it feels like my feet are sinking into fur, and wrap myself in a heated robe from the warming rack. Steam billows around me as I wipe a clear spot on the fogged mirror. The face looking back seems different somehow; cleaner, yes, but also like someone who belongs in this space, if only temporarily. My skin glows from the expensive products and rigorous scrubbing. I allow myself to enjoy this small luxury, this brief respite from the constant gnawing anxiety of the past months. The sensation is almost dizzying, like stepping off a turbulent boat onto solid ground, my body still anticipating the next lurch even as I stand perfectly still on the heated tile floor.

Wrapped in the soft robe, I head back into the main room and examine the wardrobe with trepidation. The *basics* Erin mentioned turn out to be designer clothes, of course. Cashmere sweaters. Silk blouses. Jeans that look casual, but most probably cost hundreds of pounds.

I check the jeans for a label and find they're exactly right for me. They are the size I was when Erin and I last knew each other. Not the size I was eight months ago when Daniel was still around, and I could afford proper meals. No, these clothes are sized for the new me: the one who's been on the involuntary Coke Zero and single-serving Pringles diet for the past few weeks. The me who's dropped nearly a stone without trying, courtesy of anxiety and an empty bank account.

The silver lining to destitution: I'm back to my university weight. How ironic.

I dress in the simplest outfit I can find: jeans and a white T-shirt that feels softer than anything I've worn in years. Everything fits perfectly, which is both a relief and deeply unsettling.

How did Erin know my current size?

When did she buy these clothes?

Was she that certain I would accept her invitation?

Or has she been watching me, tracking me somehow?

Damn, this paranoia is strong. I need to get a hold of myself.

One thought sticks in my mind like a fishbone in the throat: she is remembering me as I was. As though the past six years never happened

Chills ripple across my skin despite the lingering warmth from the shower. I try to dismiss the thoughts, but the question remains: how much does Erin know about the person I've become?

I have approximately two hours before dinner. Two hours to decide how to play this. Do I embrace the charity, swallow my pride, and accept whatever game

Erin is playing? Or do I maintain my guard, watching for the inevitable catch?

Because there is always a catch with Erin Blake. Always an agenda.

A soft knock at the door interrupts my thoughts. I open it to find Nicholas, his expression as unreadable as before.

My hair is still damp and piled on my head in a towel turban. Even though I most certainly look better now than I did when we met earlier, I can't stop the blush of awkwardness flooding to my cheeks.

"Settling in?" he asks, though his tone suggests he doesn't particularly care about the answer.

"Yes, thank you. The room is beautiful."

He nods, then hands me a small, plain but pretty box. "Erin asked me to give you this."

I lift off the lid; inside is a smartphone.

"She thought you might need an upgrade. Your number is the same as your old one. She transferred the SIM over."

I frown. "My phone? How did she..."

"It was in your duffle," he says with a slight shrug.

"You went through my bag?" I can't keep the indignation from my voice despite my precarious position here.

"The zipper's broken. It was right on top." He tilts his head slightly. "Your phone was broken too, so..."

"That's not the point. That was *my* phone. You had..." No right, I was going to say, but I stop myself. The gift would actually have seemed like a kind gesture if it didn't feel quite so utterly invasive.

Nicholas's expression doesn't change. "You have a new one now. A proper phone." He waves to the box in my hand as if that settles everything.

Before I can respond further, he turns and walks away, his footsteps silent on the thick carpet.

I almost step out after him.

I almost shout, '*Wait! What the hell?*'

But I don't.

I close the door and stare at the phone in my hand.

This is Erin, after all.

Boundaries have never meant much to her.

I press the power button, and the screen illuminates.

It's already set up.

Already connected to the house Wi-Fi.

Already populated with contacts, including Erin and Nicholas.

A text message notification appears as I watch.

Welcome home, Sam. Hope you like your room. Can't wait to catch up at dinner! xo

Home.

As if I belong here. As if this sterile perfection could ever be home to someone like me.

As if stealing my phone and replacing it with a new one is perfectly normal.

I've escaped one prison only to walk willingly into another. The only difference is that this one has better amenities.

CHAPTER SIX

I spend the afternoon wandering through the suite like it's a show home, every drawer neatly curated with luxury. Designer skincare. Cashmere and silk clothing. Tampons aligned like soldiers. It's more than thoughtful, it's unnerving. No one stocks this kind of precision overnight.

I stare at a row of serums worth more than my entire toiletries bag and realise: this wasn't set up for me. This is just Erin. A guest-ready life. The kind of woman who always has a cheese board and Shiraz in the kitchen and a new toothbrush on standby in every guest suite.

I run my fingers along the countertop in the en-suite bathroom, thinking about the home I lost. Our little two-bedroom apartment in Finsbury Park that I fought so hard to keep. The mortgage payments I juggled, the bills I prioritised even as my bank balance dwindled after Daniel left. All to hold onto a flat where we'd planned to raise children who never materialised.

How grimly ironic that for years we kept that second bedroom ready. First as a potential nursery, later as a home office after those dreams died. Then, in those last weeks, it became Daniel's retreat as our marriage crumbled. All that time worrying about filling and maintaining two bedrooms, while Erin casually keeps what must be at least six in this country mansion alone.

I lost my home because I couldn't manage the mortgage payments on a modest two-bedroom. And

41

Erin inhabits this life with the casual ease of someone who has never had to check her account balance before making a purchase.

I've spent the afternoon alternating between enjoying the luxury of my surroundings, questioning my good fortune and remembering the bad. I've also been avoiding the new phone as if it might bite me. Eventually, though, I cave and use it to check the time. Six thirty. Dinner in half an hour.

At precisely 6:58pm, I follow the smell of food to the kitchen. The house is unnervingly quiet. No television sounds, no music, no distant conversations. Just the soft pad of my borrowed socks on hardwood floors. Should I have worn shoes? In the house? Is that what rich people do? Is that what normal people do? I'm second guessing everything.

I have to stop this.

Downstairs, Erin stands poking at a tray of roasted vegetables with a deep red spatula. Nicholas leans against a counter, swirling amber liquid in a crystal glass. They make a beautiful tableau. Her entire life is Instagram-perfect.

"There she is!" Erin trills when she sees me, her smile dazzling. "Just in time. Wine?"

Erin appraises my outfit without expression. She herself has changed from when I saw her earlier and is wearing a floaty dream of a dress. It moves around her like water as she reaches for the wine bottle.

She doesn't wait for my answer before pouring a generous glass of red. Nicholas nods at me, his expression unchanged from earlier. Neither warm nor cold. Just watchful.

"You look great," she says, handing me the glass. "Everything fit alright?"

"Perfectly," I reply, taking a sip. It tastes like money and old vineyards. "How did you know my size?" I ask.

Erin laughs lightly, the sound like wind chimes. "Oh, I didn't really. I just assumed we'd be about the same, like we've always been. We're practically identical, aren't we?"

I manage a small snort that might pass for agreement. Same size? Eight months ago, when I was still with Daniel and could afford three proper meals a day, I was nearly a stone heavier than I am now. I've only reached this size through what a doctor would probably call '*situational malnutrition*' and what I call the '*destitution diet*'.

"Sure," I say, forcing a smile. "Always the same size."

Erin beams, clearly pleased with herself for getting it right. Meanwhile, I'm mentally calculating the difference between us: her slim figure maintained through what's undoubtedly an expensive personal trainer and meal delivery service, mine achieved by rationing tea bags and choosing between heating and eating.

"Can I help with anything?" I ask, eager to change the subject. It's either offer assistance or bring up the phone Erin had Nicholas set up behind my back, and I just can't face confrontation right now. Not about that. Not about anything.

"No," Erin says firmly. "You're our guest."

"I don't mind," I insist. "I feel useless just standing here."

"Nicholas, tell her she's being silly," Erin says with a playful lilt.

Nicholas takes a sip of his drink. "Let her help if she wants to."

Something flickers across Erin's face, a momentary tightening around her eyes, before her smile returns.

"Fine! You can set up for dinner. Everything's in that drawer." She points with her perfectly manicured index finger. "We're going to eat in the kitchen tonight. The dining room is a bit too much, don't you think, Nicholas?"

He shrugs, and I busy myself with placemats and cutlery, grateful for something to do with my hands. There's too much air between us, too many things not said.

I could say it.

I could start asking questions.

But this isn't the moment.

I need to be smarter than that.

This whole situation is weirding me out a lot more than I thought it would, and with all the skeletons that we haven't let out of the closets yet, it's only going to get worse.

The food is exquisite: roast chicken, vegetables roasted with herbs, a salad that probably has a backstory. We sit at the kitchen island like an aspirational lifestyle ad.

"So," I say, feigning casual interest, "how long have you been here?"

I already know the answer. I just can't think of anything else to say, or at least nothing I can say right now.

"A year," Erin replies, eyes bright. "The light's better. Content-wise. Out here in the country."

Of course. The business.

"You've really built something," I offer.

Her smile sharpens. "Well. It helps to have vision."

I see Nicholas glance at me, his gaze unreadable. Erin knows exactly what she's just said. And she knows I know. But neither of us breaks character. We both smile, performing civility like pros.

It's a test. A poke at a bruise she knows is still tender.

I stay on script, because breaking it now would be like handing her the spotlight all over again.

Nicholas swirls his wine. "Some of her clients pay more than most people earn in six months."

"No, darling," Erin corrects. "It's only twenty thousand pounds." She laughs lightly as though Nicholas said something oh-so-silly.

I nearly drop my fork. "Twenty thousand?"

"Worth every penny," he says. "Her success has been remarkable."

I nod slowly, tasting the wine again. It's thick, dark, and I know it's expensive. Erin watches me over the rim of her glass. Not gloating, exactly. Measuring.

I hold her gaze, still smiling. There's tension beneath it, like wires pulled too tight. An old current, still live.

I swear I can hear the elephant in the room sigh.

She opens her mouth. "I..."

I shake my head, subtle but firm.

Not now.

Not yet.

She draws in a slow breath and drops her gaze.

Nicholas takes a forkful of courgette and pepper laden chicken to his mouth, but Erin has stopped eating.

So have I.

Even exquisite meals lose flavour when tension is the main course.

Erin clears her throat and winces slightly.

"I..." she begins. "There's something I need to say." She's close-on breathless and Nicholas shoots her a sharp glance.

She puts her hand onto his and shakes her head, just slightly, just once.

I can feel my chest tighten with anticipation.

It's too soon for this. I'm not ready to have the big showdown with her.

Bygones should go bye-bye, right? That's what Erin always used to say. She always was the better philosopher.

When you're staying in the guest room of your ex-best friend's mansion, wearing her clothes, eating her chicken... There must be some Chinese proverb that sums all this up, but my mind is spinning out of control trying to think of one.

My breath is shallow, and I almost stand up, I almost walk to the door, I almost run, but then Erin speaks.

"We're expanding. Internationally. Next week."

"Oh?" I respond, shifting in my seat but not leaving it. "Europe?"

"Aruba," she says, her voice rising with genuine excitement. "A beautiful private villa, infinity pool overlooking the ocean, personal chef. The works."

"Sounds amazing," I say, and almost mean it. "When do you leave?"

"Saturday," Nicholas answers. "Four days from now."

"So soon?" I can't keep the surprise from my voice. What was Erin planning to do with me while they were gone? Leave me here alone? Send me back to the motel?

"There's actually something we wanted to discuss with you," Erin says, setting down her fork. "I've been looking for a new photographer to document everything. My last one wasn't great with people. She couldn't capture the authentic moments."

She lingers on the word. *Authentic.* Her eyes meet mine, just long enough for it to mean something more.

"You always had such a good eye," she continues. "Remember those photos you took for the university magazine? They were amazing."

I almost laugh. I haven't touched a proper camera in years.

"I've not done much lately."

"It's like riding a bike." She leans forward slightly, as if sharing a secret. "Come to Aruba. Document the retreat. All expenses covered. Plus five thousand pounds."

The number drops like a stone in my chest.

Five thousand.

She says it like she's doing me a favour. Maybe she thinks she is.

But five grand won't even the scales. She knows that.

Still, I could live again. Not comfortably. Not forever. But enough to stop drowning.

I could rent somewhere. Get off the treadmill of panic.

I look at her, trying to read the angles. Generosity? Pity? A debt being paid?

Nicholas watches me with that same blank expression. Not cold, just... removed.

"It was Nicholas's idea, actually," Erin says, following my glance.

I set my fork down. "Was it?"

Nicholas nods. "You need work. We need a photographer. It's practical."

Practical. That stings more than it should. Somehow, his bluntness feels more honest than Erin's warm delivery.

"I don't have a visa," I offer, half-hearted.

"Aruba's visa-free for Brits," Nicholas replies. "You'll need a passport."

I do have one of those. Unused. We were meant to honeymoon somewhere hot and beautiful once, but we never made it. I had plans for us to go to the Bahamas. Aruba isn't that far away, is it? I still have the passport, but not the husband.

"And a driving licence," Nicholas adds matter-of-factly. "We'll have a rental car available for errands, trips into town, whatever you need."

Erin waves a hand, breezy. "Don't worry about the visa thing. It's just *helping out*, anyway. If anyone asks, we'll say it's... informal."

Not illegal. Just conveniently undefined.

I wouldn't expect anything else from her.

"Well," I say, my voice steady, my smile not. "It's a generous offer."

Carefully spoken. A balancing act between desperation and dignity.

"You don't need to be a pro," Erin says. "It's lifestyle content. Candid, beautiful moments. The equipment does most of the work."

"And if I mess it up?"

She laughs, soft and crystalline. "You won't. But even if you did, what's the worst that happens? You get a free holiday, and I hire someone local."

She makes it sound so simple. So easy. Like none of this has any weight.

What do I have to lose? Besides my pride. My dignity. The version of myself I used to believe in.

Of course, that's not what I ask. Erin has seen enough of my desperation. Instead, I ask, "What happens after?"

"That depends," Erin says with a shrug. "If it goes well, there'll be more work. If not, you've got a bit of money to start again somewhere else."

Start again. Not here, then. Not with her.

"I need to think about it," I say, though I already know I'm running out of time... and options.

Nicholas raises an eyebrow. "What's there to think about? You need money."

His tone is flat, factual. No cruelty in it. Just basic maths.

"Nick," Erin murmurs.

"It's okay," I say quickly. "He's not wrong. I just... need to catch my breath."

And there's a lot to think about.

"Life moves fast," Erin says. "Sometimes you have to move with it."

And sometimes you just get left behind.

I smile again. I'm getting good at that.

Five thousand pounds. A tropical paradise. A second chance.

Or something that looks like one.

Erin glances at Nicholas, something unspoken passing between them. My stomach tightens, recognising the silent communication of people who share secrets.

"We need more wine," she says, her voice light but her eyes fixed meaningfully on her husband.

Nicholas sets down his napkin and rises without protest. "The Bordeaux?"

"Perfect," she replies, her smile not quite reaching her eyes.

The air seems to thicken as his footsteps fade down the hallway. This is the first moment we've been truly alone since I arrived, and the weight of our unacknowledged history settles between us like a physical presence. A warning prickles along my skin: danger wrapped in expensive perfume.

My fingers tighten around the stem of my wineglass until I fear it might snap. "You know that five thousand pounds isn't..."

Erin looks at me, her expression suddenly stripped of its practised warmth.

"I know," she says quietly.

The simplicity of her admission catches me off guard. I'd been prepared for deflection, for carefully choreographed innocence. Not this direct acknowledgment.

She traces the rim of her glass, her perfectly manicured nail making a soft, crystalline sound against the edge.

"It's been a long time. I'm sorry about what happened back then."

The apology hangs in the air between us, insufficient and yet more than I ever expected to hear. My throat constricts as memories flood back.

"I owe you for what I did," she continues, her voice hushed as though the walls might be listening. "I know that."

The kitchen's soft lighting casts shadows across her face, momentarily revealing something that looks almost like genuine remorse. Almost.

My hands tremble slightly. I place them flat against the cool surface of the table to steady them, aware that Erin misses nothing. Every reaction is catalogued, every weakness noted.

"We were close, weren't we?" she says at last. "I've never had a friend like you. Not before. Not since."

"And yet..." I say, the words carrying the weight of years of resentment.

"And yet," she nods, accepting the indictment.

She reaches across the table, her fingers hovering near mine without quite touching. "I'm still the same person you knew back then. Before everything."

I'm not sure how to respond to that. Am I the same person? In some ways, perhaps. In others, definitely not. Divorce, failure, and near-homelessness have a way of changing a person. Of hardening the soft places, sharpening the edges.

"And our history doesn't concern you? You think stepping in and offering me this..."

She studies me for a long moment, her gaze calculating behind the veneer of vulnerability. "The past is the past. I'm more interested in the present. Bygones..."

"Don't say it," I say.

I can't bear to hear her stupid phrases now.

The pressure in my chest builds as I consider the layers within her words. The things said and unsaid. The delicate dance around truths we both know but refuse to name. I can feel myself teetering on a precipice, knowing I'm about to step willingly into whatever game she's playing.

But what choice do I have? Pride doesn't keep you warm. Principles don't pay rent.

I hear Nicholas's footsteps returning, the soft clink of a bottle against the doorframe. Erin's expression shifts so quickly it's almost imperceptible: vulnerability tucked away, replaced by the polished hostess once more.

"Found it," Nicholas announces, holding up the Bordeaux as he re-enters the kitchen.

Erin turns to him with a smile so radiant and effortless that if I hadn't witnessed the transformation, I'd believe it was genuine.

"Perfect timing, darling."

She squeezes his arm affectionately as he uncorks the bottle. Not a trace of the woman who, moments ago, was acknowledging her debt to me. The ease with which she switches personas is chilling.

But somehow not unexpected.

"So," she continues, studying me with those keen eyes, her mask of warm hospitality never slipping, "have you decided? About Aruba?"

Saturday. It's not as though I have a full calendar.

This isn't exactly what I had planned, but... the Caribbean? A way out of rock bottom, even temporarily?

Who could say no?

CHAPTER SEVEN

That first night with Erin, I hardly sleep, despite the mattress being the kind that probably has its own postcode. No bedbugs. No shouting neighbours. No stained ceiling tiles. Just silence. Luxury. And a mind that won't shut off.

I turn over a hundred times, my body unable to adjust to softness after weeks of metal springs and motel gloom. The darkness is absolute: no flickering neon signs, no headlights sweeping across walls, nothing to break the perfect emptiness. But somehow, I miss the familiar hum of the vending machine outside my motel room, the creaking floors, even the faint smell of mildew. At least there, I knew who I was: a woman at rock bottom. Here, in this pristine guest suite, I am... what? And what exactly am I doing here?

When dawn breaks, I give up on sleep altogether and pad to the window. The estate stretches before me, mist clinging to manicured lawns and perfectly trimmed hedges. Everything here exists in a state of controlled perfection, like Erin herself.

I wonder if the gardens ever rebel. If weeds dare to push through her carefully planned flower beds. If anything here is ever allowed to grow wild.

I'm wrapped in one of Erin's bathrobes, still staring out at the mist rolling over the garden, when the knock comes.

Before I can say anything, the door creaks open.

"Special delivery!" Erin's voice is bright and sugary. Too bright for this early in the morning.

She steps inside holding a leather camera bag like it's a birthday present.

Erin is already immaculate, hair styled in loose waves, minimal makeup that somehow enhances her natural glow, dressed in silk loungewear. Not a hint of the aftermath of the previous night's wine visible on her face. Meanwhile, I can feel the puffiness around my eyes, the pallor of my skin.

"You're up early," I say, clearing my throat. I look like a feral cat compared to her sleek, groomed appearance.

"I'm usually up at five," she says, as if it's completely normal. "The early bird catches the Instagram light."

She sets the bag on the end of my unmade bed, and I notice her gaze lingering on the rumpled sheets. Judgement or concern? It's impossible to tell.

"Well, I know I gave Nicholas the whole spiel about how great you were at uni, but... you're going to need some practice," she says, waving towards the camera bag with a flourish. "This is what you'll be using in Aruba."

I pick it up, unzip, and lift out the camera. It's sleek, compact, and I know it's top range. It even smells expensive, like brushed metal and fresh opportunity.

The weight of it feels significant, like it carries more than just megapixels and memory cards.

"I want you to feel confident," she says, observing me. "It's yours now. For Aruba and beyond."

There it is again: her casual generosity, dressed up as friendship but always weighted. Always measured.

I look at it a little longer and then set the camera down carefully on the bedside table.

"What if I can't do it?" I ask.

She waves away my protest. "You'll be fine." Not good, not great, just fine. I try to stop my face from falling. "Besides," she carries on, "you're doing me a favour. We're here for each other. Like we always used to be."

The words hit like a slap. Of course we were. Of course nothing has changed. Is that really the way she wants to play this?

Something must show on my face because she tilts her head, studying me with those calculating eyes.

"What?"

"Nothing," I lie, forcing a smile. "Just tired."

She doesn't push it, but I can see her filing away my reaction for future reference.

"Breakfast?" she asks. "We can have those pancakes you used to like. The lemon ricotta ones. Do you remember?"

I remember.

"Bring the camera. I'll show you where to practise later."

Friday mornings in our third year, when neither of us had lectures. We'd make them in that terrible shared kitchen and drop crumbs in her bed or mine, depending on whose turn it was.

I almost smile, and my stomach growls in betrayal.

"Sure," I manage.

I assume she won't be the one cooking, but it won't be me either. And breakfast, actual breakfast, sounds wonderful after too many days of dry cornflakes.

Downstairs, the kitchen is already flooded with light. Erin moves like she's choreographing a shoot even when there's no camera on her. She pours coffee with a flourish and sets a plate in front of me.

The pancakes are already waiting: golden, fluffy, with just the right balance of sweetness and tang. Just like they used to be, except now they're served on fine china instead of chipped IKEA plates.

She knew I would want them. She knew I would accept, just like I accepted her help, the job, Aruba.

I jab a fork into the top of the pile. Let her keep thinking that I'm here to forgive and forget.

Nicholas enters the kitchen as I take my first bite, dressed in running gear, a thin sheen of sweat glistening on his forehead. He nods at me, barely acknowledging my presence, then goes to the fridge for a bottle of water.

"Pleasant run?" Erin asks, sliding a plate toward him.

"Fine," he says, uncapping the bottle. "Saw a fox by the south field."

The casual domesticity of their exchange feels performative somehow, as if they're actors in an advertisement for country living. I wonder if they practise these moments, if they rehearse their lines before I appear.

But even as his words remain neutral, I notice the way his eyes linger on me rather than Erin. There's something in his gaze, not warmth, not exactly, but a focused interest that doesn't match his aloof demeanour. When he finally turns to Erin, his expression shifts subtly, a flicker of something I can't quite name passing across his features.

"Funny how things work out," Nicholas says suddenly, breaking the silence. He's looking at his plate, but his words feel directed at both of us. "How people come back into your life at exactly the right moment."

The comment hangs in the air, innocent on the surface but somehow loaded. I catch a slight tightening around Erin's mouth before her smile reasserts itself.

"Fate has a way of bringing the right people together," she agrees, her voice light but her eyes watchful.

"Is that what you think happened?" I ask, quietly.

She sets her fork down, eyes softening. "Let's leave the past behind us. Let bygones..." This time she stops herself and chooses different words. "I want to help you, and I want to make things right. I know what I did."

The words hang in the air, heavier than the syrup between us.

Still, she doesn't elaborate. Doesn't name it. Just lets the admission settle like mist.

Nicholas pushes away from the counter.

"I need to shower. Flight arrangements are confirmed for weekend. I added Samantha to the booking. Car's coming at eight." His tone is businesslike, efficient. As he passes behind my chair, his hand brushes against my shoulder, so light I might have imagined it, yet somehow unsettling.

After Nicholas leaves, the two of us sit in the kitchen in silence as I finish my pancakes. No matter how tense the atmosphere feels, these actually are my favourites, and I haven't eaten them since Erin and I were back in our olden days, golden days.

"I'm sorry if I seem a little off," I say eventually. "I just don't want to mess this up. The photographs, I mean."

"You won't," she says, already breezing past the moment. "You've got the eye. You always did. Just point it at something beautiful and press the button."

As if it's that simple. As if any of this is.

She stands, brushing imaginary crumbs from her perfect silk trousers.

"Finish your breakfast. Then I'll show you the best spots to practise. You're going to make magic, Sam. I can feel it."

And just like that, she's gone.

I sit alone in the gleaming kitchen, wondering what exactly I've agreed to.

To be clear, I did freaking love taking photographs when we were at uni. I signed up for the photography club first term I was there and lurked around the dark room, pointed my Canon in everyone's face, and pretty much made it my only hobby. With a camera, I felt safe. I could hide behind it, but it was a passport to go anywhere, talk to anyone... or to *not* talk to anyone because *hey, I'm busy working here*.

But it was only ever a hobby. If I hadn't chosen the life of being a soon to be divorced destitute homeless woman, maybe this is the career I would have gone for.

Or maybe I would have been hosting international, glamourous wellness retreats.

If only I had been the one to think of Erin's brilliant business plan.

The camera sits on the counter, its black lens reflecting the morning light. I pick it up, turn it on, and point it at my empty plate. Through the viewfinder, even the mundane becomes artistic, a story told in pancake crumbs and expensive dishware.

I take the picture. It feels like evidence, though of what, I'm not yet sure.

Click.

The sound echoes in the empty kitchen. I take another shot, this time of the doorway where Erin disappeared. Then another of Nicholas's water bottle, left on the counter.

Click. Click.

Each image feels like a breadcrumb, a way to find my way back through this strange fairy tale I've wandered into. A way to remember who I was before Erin swept back into my life, offering salvation wrapped in cashmere and tied with strings.

I don't want to remember that.

I want to imagine a life where it was me who founded the business that brought Erin this lifestyle, that I was the one with the stable marriage and the country mansion. But the camera never lies, does it?

CHAPTER EIGHT

The next two days pass in a whirlwind of preparations. Erin moves through them with military precision, checking equipment, confirming schedules, reviewing participant profiles. I spend hours practising with the camera, my fingers gradually remembering old skills. Nicholas remains an enigma, appearing and disappearing throughout the house, always watching, rarely speaking.

Each night I lie awake in that too-perfect guest room, listening to the quiet of the countryside and wondering what exactly I've signed up for. Each morning I wake to find Erin already immaculate, already moving, as if she never truly sleeps.

By the time Saturday arrives, I've settled into an uneasy rhythm with them both. We board a private car to the airport, pass through the exclusive lounge (where Erin is recognised twice), and settle into business class seats with practised ease. Well, practised for them. I pretend this is normal, that I belong in this world of priority boarding and champagne before take-off.

Thirteen hours later, we touch down in paradise.

Aruba is exactly as beautiful as every travel vlog promises. Impossibly clear water in gradients of turquoise. Sand so white it hurts your eyes. Palm trees that look like they've been positioned by a set designer for maximum aesthetic impact.

From the moment our private car pulls up to the villa, I'm struck by the surreal quality of the entire experience. This doesn't feel like real life. It feels like I've stumbled into someone else's dream. Erin's dream, to be precise.

The villa sits on a cliff overlooking the ocean, a sprawling affair of bright stone and glass that catches the Caribbean light and transforms it into something magical. Inside, it's all open spaces and panoramic views, with cream-coloured furniture and natural wood accents.

"What do you think?" Erin asks, watching my face as I take it all in.

"It's incredible," I admit, because it is. "How did you find this place?"

"One of my followers owns it," she says with a casual wave. "She offered it at a discount in exchange for social coverage. Win-win." The way she says it is breezier than the tropical air.

Of course. Erin's entire existence seems to operate on this principle, leveraging her influence for maximum gain while making it seem like she's doing everyone a favour.

"Your room is this way," she continues, leading me down a hallway lined with local art. "It's not the master suite, obviously, but I think you'll be comfortable."

The not-the-master-suite turns out to be enormous, with a king-sized bed and a private balcony overlooking the sea. A fresh arrangement of tropical flowers sits on the dresser, and the bathroom features a glass-walled shower with a rainfall showerhead.

"This is... more than comfortable," I say, setting down my luggage.

My old duffle has finally met its fate: trash or incinerator, as I once feared when Nicholas first examined it only a few days ago. I don't know which way it went, but it has gone. In its place, a sleek new case Erin has provided, along with a complete wardrobe for the trip. The speed of these changes is dizzying, but I can't pretend I'll miss that broken zipper or the lingering motel smell.

She checks her watch: a slim gold Cartier that catches the light.

"You should have time for a quick swim before the team meeting. The participants arrive tomorrow, so tonight is our chance to go over the schedule and get you properly briefed."

"Team meeting?" I'm already exhausted after the flight. I tried to nap, but even with the lay-flat seat, I couldn't stop my racing thoughts long enough to sleep.

"Just you, me, Nicholas, and my assistant Layla. She's handling the logistics while you focus on being creative." Erin flashes her perfect smile. "Meet downstairs in an hour? The pool deck has the best light this time of day."

She's gone before I can respond, leaving me alone. I step onto the balcony and let the warm Caribbean air wash over me. The view is breathtaking: endless ocean meeting endless sky, the rhythmic crash of waves below. I allow myself to simply enjoy it. To pretend this is my life now. That I've earned this.

I deserve this just as much as Erin does. Maybe more.

I could have had her life. All of this could have been mine.

But then I catch my reflection in the glass balcony door. I'm not her. I'm still me: still uncertain, still an imposter in this world.

The heat, suddenly unbearable, drives me back inside. I don't want a *quick swim*. I want stillness. I need a moment to think, to breathe, to let my mind catch up with the whirlwind I've stepped into.

First things first.

I unzip the new suitcase and begin unpacking, carefully hanging each item in the empty closet. The fabrics whisper expensively between my fingers: flowy linen in neutral tones and bright whites, delicate sandals stamped with discreet designer labels, swimwear that somehow manages to be both modest and provocative.

Everything looks like it belongs on Erin's Instagram feed, not in my life.

At university, our identical sizes made our wardrobes communal territory. I'd wear her baggy jumpers while she borrowed my vintage jeans, tossing clothes back and forth without thinking. We'd fall asleep still wearing each other's party dresses, wake up and carry on in whatever was closest to hand.

Now, through very different routes - her disciplined regimen and private trainers, my involuntary poverty diet - we've arrived at the same dimensions again. I hold a gauzy white cover-up against myself, the material so fine it feels like it might dissolve between my fingers. It will fit perfectly, like everything else Erin has provided.

I'm being unfair. She opened up the web browser and let me choose what I wanted from a variety of exclusive sites. It's not as though I am her doll. Pet project, maybe. Doll, absolutely not.

Still, this isn't the casual '*what's mine is yours*' of our university days. This is us now. This is a different dynamic.

This is Erin saving me.

And, apparently, despite everything, it is me letting her.

The villa is empty as I finally make my way downstairs. No sign of Nicholas or this Layla person Erin mentioned. I follow the sound of voices to the pool deck, an expansive area of pale stone surrounding an infinity pool that appears to merge seamlessly with the ocean beyond.

Erin is already there, reclining on a lounger in a white bikini that's practically identical to the one from her Instagram photo: the one in the post I liked that started this whole strange journey. She's talking to a young woman I assume must be Layla, because she is taking rapid notes on an iPad and looking at Erin as though her every word is nectar.

Layla wasn't on our flight, or at least she wasn't in the business class section Erin had insisted on booking *'for people like us*' - a comment that made me wince even as I sank into the luxurious seat.

I've never been served a three-course dinner with fine china and silver cutlery on a plane before; I've only ever had the blinged up ready meals that come out all on one tray with a plastic knife and fork set.

I can only guess Layla came on ahead to make sure everything was perfect for our – or rather Erin's – arrival.

"There she is!" Erin calls when she spots me. "Doesn't she look amazing? Sweetie, come and meet Layla."

Layla turns to assess me, her expression professional but evaluating. She's sleek and polished in a way that suggests she's studied Erin's aesthetic and adapted it to her own purposes.

"Oh, the resemblance is remarkable," she says, which strikes me as an odd greeting.

"Resemblance?" I ask, suddenly self-conscious.

Erin laughs. "She means we could be sisters in these outfits. We have similar colouring, don't we?"

We don't, actually. Erin's blonde is expensively maintained, while my hair was dishwater brown before Erin's shampoo took effect. Her skin seems perpetually golden; mine is pale with a tendency to burn.

But in these clothes, with this backdrop, I can almost see what Layla means. We're playing the same role, just different versions of it.

I let the comment slide, and give Layla a smile.

"Where's Nicholas?" I ask instead, choosing a lounger that keeps me partly in the shade.

"Taking a call," Erin says dismissively. "Business stuff. Boring. He'll join us later."

Layla hands me a folder without being prompted. "The schedule for the week," she explains. "You'll need to be familiar with all the activities to anticipate the best photo opportunities."

I flip through pages of meticulously planned activities. Sunrise yoga. Mindfulness journaling. Group therapy sessions disguised as '*narrative exploration*.' One-on-one coaching with Erin. I'm surprised there are no excursions to local beauty spots carefully selected for their Instagram potential.

I grip the folder tighter, my knuckles going white as I scan each page.

"This is... comprehensive," I say, fighting to keep my voice neutral. "They won't even have time to think."

"They're paying for transformation," Erin explains. "That doesn't happen with downtime."

She watches me as she says it, and I feel the weight of her gaze. There's a challenge there, a test. As if she's waiting to see what I'll do, if I'll say something, here, now, in front of Layla.

I don't. Not yet.

She lifts a hand toward a nearby staff member, skin sun-kissed and expression unreadable. "Mateo makes the best mojitos on the island. Would you like one, Sam?"

"Sure," I say with more enthusiasm than I feel.

We sit in silence as Mateo muddles the mint. The rhythm is slow, methodical. Too slow.

I can feel Erin watching me, her gaze heavy with expectation. The tension between us stretches like elastic, pulled taut by six years of distance. Still, I say nothing.

The citrus tang of lime hits the air, sharp and bright. It twists in my stomach.

Mateo drops ice into the shaker and the clatter jolts me.

Erin doesn't flinch. Her smile remains serene, but her fingers are curled tightly around her glass.

She's not sipping anymore.

She's waiting.

The mojito is perfect. Of course it is. Just the right balance of sweet and sour, with fresh mint that must have been picked minutes ago.

"So, what exactly do you want me to capture?" I ask, letting the question land softly.

"The journey," Erin says, and it's almost comical how serious she sounds. "The before and after. The moments of breakthrough. The connections between the women." She leans forward like she's delivering sacred truths. "These aren't just wealthy women on vacation, Samantha. They're seeking something profound. Your job is to frame that search, that discovery."

My eyes turn down to the folder. The schedule, the structure, the polished language. My thumb presses into the edge of the page until it curls.

I look up. Nicholas is in the doorway, silent. Watching. His face gives nothing away, but there's something in his gaze, sharp, assessing.

Erin follows my line of sight, then lights up with practised charm. "Nick, darling, join us. Sam was just getting acquainted with the programme."

Nicholas moves toward us with that same measured grace, taking the seat next to Erin rather than next to me.

"And what do you think?" he asks, his eyes never leaving my face.

"It's..." I search for a word that won't betray the storm inside me. "Impressive. Very thorough."

Something passes between Erin and Nicholas, a glance so quick I almost miss it.

"I think I understand what you want," I say. "Beautiful moments, transformations, connections. Capturing women at their most vulnerable."

I feel the word like a stone in my stomach.

"Their most authentic," Erin corrects, smile never faltering. "There's a difference."

Is there? I wonder. Or is authenticity just another product being sold here?

"You always did understand what people needed," I say, the words carrying a weight only Erin might catch.

She tilts her head slightly, studying me. "We all have our talents."

I sip my mojito. Erin raises her glass in a silent toast, our eyes meeting over the rims. A perfect picture of old friends reunited. Only we both know what lies beneath the surface, what happened between us, what led to six years of silence. And as Nicholas watches us with that calculating gaze, I realise I have no idea which one of us he's really studying.

CHAPTER NINE

Dinner is served on the terrace as the sun bleeds into the horizon, painting everything in gold and crimson. Fresh seafood that was no doubt caught earlier today, tropical fruits arranged artistically on platters, and wine that flows as endlessly as the waves below. The conversation revolves entirely around the retreat: the participants Erin has enrolled, the transformations she envisions for each of them, the content goals for the week.

Content that I am going to be key to providing.

"Petra Grady. Alessandra Moore. Yes, yes," Erin says, scrolling through her phone. "Sarah Templeton. Forty-two, recently divorced, inherited her father's manufacturing company but lacks confidence in running it. Classic imposter syndrome."

Layla nods approvingly. "Perfect candidate for the Authentic Self Framework."

"The Authentic Self Framework?" I ask, leaning in. "What's that?" I try to keep my tone as natural as possible, but I can still hear the tension running through my words.

Erin hides her face by dipping below the brim of her hat, but she makes it look like a natural movement.

"Erin's trademarked transformation model." Layla smiles without missing a beat.

"Trademarked," I repeat, my eyes never leaving Erin. "It must be good, then."

"All of the customers seem to think so," Layla says, her voice light and soft.

I maintain my neutral expression, but my lips tighten. Nicholas notices. I catch his quick glance at my face before his eyes return to Erin.

"And Maya Lawson," Erin continues. "Finance executive, workaholic, relationship issues. She needs to reconnect with her feminine energy."

Don't we all?

"Lawson?" Nicholas asks, his first contribution to the conversation in ten minutes. "I recognise that name. She's back again?"

Erin nods. "With add-ons for the private coaching sessions and the exclusive content package."

"Good," he says, and falls silent again.

I listen more than I speak, watching the dynamic between the three of them. Erin dominates, naturally. Layla supports and amplifies, occasionally offering a suggestion that Erin either embraces as brilliant or dismisses without consideration. Nicholas observes, speaks only when necessary, his contributions brief but precise.

It's a well-rehearsed dance, and I'm the only one who doesn't know the steps.

What I do know, though, is the Authentic Self Framework.

"The transformation photos are crucial," Erin says, pivoting her attention to me. "We need before and after imagery that shows a visible shift. Lighting, expression, body language: they should all tell the story of profound inner change."

"Even if that change hasn't actually happened?" The question slips out before I can stop it.

The table falls silent. Layla looks horrified, her fork frozen halfway to her mouth. Nicholas's expression, interestingly, doesn't change at all, but his eyes fix on me with new intensity.

Erin's laugh breaks the tension, though it doesn't reach her eyes. "Oh Sam, always the sceptic! The change happens precisely because we visualise it first. We're just helping them see what's possible."

"It must be an incredible framework," I say.

Erin turns to Layla, smoothly changing the subject, and the moment passes. But I catch Nicholas watching me for several minutes afterward, his expression unreadable in the fading light.

After dinner, Erin announces she needs to prepare for tomorrow. Layla immediately stands to assist her, leaving me alone with Nicholas on the terrace. An awkward silence falls between us as the staff clears the dishes with calm efficiency.

"This is quite an operation," I say finally, gesturing vaguely at the villa, the view, the invisible machinery of Erin's business.

Nicholas takes a slow sip of his whiskey. "You have no idea."

Something in his tone makes me look at him more closely. "You don't seem particularly enthusiastic about it."

He shrugs. "It's not my passion. It's hers."

"But you're still part of it. Actually, couldn't you take the photos? The camera does all the work, after all." I say it as if I'm joking, but really I'm not. The more time I spend here, the more I wonder why they need a tag-along as a photographer at all.

Is Erin really doing this to try to make things up to me?

And just how long does she expect me to stay silent?

"I handle the business side," Nicolas sighs. "Structure, finances, legal." He swirls the amber liquid in his glass. "Erin provides the vision, the content, the performance."

The way he says '*performance*' catches my attention.

"You make it sound like she's acting."

Nicholas looks at me directly for the first time that evening.

"Aren't we all?"

I don't answer immediately, taking a moment to study him. In this setting, he seems different from the rigid man I met in the Cotswolds. His linen shirt hangs open at the collar, revealing a sliver of tanned skin. His posture is looser, less controlled. The Caribbean setting suits him in a way the English countryside didn't.

It's time for *me* to change the subject.

"How did you two meet?" I ask.

He almost smiles. Almost. "Oh, in London. She was just starting to gain attention for her work."

"And what did you do before... this?" I wave my hand to encompass the villa, the business, their life together.

"Finance." His answer is clipped, but then he surprisingly elaborates. "Private wealth management. I helped rich people become richer."

"And now?"

"Now I help one rich person become richer."

There's a dry humour in his voice I haven't heard before.

I take a sip of wine.

"You must have been good at your job. This is quite a step up from wealth management."

Nicholas studies me, then sets his glass down deliberately. "Erin didn't tell you, did she?"

My heart beats faster.

"Tell me what?"

He leans forward slightly. "I was one of her first clients."

The revelation sits between us, unexpected and loaded with implications. "A client? For...?"

"Personal transformation coaching. Before the retreats, before the social media empire." His voice remains neutral, but something flickers in his eyes. "I was successful, but miserable. Classic burnt-out executive. She promised to help me find purpose."

I try to imagine Erin, pre-fame, coaching Nicholas. It's difficult to reconcile. "And did she? Help you find purpose?"

His laugh is so quiet I almost miss it. "She certainly changed my life." He stands abruptly, moving to the terrace railing to look out at the darkening sea. "Have you known many happy people, Samantha?"

The question catches me off guard. "I... I suppose so. Why?"

"I've found they're quite rare." His back is to me now, his silhouette sharp against the twilight sky. "True happiness. Not the performed kind that fills social media feeds."

I stand too, drawn to this unexpected philosophical turn. "Is that what bothers you about all this? The performance?"

He doesn't answer directly. Instead, he asks, "How much do you know about the Authentic Self Framework?"

I stumble for words, and I'm flooded with relief when we are interrupted.

"Nicholas." Erin's voice floats out from inside the villa, sharp despite its melodic quality. "Can you come here for a minute?"

Whatever he was about to say, it's lost in the Caribbean night.

He drains his glass and sets it down with deliberate care. "Get some rest, Samantha. Tomorrow the real show begins."

He moves toward the door but pauses beside me. For a brief moment, his hand touches my arm, light but unmistakable. "Be careful, okay?"

Careful?

I don't have time to ask him what he means, or to tell him that he doesn't need to worry about me.

I remain on the terrace long after he's gone, watching the stars emerge over the Caribbean Sea. The breeze carries something from inside: the sound of raised voices, just for a moment, before falling silent again. Erin and Nicholas, disagreeing about something?

75

About me, perhaps? The thought sends a chill down my spine despite the warm tropical air.

Tomorrow the real show begins, Nicholas said.

But I know it's already started.

I know that the next few days on this island are going to be anything other than a paradise.

Because the Authentic Self Framework was my idea.

And Erin's life should have been mine.

CHAPTER TEN

The next morning arrives in a burst of hazy sunshine. I wake disoriented, momentarily forgetting where I am until the sound of waves reminds me: Aruba. Paradise.

Erin's world.

I slept fitfully, plagued by a dream where I stood before a mirror that refused to show my reflection. Instead, Erin stared back at me, mimicking my movements with perfect precision. When I reached to touch the glass, our hands met, and suddenly I couldn't remember which side of the mirror I stood on. Which one of us was real.

I shake off the unease and stumble to the bathroom. Even half-asleep, I notice that someone has entered my room while I slept. An outfit has been laid out for me on a hanger behind the bathroom door: a white linen dress with a delicate gold belt. My toiletries have been rearranged, lined up with mathematical precision. Even my camera has been moved, placed on the dresser at a perfect right angle to the edge.

This should disturb me more than it does.

It should surprise me more than it does.

After the past few days, I'm becoming accustomed to having my boundaries silently crossed.

I accept the wardrobe choice and after a swift shower, I prepare for the day.

The white linen dress feels cool against my skin as I examine myself in the mirror. For a second, I do almost mistake my reflection for Erin: same clothes, similar silhouette. It's as if I'm slowly being erased and redrawn in her image. Last night's dream echoes in my mind and I shake it off.

"You're not her," I whisper to my reflection. "Remember that."

But as I stare longer, the differences between us seem to blur. My hair, lightened by yesterday's sun, looks more golden than its usual dishwater brown. My skin has already taken on a glow from the Caribbean light. Even my posture has changed, unconsciously mimicking Erin's confident stance.

Part of me is repulsed by this transformation. But another part – a part I don't want to acknowledge – is thrilled by it. After months of feeling invisible, worthless, it's intoxicating to step into a life where people notice me and value me. Even if it's only as Erin's echo.

Downstairs, the villa has transformed overnight. Fresh flowers everywhere. Infused water stations. Meditation cushions arranged in a circle. Personalised welcome baskets waiting by the front door, each tied with a ribbon bearing a participant's name in elegant calligraphy: Sarah, Maya, Alessandra, Petra and the others. These are the names I memorised from last night's team meeting. I want to treat these women as the individuals that they are. To me, they aren't just clients, they are women who deserve the authentic changes that they've come here for.

Everything is immaculate, camera-ready, and arranged to a tee. The Authentic Self Framework in physical form; a stage set for transformation.

My Framework. My concept. My vision for authentic change, now twisted into this Instagram-perfect performance.

Erin stands in the centre of it all, channelling staff with the precision of a film director. She's wearing linen pants that could have been cut from the same cloth as my dress, styled with a silk blouse. Her hair is swept into an effortless looking updo that probably took an hour to achieve.

I wonder for a moment whether that style would suit me, and curse myself for thinking it.

"Samantha!" she calls when she spots me. "Perfect timing. Everything is set up in the main room. I need you to get some establishing shots before everyone arrives."

I spend the next hour photographing the villa, trying to capture the atmosphere Erin has so carefully created. The camera she gave me is indeed intuitive enough that even my rusty skills produce decent results. I find myself enjoying the process, rediscovering an old pleasure in framing shots, seeking interesting angles, playing with light.

Despite everything.

"These are fantastic," Erin says, reviewing my work on a tablet. "You haven't lost your touch at all."

The praise shouldn't matter to me, but it does. I've been starved for validation for so long that even this small acknowledgment feels significant.

Despite everything.

The warmth that spreads through me at her words is embarrassing – like a stray dog wagging its tail at the first person who offers it scraps.

"I had a good teacher," I say, and immediately regret the words. We both know I taught her photography, not the other way around. Back in university, when we'd wander London with my camera, me showing her how to frame a shot, how to work with natural light.

She pauses, and I think she'll acknowledge it. Instead, she smiles as if I've said something charming. "We taught each other so many things, didn't we?"

When I don't answer, she clears her throat and changes tack.

"The guests will be arriving soon. Why don't you get some shots of the entrance? I want to capture their first impressions."

I nod and make my way to the villa's grand hallway, positioning myself to capture both the approaching cars and the reactions of the women as they step into Erin's carefully constructed world. As I adjust the settings on the Leica Q2, I can't help but wonder how many other things from our shared past Erin has rewritten in her mind.

The participants begin arriving at eleven, chauffeured in a fleet of luxury SUVs. Eight women, exactly as the dossiers described them. Successful, affluent, seeking something they believe Erin can provide. They greet her with the reverence usually reserved for celebrities or spiritual leaders, their expressions a mixture of excitement and nervous anticipation.

I circulate among them, camera in hand, invisible behind the lens. I capture their arrival, their first impressions of the villa, their interactions with each other. Erin has instructed me to focus on '*authentic moments,*' though nothing about this feels authentic to me.

As I review the images on my camera's display, something catches my eye. In the background of several shots, almost out of frame, Maya Lawson appears to be watching Erin with an intensity that borders on fixation. Not with the adoration of the others, but with a focused scrutiny that seems almost... analytical.

I recall Nicholas mentioning last night that Maya had attended one of Erin's retreats before. That would explain the recognition in her eyes, perhaps even her comfort in this environment, compared to the wide-eyed newcomers. Still, there's something in her observation that seems different – not the gaze of a returning devotee, but something more calculating.

Interesting.

I make a mental note to keep an eye on Maya. Previous attendee or not, her attention feels more deliberate than casual familiarity would explain.

Once all eight women have arrived and been given welcome drinks, Erin leads them toward the beach, gesturing for me to follow. The morning light is perfect – golden and warm, casting everyone in the most flattering glow. Despite myself, I find satisfaction in capturing these beautiful images.

Whatever else is happening here, there's no denying that Erin has created a visually stunning experience.

I wonder for a brief moment if I would have created anything nearly as impressive with my idea, if she hadn't stolen my plan and run with it. Could I really ever have pulled something like this off?

I hate myself for even thinking it.

But a part of me – the part of me that thought maybe I could get used to living in a motel and eating pasta a la ketchup as a treat meal – thinks that there's no way I could ever have made the Authentic Self Framework a success like Erin has.

The thought settles like poison in my stomach as I continue taking photos, capturing expressions of wonder and anticipation as the women follow Erin toward the beach. Even my bitterness can't deny that she's good at this: the performance, the attention to detail, the way she makes each woman feel like the most important person in her orbit.

The welcome ceremony takes place beyond a line of thatched roof tiki huts. The tropical vibes could hardly be stronger. The women form a circle around Erin, who leads them through a ritual involving burning sage on a small fire-pit in the sand, setting intentions, and sharing their '*transformation goals*'. I photograph it all, moving quietly around the periphery, catching expressions of hope and vulnerability.

My self-doubt evaporates when Erin speaks.

"The Authentic Self Framework begins with recognition," Erin tells them, her voice carrying easily over the sound of waves. "Recognising the masks we wear. The false selves we present to the world."

My finger freezes on the shutter. My words. Verbatim from the concept document I drafted six years ago. The document that mysteriously disappeared from my laptop after Erin used it for '*research*'.

Maybe she's better at executing my vision than I would have been, but they're still my words. My concepts. My framework.

I lower the camera, momentarily unable to continue. The audacity of it – not just stealing my idea, but reciting my exact words while I stand here documenting it. Whatever doubts I had about my own abilities fade beneath the resurgence of anger and betrayal.

"Sam?" Nicholas appears at my side, his voice low. "Everything okay?"

I didn't notice him approach.

"Fine," I say, raising the camera again. "Just taking a moment."

Before I can say anything else, he's gone, moving back towards the villa with his usual quiet efficiency.

I force myself to continue photographing the ceremony, focusing on my breathing to stay calm. With each familiar phrase Erin speaks – my phrases, my ideas – my grip on the camera tightens. By the time the ritual concludes, there's a dull ache in my jaw from clenching my teeth.

Erin announces that lunch will be served on the terrace, and the group makes their way back to the villa. I hang back, genuinely needing a moment alone to compose myself. As I stand there, watching the waves, I wonder how I'll make it through the entire retreat. Watching Erin perform my ideas as if they were her own, all while I document it for her marketing materials.

Five thousand pounds, I remind myself.

Five thousand pounds to restart my life.

Both of us know it's nowhere near enough.

During the lunch break, one of the women, Julia according to her name badge, approaches me.

"You're Erin's friend from university, right?" she asks. According to her dossier, she's the CEO of a tech startup, here to '*recalibrate her personal and professional boundaries*'.

How very.

"That's right," I confirm. I'm not good with new people, and I suddenly feel awkward and vulnerable without my camera to hide behind.

Erin told me to take a break with the rest of them, but perhaps I would have been more comfortable with the Leica Q2 around my neck. I'm not one of them. I'm not one of the participants, and I'm not really one of the crew.

What am I even doing here at all?

I know what Erin did to me.

She knows what she did to me.

And yet, here I am, watching her living my dream – even if that dream has been twisted into something I never intended it to be.

She studies me with interest. "You look so much like her. Has anyone ever told you that?"

"Not until recently," I admit.

"It's uncanny," she continues. "Especially from certain angles. Are you related?"

"No, just... friends." The word feels strange in my mouth.

"Well, she speaks very highly of you. Says you're incredibly talented."

This surprises me. "She talked about me?"

Julia nods. "During our preparatory call yesterday. She mentioned her dear friend would be documenting the retreat. Said you had an extraordinary eye for capturing authentic moments." She lowers her voice slightly. "She seemed really excited you were here. Called it a '*fortuitous alignment*' that you could join us."

My chest tightens. Fortuitous alignment? As if my desperate situation was some kind of cosmic convenience.

"She mentioned you'd been through some challenges recently," Julia continues, oblivious. "And that watching people navigate life's obstacles inspired her to develop the Authentic Self Framework in the first place."

The world seems to tilt beneath my feet. This is a whole new level of manipulation – not just stealing my idea but weaving my personal struggles into her origin story. Making my failures part of her brand narrative.

I'm saved from responding by Erin herself, who materialises at my side with the silent grace of a cat.

"Julia! I see you've met Samantha." She loops her arm through mine in a gesture of casual intimacy. "We've known each other forever, haven't we, Sam?"

"It feels that way sometimes," I reply, which isn't quite a lie.

"You two could be sisters," Julia observes.

Erin laughs, squeezing my arm. "People used to confuse us all the time at university. Remember that professor who could never keep us straight?"

No such professor ever existed. We didn't look alike then, and we don't look alike now. But I smile and nod, playing along with this fiction Erin is creating.

"Anyway," Erin continues, "I need to borrow my photographer for a moment. Technical discussion."

She leads me away from Julia, her grip on my arm firmer than necessary. "You're doing beautifully," she says once we're out of earshot. "The women are responding to you."

Her compliment glides over me.

"So apparently we look alike now," I say, testing her reaction.

"People see what they want to see," Erin replies with a dismissive wave. "Anyway, it's useful."

"Expect? Useful how?" I have no idea where she is going with this.

She stops walking, turning to face me fully. "Trust is transferable, Samantha. If they trust me, and they see *you* as an extension of *me*, they'll open up to you. Give you better shots. More authentic moments. That's why I chose an outfit for you that's similar to mine. We give off the same energy. It relaxes people."

I'm not sure how relaxing it is for me.

I frown. "So you *want* me to... pretend to be like you?"

86

"I want you to be yourself," she says, though her expression suggests otherwise. "But creating a calm, uniform, relaxing environment for the women is..."

"A step towards the perfect authentic framework." I look her dead in the eyes while I finish the sentence that I wrote.

It's not like I can disagree with my own philosophy. Not when it's working so very well for Erin.

I should confront her. Ask her why she's rewriting our history. Ask her why she hasn't even had the balls to apologise yet.

But the words stick in my throat.

Five thousand pounds.

I need that money.

I need this job.

I need to play along.

For now.

I know I've let her off the hook again as she glances at her watch, that same elegant Cartier.

"The afternoon session starts in fifteen minutes. The light in the meditation room should be perfect right now if you want to get some setup shots."

And just like that, the conversation is over. Erin glides away to prepare for the next activity, leaving me with the unsettling feeling that I'm being moulded into something or someone I'm not.

CHAPTER ELEVEN

The day passes in a steady stream of back-to-back activities. Guided meditation. Vision boarding. A *'vulnerability circle'* where the women share their deepest insecurities while Erin nods compassionately and offers tailored wisdom. I document it all, increasingly uncomfortable with my role as witness to these intimate moments.

The shimmer of late afternoon transforms the villa, bathing everything in a honey-gold luminescence that makes even the most ordinary objects appear precious. Erin gathers the women for the day's final session. They sit cross-legged on cushions arranged in a perfect circle, their faces glowing with the particular sheen that comes from equal parts tropical humidity and expensive serums.

"As we end the day, we focus on visualisation," Erin announces, her voice melodic yet authoritative. "The secret to transformation isn't about becoming someone new," Erin says, her voice carrying effortlessly across the circle of women seated on cushions around her. "It's about reconnecting with your authentic self, the person you were always meant to be."

She catches my eye as I adjust my camera settings, a slight smile playing at the corners of her mouth.

"Close your eyes," she instructs the group. "Picture that version of yourself. The authentic *you*. The you that lives beneath the masks and the compromises. See her clearly in your mind."

The women obediently close their eyes, their expressions softening as they follow her guidance. I continue taking photos, moving silently around the circle.

"Now," Erin continues, her voice dropping to an almost hypnotic cadence, "this is the crucial part. You have to *wish* you were *her*. You have to want it with everything inside you. Desire creates reality. You have to wish so deeply to be her that the universe has no choice but to make it happen."

Something in her tone makes me look up from my viewfinder. Erin is staring directly at me, her eyes unnervingly intense, as if the words are meant to penetrate my skull, to burrow into my brain and nest there. Not some benign guidance for her adoring clientele, but a message carved specifically for me, serrated and personal.

You have to wish you were her.

Do I wish I were Erin? Once, perhaps. Before I saw what she's done with my framework, how she's twisted it into this exclusive playground for the wealthy elite.

This isn't what I intended when I first sketched out the Authentic Self Framework. It came to me during my first real adult heartbreak, a breakup that left me eating instant noodles every night, scrambling to make rent, crying into the cheap wine that Erin provided.

Plus ça change, plus c'est la même chose.

My circumstances in the motel room eerily mirrored those that inspired the framework in the first place. *Navigating life's obstacles*, wasn't that what

Julia said? It sounds so much more sanitary phrased that way.

"There must be more to life than this," I told Erin back then, huddled in our tiny university flat.

"You don't have to dream bigger," she replied, refilling my glass. "You have to dig deeper. The person you want to be is already inside you. You just need to find her."

Those words, Erin's words, sparked something in me that night. I couldn't sleep, couldn't stop thinking about the concept. I spent weeks expanding it, developing methodologies, creating exercises, building a framework around that core idea. The Authentic Self Framework was born from Erin's seed, watered by my sweat and tears, grown into something that could help others like me, regular people struggling with confidence, with direction, with believing they deserved better. The girl next door, not the woman with the private villa.

I developed the framework for people who couldn't afford luxury retreats in tropical paradises. For people eating on a pound a day and wondering how they'd make rent. For people who needed actual authentic transformation, not Instagram-worthy performances of it.

Now I'm here, in this Aruban paradise, watching Erin profit from my rock-bottom epiphany.

I'm here for a reason.

I have to focus.

Instead of showing Erin my reaction, I snap another photo, adjusting my position to capture the expressions of the participants. They hang on Erin's every word. The Aruban sunlight filters through the villa's enormous windows, casting everything in a golden glow that makes the scene look almost holy. Erin is at the centre, radiant. Her disciples gather around her, eyes closed, deep in personal reflection.

Each of them apart from Maya. Her eyes are slightly open, her gaze fixed on Erin rather than turning inward as instructed. She almost looks as though she is studying Erin's performance.

I know I'm projecting my own feelings, and I'm worried that my negativity will seep into the women who have paid to be here. It's not their fault. None of this is their fault.

I take a deep breath, trying to ground myself, and I focus.

"This idea of reconnection," Erin continues, "is why I developed the Authentic Self Framework. It's not about adding something to your life, it's about removing the barriers between who you are now and who you *truly* are."

Despite myself, I find my own eyes closing, following Erin's instructions. I picture the Samantha I might have been: confident, successful, running my own business based on *my* Authentic Self Framework. In this visualisation, I'm the one leading a retreat, while Erin sits in a dingy motel room, scrolling through *my* life with bitter envy.

The image is so vivid, so satisfying, that when I open my eyes, reality hits me like a fist. For just a second, I'd been seduced by my own fantasy.

"Share what you saw," Erin encourages the group. "What does your authentic self look like? How does she move through the world?"

One by one, the women describe their visualisations. More confident versions of themselves. Happier. Freer. Unburdened by the expectations of others.

Sarah, the recently divorced CEO, describes her authentic self standing at a podium, addressing shareholders without a tremor in her voice. Alessandra envisions herself creating boundaries with her demanding family.

When it's Maya's turn, she opens her eyes fully, her expression contemplative.

"I saw myself recognising patterns," she says, her finance background evident in her analytical approach. "Seeing the connections between past and present that others miss."

The other women nod politely, though some look slightly confused by her less emotional response.

"And in this vision," Erin prompts, "how does that make you feel?"

Maya's gaze meets Erin's directly. "Powerful," she says simply. "There's nothing more valuable than recognising something when others don't."

Something flickers across Erin's face, so brief I almost miss it.

"Interesting perspective," Erin says, smoothly turning to Judith. "And you, Judith? What did you see?"

The silver-haired publishing executive describes her authentic self as "*finally brave enough to write the novel I've always dreamed of.*"

Erin's smile tightens almost imperceptibly. "Beautiful," she says, but there's a hollowness to the word. "Remember, the path to authenticity isn't about becoming someone else. It's about shedding the false self to reveal what's always been there."

My own words. Again.

I lower my camera slightly, the weight of it suddenly oppressive in my hands.

"I think that's the perfect note to end our first day," Erin announces, her voice shifting to a more practical tone. "Take some time before dinner to reflect on your visualisations. We'll meet on the terrace at eight."

The women rise, murmuring appreciatively to Erin as they disperse. Maya lingers, her gaze moving between Erin and me before she follows the others.

Within minutes, the room is empty. Erin gathers the scattered cushions, piling them methodically in the corner.

"So, how was that for you?" she says without looking up.

I remove the camera strap from around my neck, setting the expensive equipment carefully on a side table.

What does she want me to say?

"I got some good shots, I think."

"And?"

"And what?"

She straightens, finally meeting my eyes. "What do you think of all this? The retreat. The framework in action."

The question hangs between us. My heart beats faster, my palms suddenly damp.

"I think you've done very well with it," I say carefully. "It's certainly profitable."

She tilts her head, studying me. "That sounds like criticism."

"Does it? I meant it as an observation."

"You've never been good at hiding your thoughts, Sam." She moves to the windows, adjusting the blinds against the late afternoon sun. "If you have something to say, just say it."

Of course I have something to say.

I have so much to say.

Too much to say.

The moment stretches between us, taut with unspoken accusations. Six years of silence, and now she wants me to speak first.

"Fine," I say finally, my voice trembling despite my efforts to sound controlled. "Are we really going to keep pretending? You didn't just take the framework, Erin. You stole my words verbatim. *'Shedding the false self to reveal what's always been there.'* That was from my original draft, word for word." I step closer, heart hammering against my ribs. "You didn't just take my ideas. You erased me from them entirely. Built your entire career, this whole perfect life, on something we both know you didn't create."

The golden Caribbean sunlight slices through the windows, illuminating dust particles between us like a physical manifestation of our shared, suspended history.

Erin turns from the window, composing herself before facing me fully. When she speaks, her voice carries a measured calm, but there's a tightness around her eyes that wasn't there before.

"I was wondering how long it would take," she says, examining her manicured fingernails as if we were discussing the weather.

"For what?" I demand, my fingernails digging half-moons into my palms.

"For us to have this conversation."

She moves toward me with that effortless grace, stopping just far enough away to maintain her advantage. I catch a subtle tremor in her left hand before she tucks it behind her back.

"It's been, what, four days since you arrived at my home? Longer than I expected, honestly."

I want to scream at her, to grab her by those perfectly toned shoulders and shake the smug composure from her face. Instead, I swallow hard, tasting metal. "And what did you expect? That I'd stay quiet forever? That I'd be so grateful for your charity I'd forget what you did? Of course we were going to have this conversation!"

She tilts her head, studying me with the clinical detachment of someone observing an insect under glass. But there's something else there too, a wariness that wasn't present before. The careful distance she maintains between us suddenly seems less about power and more about protection.

"Of course," she says, calmly.

The casualness of her response ignites something in me. "Your whole *authentic* life is built on screwing over someone who was supposed to be your best friend," I say, my voice low but sharp. "You stand there talking about removing barriers to authenticity while living the most inauthentic life imaginable."

"And yet you're here now."

"As what? Your photographer? Your assistant?" I gesture at the clothes she's provided, the camera she's given me. "I have to wear your clothes to look like you, so people are '*relaxed*'... but did you ever think about how it feels for me? Watching you up there, spouting my words, my ideas, while I document it all like some... some shadow."

Erin's head tilts slightly, her expression softening into something that resembles pity. "Did you not consider any of this when you accepted my offer to come to the Cotswolds? I thought with you accepting that you'd put the past behind you." She shrugs elegantly. "Bygones should go bye-bye."

"Just like that?" I stare at her, incredulous, wincing at her words.

"Just like that." Her voice is light, dismissive.

"Why would you think I'd ever let this go?"

"Because you have nothing else." The words fall between us like stones. She doesn't say them cruelly. She speaks almost gently, in fact, which somehow makes it worse. "Your husband left. Your job disappeared. You were living in a motel with what, three pounds to your name? And I offered you a way out."

The accuracy of her assessment stings more than any insult could. I take a step back, suddenly aware of how close we've been standing, how much space she occupies in the room despite her slender frame.

"So this is charity? Your way of making amends?" I ask.

Erin sighs, moving to a plush chair and sinking into it with effortless elegance. "Does it matter? I'm offering you a chance, Sam. Five thousand pounds."

Before I can protest that it's nowhere near enough, she raises a hand. "Not enough. I know. But there's exposure to my network. A foot in the door of an industry you once wanted to be part of."

"Once," I say. Am I still even the slightest bit interested in this? Maybe in my version, not hers. "You've twisted all of my ideas."

"Ideas you never would have implemented." Her voice sharpens slightly. "Let's be honest, how many brilliant concepts did you start and abandon at university? The app for student meal sharing. The vintage clothing exchange. The mindfulness journal that lasted exactly three entries."

Each example lands like a slap. She's right, of course. I had ideas, always ideas, but never the follow-through. Never the ruthless determination that Erin possesses.

"That doesn't make what you did right," I say, but my voice lacks its earlier fire.

"No," she agrees, surprising me. "But I made it successful. And now I'm offering you a piece of that success." She leans forward, her expression suddenly earnest. "Not just the five grand, Sam. We could work together. Officially. Beyond this retreat."

She gestures around the luxurious space, then at herself: the perfect hair, the designer outfit, the aura of success she wears like a second skin.

"All of this could be yours too," she says, her voice taking on that hypnotic quality she uses with her clients. "You created the framework. You understand it better than anyone. In some ways, you might even be better suited to this life than I am."

My eyes fix on her, trying to read the truth behind her words. Is this another manipulation? Or a genuine olive branch?

"Why would you offer that?" I ask. "Why now? If you wanted me in on it, you wouldn't have..."

She knows what she did. We both do.

Something shifts in her expression; there's a flicker of vulnerability so brief I might have imagined it.

"I told you before. I miss having someone who calls me on my bullshit. I want someone to make sure I stay true to..." Her eyes turn away for a split second, and then she's back. "I want the framework to be everything you thought it would be. Maybe only *you* can make that happen."

Before I can respond, the door opens and Nicholas appears, his timing impeccable as always.

"Everything okay in here?" he asks, his gaze moving between us. "We need to start getting ready for dinner."

Erin stands smoothly, her mask sliding back into place. "We're fine. Just catching up on old times." She turns to me with a smile that doesn't quite reach her eyes. "Think about what I said, Sam. The offer's genuine."

As she follows Nicholas out of the room, I'm left with the distinct impression that I've just been offered something significant. Whether it's an opportunity or a trap, I'm not entirely sure.

CHAPTER TWELVE

When I return to my room to prepare for dinner, I find yet another outfit laid out on my bed. This time a white silk dress with a subtle shimmer that catches the evening light streaming through the windows. It's elegant in its simplicity, the fabric looking impossibly expensive, with a delicate gold bracelet placed beside it like an exclamation point. The choice doesn't feel random. Our matching outfits during the day caused more than one retreat participant to comment on our *coordinated auras*. Now it seems the twinning is to continue into evening, with an upgrade from casual resort wear to something more formal.

I'm not sure how easy it will be to give off the same energy as her when she is Queen Bee and I'm more of a tatty hornet. Still, for now, I'm choosing to go along with it.

Let there be no mistake. I am choosing this.

But I'm still reeling from Erin's proposition. Collaboration. A piece of her empire. After everything she did. After stealing my framework and cutting me out completely. Now she wants me involved? Am I going to go along with that too?

The thoughts circle as I slip the dress on, the cool silk sliding against my skin with a whisper. It fits as if it were made for me - another unsettling reminder that Erin knows my dimensions, my tastes, perhaps more about me than I'm comfortable with. The neckline frames my collarbones exactly as it would frame hers. The hemline hits at precisely the most flattering point of my legs. In the full-length mirror, I meet the gaze of someone vaguely familiar: me, but polished, refined, curated. The Sam Foster Deluxe Edition.

I fasten the gold bracelet around my wrist, the clasp clicking shut with a finality that makes me shiver. It feels like a shackle, binding me to choices I haven't fully made yet. The gold catches the light, beautiful but slightly uncomfortable against my skin. Just like this entire situation, dazzling on the surface, unsettling underneath. I could remove it, of course. I could change back into my own choice of clothes.

I could walk away.

But where would I go? Erin's earlier assessment echoes in my mind: I have nothing else. And we both know it.

The dinner is exactly what you'd expect from a luxury retreat: exquisitely presented, lovingly described by the private chef, and achingly pretentious. Eight women in designer resort wear hang on Erin's every word as she discusses '*embodied authenticity*' and '*integrated wholeness*'. Even as she daintily cuts into her perfectly seared scallop, Erin never breaks character. Every gesture is a performance, every anecdote carefully calculated to inspire or impress. The Authentic Self guru giving her disciples exactly what they paid twenty thousand pounds for.

Meanwhile, Nicholas watches the women from the head of the table with that same inscrutable expression. He's wearing a black shirt that's the perfect contrast to Erin's white dress, the two of them looking like opposite chess pieces positioned side by side at the end of the table.

I push grilled mahi-mahi around my plate, appetite diminished by the growing knot of resentment in my chest. The irony is suffocating: here I am in paradise, eating food I could never afford, surrounded by beautiful, accomplished women who have paid thousands to learn concepts I developed... yet none of them know I'm its true creator. Meanwhile, Erin smiles benevolently beside me, reaping the rewards of my intellectual labour.

I agreed to this arrangement, true, but each moment makes the price of my desperation feel steeper.

"Samantha has such an eye for authenticity," Erin says, gracefully redirecting the conversation my way. "Some of the photographs she's taken today genuinely capture the transformation process beginning in each of you."

She hasn't even looked at them yet. They could be terrible. But of course, that wouldn't matter. Erin is building me up to these women, adding another layer to her performance. I'm being woven into the tapestry of her retreat, another tool for creating the perfect experience these women have paid for. Authenticity expert by proxy.

All eyes turn to me, expectant. I manage a modest smile, though it feels like my face might crack from the effort.

"I just focus on the genuine moments," I say, surprised by how easily the words roll off my tongue. The affected wisdom, the gentle smile... I'm slipping into the role of collaborator with disturbing ease.

Perhaps I've already seen enough of Erin's performance that I've absorbed the rhythm of her show.

Maya tilts her head.

"And how do you determine what's genuine?" she asks.

"You can feel it," I reply after a pause. "There's a quality to authentic emotion that can't be manufactured."

I glance at Erin as I say this. Her smile remains fixed, but something flickers behind her eyes.

"Exactly right," she agrees smoothly. "Authenticity resonates at a frequency we can all sense, even if we can't articulate why. It's why the Framework is so powerful. It doesn't teach you something new; it helps you reconnect with what was always there."

My framework. My words. My ideas.

Nicholas slices into his fish with the side of his fork, the movement drawing my attention towards him. He's been mostly silent throughout dinner, observing rather than participating.

"What fascinates me," he says suddenly, his voice cutting through Erin's monologue about authentic connection, "is how differently people present themselves in different contexts." His gaze travels deliberately around the table before settling somewhere between Erin and me. "The person we show to strangers versus loved ones versus... old friends."

There's something in the way he emphasises *old friends* that makes me wonder how much he knows about my history with Erin. The women nod thoughtfully, taking his comment as another profound insight to contemplate, but I notice Erin stiffen beside me.

"Nicholas has a background in behavioural economics," she explains smoothly, reclaiming control of the conversation. "He's always analysing people." Her tone is light, affectionate even, but there's a current of tension underneath.

I'm almost waiting for her to tell everyone how *he* was involved with the development of my framework, but of course that particular truth isn't part of the origin story she sells. Instead, she places her hand over his, the diamond on her ring catching the light as she gives him a smile of such practised adoration that the women around the table practically melt. Several exchange glances, visibly charmed by this display of marital harmony. I wonder if I'm the only one who notices how Nicholas's fingers remain perfectly still beneath hers, neither reciprocating nor pulling away.

The conversation shifts to tomorrow's activities as dessert is served. It's a delicate tropical fruit pavlova that tastes like clouds and sunshine. I take a bite, letting the sweet meringue dissolve on my tongue while Erin outlines the beach yoga that will '*realign everyone's energy centres.*' But my attention keeps drifting from her words to the undercurrents pulsing beneath the polite dinner chatter.

Nicholas has barely touched his dessert, his eyes tracking Erin's movements with the focus of someone monitoring for irregularities. Twice now, Erin has checked her watch with subtle flicks of her wrist that wouldn't register unless you were looking for them. And Maya, seated diagonally across from me, alternates her attention between Nicholas and Erin with unsettling precision, as if cataloguing their interactions. When she catches me observing her, she doesn't look away. Instead, she raises her eyebrows slightly, a silent question or perhaps acknowledgment that we're both witnessing something beneath the surface.

"Samantha will be capturing key breakthrough moments during tomorrow's revealing exercise," Erin announces, startling me back into the conversation. "It's fascinating how often people don't recognise their own transformation until they see it reflected back at them." Her eyes meet mine, holding just a beat too long. "Sometimes we need someone else to show us who we really are."

The weighted significance of her words lands like a stone in my stomach. Is she talking about the retreat participants, or is she talking about me?

A memory surfaces of Erin's voice from our earlier conversation: *I miss having someone who calls me on my bullshit.* The intimacy of that admission felt genuine, a rare crack in her polished facade. Could she actually be talking about herself? Asking me, in this coded way, to be that mirror for her?

I search her face for clues, but Erin's expression remains perfectly calibrated for her audience: open, wise, benevolent. Whatever vulnerability she showed me earlier has been tucked away, hidden beneath layers of performance so convincing that I wonder if I imagined that moment of honesty between us.

I glance around the room at the others, suddenly hyperaware of everyone's performance: Nicholas's detached efficiency, Maya's studied intensity, the other women's affected vulnerability. In this paradise of forced authenticity, I realise I know nothing certain about any of them, or perhaps even myself.

The framework was built on truth-telling, but as I watch Erin work the room with calculated precision, I can't shake the feeling that I've walked willingly onto a stage where everyone knows their lines except me. And in my experience, that's when accidents happen.

CHAPTER THIRTEEN

The dinner concludes with polite smiles and promises of transformation, the participants floating back to their rooms in a haze of wine and validation. I linger on the terrace, the night air warm and heavy with the scent of frangipani. The rhythmic chirping of cicadas creates a pulsing soundtrack to the evening as I watch palm fronds sway against the star-filled Caribbean sky.

"Walk with me?" Erin's voice materialises beside me, that familiar blend of request and command.

After our confrontation earlier, I'm surprised she wants to be alone with me, but curiosity propels me forward.

We descend to the beach in silence, both removing our sandals at the edge where travertine meets sand. The moon carves a silver path across the water, so bright I can make out the silhouettes of fishing boats on the horizon. For several minutes, we walk without speaking, my toes sinking into sand still warm from the day's intense Aruban sun, the gentle waves leaving lacy patterns of foam that dissolve almost as quickly as they form.

"Earlier," Erin finally says, "we were interrupted."

We continue walking, leaving parallel tracks in the wet sand.

"Nicholas has convenient timing," I say.

"He's protective." She stops, turning to face the water. The Caribbean stretches before us, seemingly endless. "Of the business. Of me."

"How much does he know?" I ask. "About the framework? About what happened between us?"

A warm breeze lifts her hair, carrying the salt-sweet scent of the sea. For a moment, she looks almost vulnerable against the backdrop of endless horizon.

"Things are... complicated right now," she says, her voice barely audible above the waves.

"Complicated how?" I press, sensing an opening.

Erin kneels, sifting coral-white sand through her fingers, a gesture incongruously childlike against her polished appearance.

"Nicholas is... invested in maintaining our current trajectory." Her voice carries a note I haven't heard before, something almost like hesitation. "He's built a lot around the framework's success."

"Does he know the whole story?" I ask carefully, watching her expression in the moonlight.

Her eyes meet mine briefly before sliding away. "He knows enough."

"Enough," I repeat, the word hanging between us like the humid Aruban air. "That's convenient."

"I was already building the business when I met him," she says, rising and brushing sand from her white dress. "He was..."

"A client. I know. He told me."

She looks surprised, momentarily thrown off balance. Something passes across her face. Perhaps she can't quite believe Nicholas would lower himself to have a conversation with me.

I hear her swallow before she continues. "I couldn't exactly tell him I'd only had the seed of the idea... that..."

"The seed?" I turn to look at her fully, disbelief sharpening my voice. "Is that what you call it?"

"You were having one of your moments," Erin says, a defensive edge creeping into her voice. A small wave breaks closer than expected, forcing her to step back. "Some pretty boy had dumped you or stood you up or... I don't even remember which crisis it was, but you were in one of those moods."

She gestures vaguely, as if summarising years of friendship with a dismissive wave. "Classic Samantha. '*Woe is me. Life is over.*' I suggested that maybe the person you wanted to be was..."

"Inside of me all along," I finish quietly. "Yes. I remember."

Perhaps Erin felt justified in taking the framework. After all, hadn't she provided that initial spark? But a spark isn't a fire. They weren't her late nights that were spent researching psychological techniques, her careful development of exercises and methodologies, her meticulous organisation of it all into a comprehensive system. She gave me a match; I built the bonfire.

And then, I suppose, I let it burn out.

I watch a distant fishing boat drift across the horizon, its lights tiny against the vast darkness.

"So that's how you justify it to yourself? You gave me a throwaway line of comfort, so you deserved the framework I spent months developing?" My voice rises. "And what do you mean, '*Classic Samantha*'? What are you trying to say?"

Erin sighs, as if explaining something obvious to a child. "You hang all of your dreams onto men that are

109

just no good for you," she says. "Back then, and clearly more recently." Her gaze flicks over me, a subtle reminder of the state in which she found me: abandoned and destitute.

The casual cruelty of her assessment leaves me momentarily speechless.

"Wow," I finally manage. "Just... wow."

Erin's expression shifts immediately, her features softening in the moonlight. "Look, I'm sorry," she says, her voice gentling. "I want to make things right. I've been thinking about it for a long time." She steps closer, her voice dropping to something intimate, almost confessional. "When I saw the notification that you liked my picture, I thought it was fate. That we were meant to get back in touch."

The hairs on my arms rise despite the warm night air.

"I *do* owe you a lot," she continues. "I know that. The five grand for this week? It was just to get you onboard. I meant what I said earlier. You could become a part of this. You could finally get the benefit of what I've built."

I don't answer. The twisted divi-divi trees cast strange shadows in the moonlight, their shapes distorted by the constant wind into something almost menacing.

Erin fills the silence, her words tumbling out faster now. "Look, you would never have turned that idea into this success, and you know you wouldn't."

The bluntness of her statement lands like a slap.

"Because I didn't have the chance," I say finally. "You made sure of that."

110

"No," she insists, "because you never follow through on anything. How many brilliant ideas did you have at university? How many business plans sketched on napkins? How many did you actually pursue?"

I clench my jaw, hating that there's a grain of truth in her assessment. Hating that she's already told me this during our confrontation earlier. Hating, most of all, that it's exactly what Daniel, my ex-husband, said when he was packing his bags to leave.

"Always dreaming up businesses, never following through. Always comparing yourself to everyone else."

I was always full of ideas, always starting projects with enthusiasm, only to abandon them when the next inspiration struck. The accusation feels like a splinter under my skin: painful because I can't entirely extract it.

"The framework was different," I say, but my voice lacks conviction.

"Was it?" Erin presses. "Or was it just the latest in a long line of Samantha Foster's brilliant concepts? If I hadn't taken it and run with it, it would be sitting in a drawer somewhere with all your other unfulfilled potential."

I want to argue, but doubt creeps in like the tide, gradually erasing our footprints. Would I have developed the framework into a successful business? Or *would* it have joined my other abandoned projects, forgotten until someone else had a similar idea?

"You had the concept," Erin continues, her voice softening. "I had the drive to make it real. We could

111

have been partners from the beginning if you'd been more... reliable."

"Don't you dare," I warn, finding my voice again. "Don't you dare rewrite history. You didn't offer partnership. You took everything and disappeared."

Erin's shoulders sag slightly. For the first time, she looks genuinely regretful.

"I made mistakes," she admits. "I was young, ambitious. Scared."

"Scared?" I repeat incredulously. "Of what?"

"Of needing you more than you needed me." The admission seems to surprise her as much as it does me. She turns away slightly, staring at the dark horizon. "You were always the talented one, Sam. Ideas came so easily to you. I was afraid if we were partners, you'd eventually realise you didn't need me."

I almost laugh at the absurdity of it. "So your solution was to steal my framework and cut me out completely?"

"I told myself I was being practical," she says. "That I was protecting myself. And then it worked, really worked, and suddenly there was money, recognition. It all happened so fast." She kicks at the sand, disrupting a tiny crab that scuttles away in alarm. "By the time I realised what I'd done, it was too late to go back."

The sincerity in her voice makes something twist inside me. Is this the truth, finally? Or just another performance?

"And now?" I ask, trying to keep the waver from my voice.

112

"Now I need you," she says, turning to face me fully. The moonlight casts half her face in shadow, making it impossible to read her completely. "You planted this seed, Sam. I may have taken it, nurtured it, made it grow. But I know it's your philosophy at the core."

She moves closer. "The framework is flourishing, but it's growing in directions I never anticipated. It needs to be guided back to its roots." She gestures toward the distant lights of the villa. "Those women deserve the real transformation you envisioned."

A wave larger than the others surges up the beach, nearly reaching our feet. The water recedes, leaving bubbles of foam that glimmer in the moonlight before dissolving into nothing.

Her words hang between us, seductive in their apparent honesty. Part of me wants to believe her, the part that remembers our friendship before everything fell apart. But another part, the part forged in the aftermath of her betrayal, remains wary.

"If that's true," I say carefully, "why didn't you reach out before now? Before you saw me at rock bottom?"

Erin's gaze drops to the sand. "Pride. Fear." She looks up, meeting my eyes. "And shame, I suppose. The longer it went on, the harder it became to imagine making it right. And... I wasn't sure you would accept it."

I'm not sure either. I'm not sure about anything.

Movement catches my eye further up the beach. A figure standing in the shadows of a cluster of palm trees, watching us. As they step slightly into the moonlight, I recognise Maya's silhouette, the distinctive curve of her shoulders unmistakable even at this distance.

"We're being watched," I murmur, suddenly aware of how isolated we are on this stretch of moonlit beach.

Erin follows my gaze, her body tensing. "Maya."

"Was she listening to us?"

"I don't know." Erin's voice tightens with controlled panic. "But this is meant to be a sacred environment. Peace. Relaxation. Safety. Hearing us argue isn't good for her journey."

As Maya turns and hurries back toward the villa, I realise I've reached a crossroads. I can walk away from Erin and the game we are playing, or I can step deeper into this tangled web.

The problem is, I'm not entirely sure which option I want anymore.

I say nothing, waiting. The waves continue their rhythmic pattern against the shore, filling the silence between us.

"I need to think about everything," I say finally. "And I'm tired now. I need to go back to my room."

"Of course." She smiles, confident in a way that makes me wonder if she ever doubted my response. "Take all the time you need."

We walk back toward the villa in silence, my mind churning with unanswered questions. What does she really want from me? Why this sudden desire for reconnection? And how exactly does Nicholas fit into all of this?

Erin squeezes my arm lightly. "Get some rest. Tomorrow is another day of transformation."

I watch her glide back into the villa, graceful and self-assured, before making my way to my room. The night air wraps around me like a damp blanket as I climb the stone steps, the scent of salt and tropical flowers mingling with my confusion. Behind me, the ocean continues its ancient rhythm, indifferent to the human dramas playing out on its shores. I can't shake the feeling that beneath Erin's perfect paradise, dangerous currents are stirring, and somehow, I've been pulled into their path.

CHAPTER FOURTEEN

Back in my room, I peel off the white silk dress, letting it pool at my feet like spilled moonlight. Sand clings to my ankles, tiny crystals that catch the light as they scatter across the marble floor. My skin feels tight with dried salt and secrets.

The shower calls to me, promising to wash away more than just the beach. I step into the bathroom, automatically reaching for the shower handle with the tentative touch I'd developed at the motel. For weeks, I'd performed a delicate dance with that temperamental fixture: turn it thirty degrees left, wait five seconds, then ease it back fifteen degrees to coax lukewarm water from rusted pipes. The muscle memory lingers even as my fingers meet sleek brushed metal that turns with buttery resistance.

Water cascades instantly from the rainfall showerhead, a perfect temperature without adjustment. Steam billows around me as I step beneath the spray, and for the first time in hours, my shoulders begin to relax. No rust-coloured water. No sudden icy blasts. No need to plead with ancient plumbing.

As I close my eyes and let the water sluice away the sand and salt, Erin's words from the beach replay in my mind: *Now I need you.*

Aruba's finest bath products line a teak shelf within arm's reach: artisanal soaps infused with local botanicals, shampoo that boasts bond maintenance and cuticle restructuring technology, and a conditioning mask containing rare Aruban black coral.

I didn't even know my hair had cuticles. The bottles are minimalist, matte black with gold lettering, the kind that don't even need to mention they're paraben-free because anyone who can afford them already knows.

The luxury surrounding me feels different now. Not like charity. Like restitution.

This is the world Erin lives in. The one I helped create and was written out of. But as I massage an oversized blob of shampoo into my scalp, a revelation settles over me like the steam filling the bathroom. All of this exists because of something I created. My framework. My concept. My vision.

I rinse my hair, watching suds swirl down a drain that doesn't clog. As the water spirals away, so does any last illusion I might've held. A bitter laugh escapes me, echoing off marble tiles. My intellectual property is funding this paradise.

Don't I *deserve* some of this? A taste of the success that should have been mine?

Erin's offer plays on repeat in my mind. A partnership. A place in this empire she's built on my foundation.

I step out onto a bathmat thick enough to sink into, wrapping myself in a towel that feels like it's been woven from clouds. The mirror has fogged completely, hiding my reflection, which feels oddly fitting. Who am I in this scenario? The rightful creator seeking justice? The desperate woman grasping at any lifeline? The fool walking straight into another trap?

117

I drift back into the bedroom, moving automatically, limbs heavy, as if carrying the weight of too many unasked questions.

I slip into cotton pyjamas provided by Erin, another reminder of my dependence, of how thoroughly I've stepped into the world she controls. The bed beckons with its crisp white duvet and mountain of pillows, a far cry from the thin, suspicious mattress I'd endured for weeks.

The contrast between silk and cotton mirrors everything else: luxury and comfort, performance and rest, her world and mine somehow blending at the edges.

Yet despite the comfort, despite the physical exhaustion weighing my limbs, I toss on the plush mattress, replaying my conversation with Erin, searching for hidden meanings, for what she might really want.

Now I need you.

But why? What has changed?

The ceiling offers no answers as I stare upward, tracing patterns in the textured plaster. No water stains here. No cracks. No mysterious shadows that look like faces. Just perfect, unblemished white.

The room grows smaller with each passing thought. Erin's offer. Nicholas's warning to be careful. Maya watching us on the beach. By three in the morning, the walls feel like they're pressing inward, and I need air.

I pull myself from the bed and step onto the balcony, hoping the night breeze will clear my head. The tropical humidity has lifted, leaving something clearer, sharper. Stars pierce the darkness with impossible brilliance, no city lights to dim their glow. Below me, the villa sleeps in apparent peace - no lights in windows, no voices carrying across the manicured grounds.

But as I lean against the rail, movement on the beach catches my eye.

Two figures walking close together, partially hidden by shadows cast by a row of palm trees that line the property's edge.

The moonlight catches blonde hair, the distinctive silhouette I've come to know well over the past days: Erin. But who is she with? The second figure is taller, broad-shouldered. Nicholas, I assume at first. But something about the way they move together seems off, too cautious, too secretive for a married couple.

They pause where the beach curves, heads bent close in what appears to be intense conversation. I strain to make out details, but the distance is too great, the darkness too complete.

As they pass beneath one of the solar-powered path lights that dot the beachfront, I catch a clearer glimpse of the second figure. It's definitely not Nicholas. This man is heavier, with different posture, different movements. He gestures emphatically with his hands as he speaks: a habit I haven't observed in Nicholas's careful, controlled movements.

They pause again. This time, the stranger hands something to Erin, a small object I can't identify from this distance. She pockets it quickly, then glances around as if checking they're unobserved.

I instinctively step back into the shadows of my balcony, heart suddenly racing, though I'm clearly too far away for them to spot me. The night air, pleasant moments ago, now feels charged with something dangerous.

What am I witnessing? A business meeting? A romantic rendezvous? Something else entirely?

The stranger points toward the villa, saying something I can't hear. Erin shakes her head emphatically, her hand on his arm in what looks like restraint or warning. Their body language suggests disagreement, tension. After another minute of conversation, they part ways, the stranger walking down the beach towards a path that leads to the road, Erin returning to the villa.

I watch her progress along the moonlit sand, her white dress billowing slightly in the ocean breeze, making her look like a ghost gliding across the surface. She moves with purpose, shoulders set in determination rather than her usual fluid grace.

Only when she disappears into the villa's shadows do I retreat into my room, closing the balcony door quietly behind me. The cool air conditioning raises goosebumps on my skin after the tropical warmth outside.

I lie back on the bed, mind racing with possibilities, none of them reassuring. Why would Erin meet someone secretly in the middle of the night? What did he give to her?

The pieces refuse to fit together. The perfect wellness guru with her perfect husband and her perfect business meeting a stranger like a character from a spy novel. The woman who stole my framework and built an empire now claiming she needs me to save it. The successful entrepreneur, who could have reached out at any time, choosing the moment of my absolute desperation to reconnect.

What game is Erin playing? And what role has she cast for me in whatever drama is unfolding in this paradise?

CHAPTER FIFTEEN

I wake to insistent knocking, the kind that suggests the person on the other side of the door won't be going away. Sunlight streams through the windows, much too bright for early morning. A glance at my phone confirms what the light is telling me: 8:47am. I've overslept by hours.

"Samantha?" Layla's voice carries barely contained panic. "I need to speak with you. Now."

"Just a minute," I call, scrambling out of bed.

I straighten my pyjamas and flatten my hair on the stumble across the room.

When I open the door, I find Layla looking uncharacteristically dishevelled, her usual polished appearance fraying at the edges.

"Have you seen Erin this morning?" she asks, without preamble.

Something cold settles in my stomach. "No. Why? What's happened?"

"She didn't show up for the eight o'clock yoga session." Layla's voice is tight but controlled. "I checked her room, of course. Nicholas said she wasn't there when he woke up at seven, but that's not unusual for her."

Through my sleepy haze, I'm already remembering seeing Erin on the beach last night and putting pieces together. I open my mouth to tell Layla what I witnessed, then stop. I don't actually know *what* I saw.

Erin meeting someone secretly at 3am, then missing by morning? I don't know what that means yet. I saw her return safely to the villa. Whatever happened after that, I wasn't involved. And knowing Erin, this disappearance is as deliberate as everything else she does.

"I'm sure she's fine," I manage instead.

"Oh yes," Layla says in bold agreement. "I'm certain of it. It's the damage limitation that I have to deal with. I've told the women that Erin received an urgent call from her publisher in New York - some crisis with her upcoming book launch that required an early morning video conference. They're not entirely convinced, but it's bought me time."

A book. Of course there's a book. Another milestone in Erin's meteoric rise that she never mentioned, another success built on foundations I helped lay. The familiar sting of exclusion twists in my chest, but I push it down. This isn't the time to catalogue fresh wounds. Not when I don't yet understand what's really happening here.

Instead, I focus on the relief that floods through me knowing Layla thinks Erin is all right, and that she hasn't told the retreat attendees the truth about her being off grid. If Layla can't find Erin, the group doesn't need to know yet. Eight wealthy women learning their guru has vanished without explanation would be absolutely catastrophic - not just for Erin's reputation, but for these women who've invested so much hope in their transformation journey.

"What about Nicholas?" I ask. "He's not worried?"

"He said she probably went for a walk on the beach and lost track of time." Layla's tone suggests she finds this as implausible as I do. "He's not concerned, which honestly makes this easier to manage."

The walk on the beach seems accurate enough, after what I saw this morning. I wonder how much Nicholas knows.

"She wouldn't lose track," I say, with a frown. "She..."

Layla cuts me off.

"Erin has a lot on her mind right now. I'm not sure any of us know exactly what is going on in her head, but you really shouldn't worry yourself about her," she says.

My stomach clenches, but not from fear for Erin's safety. My first instinct is suspicion, not concern. The rational part of my mind insists that nothing happens to Erin Blake unless she wants it to. She's always been the one pulling strings, orchestrating outcomes. Maybe this disappearance is just another performance, another way to test loyalties or manipulate situations to her advantage.

I should at least seem more concerned, so I ask, "How can I help? Should we split up to search the beach? Check with locals in town? Is it too soon to call the police?"

Layla frowns and gives me a tight-lipped smile.

"The women are expecting a full day of programming. Meditation at ten, followed by the barrier identification workshop, then this afternoon..." Layla pauses, looking visibly shaken. "I can't lead these sessions, Samantha. I manage logistics, not transformation work."

124

I stare at her, the implication slowly sinking in. She's not asking me to help search for Erin. She's asking me to *replace* her.

"What are you suggesting?" I have to hear it from her.

"You've been observing Erin's sessions since we arrived. You understand her methods, her approach." She turns her eyes downward as she continues. "You know the material..."

Of course I do. It's my material.

Until now, I didn't know that Layla knows that too.

The realisation hits me like ice water. My breath catches, and I have to grip the doorframe to keep from swaying.

How long has she known? Since she started working for Erin? Is this common knowledge among Erin's inner circle, or does only a select few know the truth about how the Authentic Self Framework really came to be? My mind races through every interaction I've had with Layla, searching for signs I missed, clues that she knew exactly who I was and what I represented.

Seemingly impervious to the revelation she's just dropped, Layla's voice takes on a pleading quality. "Could you step in? Just for today? Until she comes back?"

The request hangs between us like a live wire. Here it is - my chance to see what life would have been like if I'd had the courage to build my own business instead of letting Erin steal my framework and run with it. What if I'd been the one to take that leap? Would I have thrived or crumbled under the pressure?

The circumstances are terrible, but the opportunity to finally know feels both thrilling and terrifying.

"I'm not qualified to..."

But I want to. The thought surprises me with its intensity. Despite Erin's disappearance and my complete lack of credentials, I want this chance more than I want to admit.

"It's not therapy, it's life coaching. Motivational work." Layla's voice takes on desperate urgency. "I have all of Erin's session plans - her talking points, the exercises she uses, even suggested responses to common questions. I can send them over to you. These women paid twenty thousand pounds each, Samantha. They came here for transformation. If we cancel their sessions, if word gets out that Erin Blake simply... disappeared during her own retreat..."

Just because everyone who knows Erin seems to be treating this as business as usual doesn't mean the participants would see it that way. To them, their expensive guru simply vanishing without explanation would look like abandonment - or worse. The implications are clear. Lawsuits. Media attention. The complete destruction of everything Erin has built - including the business based on my stolen framework.

"I don't know if I can pull it off," I say, my mind already racing through possibilities despite my protests.

"You can do this," Layla insists. "You just need to follow the script."

Follow the script. Use my own concepts, filtered through Erin's interpretation, to guide women through

126

transformations they desperately want. The irony is almost suffocating.

"What if someone asks where she is? What if they want to speak with her directly?"

"Tell them she's handling the publishing crisis, but will rejoin the group as soon as possible. That she specifically asked you to maintain the program's integrity in her absence." Layla's voice carries desperate hope. "Please, Samantha. I don't know what else to do."

The weight of the request settles over me. Somewhere in those session notes are my ideas, my techniques, my life's work - packaged and presented as someone else's expertise. Using them now feels like a betrayal of something I can't name. But what choice do I have?

"Alright," I hear myself saying. "I'll try."

"Thank you. I'll get the info to you right away. I know it's too short notice for you to handle the 9am workshop; I'll have to cancel that and make excuses, but the next session starts at ten. I'll tell the women you're stepping in as Erin's replacement facilitator." Relief floods Layla's voice. "Actually, this might work better than I hoped. Erin's been introducing you as her dear old friend all week. The participants already trust you. And with how much you two look alike, especially in her clothes..." She trails off, but the implication is clear.

All those comments about our resemblance. The matching outfits. Erin positioning me as her long-time confidante. Was she preparing for this moment? Did she know she might need someone to step into her shoes?

"And Samantha?" Layla pauses at the doorway. "Try to keep them focused on their inner work. The last thing we need is them asking too many questions about where Erin has gone."

I force my expression to remain neutral, nodding as if this is all perfectly reasonable. As if my world hasn't just tilted on its axis. "Of course. I understand."

Before I can say anything else, she's gone, hurrying down the hallway with the nervous energy of someone whose carefully orchestrated plan is unravelling.

I take thirty seconds to splash water on my face and change into fresh clothes: another outfit from Erin's curated wardrobe, this one a simple linen dress in a shade of blue that deepens my eyes. With no time for makeup or proper styling, I pull my hair into a loose knot.

In the bathroom mirror, I pause. The woman staring back looks polished, confident, like she belongs in this world of luxury retreats and transformation coaching. Like Erin. The resemblance everyone keeps mentioning suddenly seems more pronounced, as if I'm slowly morphing into her image.

Cleaner, well-dressed, a hint of sun to my skin: we *could* be sisters.

The admission unsettles me more than I expect.

Is this what she wanted? For me to become her replacement so seamlessly that no one would notice the difference?

Or at least no one who cares.

I touch my reflection, half-expecting to see Erin's hand move instead of mine. The blue dress, the expression, even my posture. Everything has been carefully reinforced to create this illusion. But am I her equal or her puppet?

My reflection offers no answers, only more questions. The stranger staring back at me tilts her head, and I realise I'm unconsciously mimicking Erin's mannerisms. When did that start?

I force myself to look away and hope I look presentable enough to face eight women who paid twenty thousand pounds each to hear Erin speak my words.

CHAPTER SIXTEEN

The main meeting area of the villa buzzes with subdued conversation as I gather the women for the ten o'clock session. They settle onto cushions in a loose circle, some still clutching coffee cups, their expressions a mixture of anticipation and uncertainty. Without Erin's commanding presence, the energy feels different: less polished, more human somehow.

"Thank you all for your patience today," I begin, settling cross-legged in the spot where Erin sat yesterday. The tablet with her session notes rests beside me, though I find I barely need to glance at it. "I know Erin's absence for your first sessions was unexpected, and I'm sorry that you have missed them." I almost throw in the offer of a refund for the skipped yoga and meditation; it's what I would have done if this were my retreat. Instead, I give them another untruth. "Erin specifically asked me to lead this section on barrier identification."

The lie flows smoothly, more easily than it should.

"Now, I've been observing Erin's work closely," I continue, "and I actually collaborated with her on developing some of these concepts."

Not entirely untrue, just a matter of who collaborated with whom.

Julia raises her hand tentatively. "Will Erin be joining us later? I had specific questions about the authenticity exercise from yesterday."

My heart beats faster, but I keep my voice steady. "She's handling the media issues, but she'll rejoin us as soon as possible. In the meantime, let's focus on your breakthrough work."

I guide them through the opening meditation, surprised by how naturally my voice takes on Erin's cadence. The breathing exercises, the gentle instruction to '*release your anxieties*' - it all feels familiar.

"Barriers," I say, once they've opened their eyes, "are rarely what they appear to be on the surface. We think our barrier is fear of failure, but really it's fear of success. We think it's about money, but it's about worth. It's about value."

The women lean forward, engaged. These concepts flow from somewhere deep in my understanding - not from Erin's notes, but from the original place where I developed them years ago.

"Sarah," I say, "yesterday you mentioned feeling like an imposter in your own boardroom. What if that feeling isn't a barrier but a signpost?"

She blinks, considering. "A signpost to what?"

"To the parts of yourself you've been hiding. The authentic leader you are, not the one you think you should be."

Her eyes widen with recognition, and I feel a surge of satisfaction I haven't experienced in years. This is what I imagined when I first developed the framework - these moments of genuine breakthrough, of helping someone see themselves clearly.

I move through the group, offering insights that seem to come from nowhere and everywhere at once. With Alessandra, I explore how her people-pleasing patterns mask a deep creativity she's afraid to express. With Judith, we uncover how her perfectionism protects her from the vulnerability required for the novel she dreams of writing.

Each conversation feels electric, charged with possibility. The women respond to me differently than they did to Erin - less reverent worship, more genuine connection. I'm not performing transformation; I'm facilitating it.

The work feels effortless, intuitive. For the first time in months - maybe years - I feel competent. Valuable. Like I'm exactly where I'm supposed to be.

A flash of guilt cuts through my satisfaction. I *should* be worried sick about Erin. I should be out there searching for her, not sitting here basking in the attention that rightfully belongs to her. But the guilt fades as quickly as it rose, replaced by a rationalisation that feels almost virtuous: I'm helping these women. I'm keeping the retreat on track. I'm doing what Erin would want me to do.

Aren't I?

And if I'm honest with myself - brutally honest - there's a small, dark part of me that whispers this is where I should have been all along. These are my concepts, my insights, my framework. Maybe Erin's absence is simply the universe correcting itself.

The thought should horrify me, but it doesn't. It feels like truth.

What if she doesn't come back? The question surfaces unbidden, and I'm shocked by the thrill that accompanies it rather than dread. What if whatever happened to her last night was... permanent? Could I step into her life completely? These women already trust me. Layla sees me as a viable replacement.

I could be Erin Blake. I could have the life that should have been mine from the beginning.

The realisation should terrify me. Instead, it feels like an awakening.

The women's voices bring me back to the moment, their engagement proof that my dark thoughts might not be so unreasonable after all.

"This is remarkable," Julia says during a brief break. "You have such insight into these patterns. Have you done this kind of work before? Thank you, Erin - oh God, sorry! You're just so... you remind me so much of her."

Maya speaks up from across the circle. "Yes, *Samantha*, tell us more about your background. How long have you been working with these concepts?"

There's something in her tone - not accusatory, but probing. And the way she stresses my name feels deliberate, pointed. I feel heat rise to my cheeks, my moment of confidence wavering.

"I've been... studying personal development for years," I say carefully. I've certainly read enough self-help books in my time. None of them did much for me, though. Although to be fair, after googling *'how to get your life back on track'* from that godforsaken motel room, I ended up here, so maybe there's something to be said for the power of the universe's twisted sense of humour. "Working with Erin has deepened my understanding."

"Studying where?" Maya presses gently. "Do you have certification in coaching or therapy?"

My mouth goes dry. "I'm not a licenced therapist, no. This is more... life coaching. Motivational work."

"Of course," Maya says with a smile that doesn't reach her eyes. "I'm just curious about your training. These insights seem so natural to you."

Because they are natural to me. Because I created this framework. Because every word coming out of my mouth originated in my mind years ago.

But I can't say that.

"Experience is the best teacher," I manage, then quickly redirect. "Shall we continue with the paired exercises?"

I have the women couple up to identify their three primary barriers, just as Erin's notes suggest. As they work, I move between the pairs, offering guidance and asking clarifying questions. My confidence returns as I watch the breakthroughs happening around me. This is what I was meant to do. This is what the framework was designed for.

But as I crouch beside Maya and her partner, I notice something that makes my pulse quicken. Maya has a small leather journal open beside her, and she's been writing throughout the session. Not just personal reflections - I catch a glimpse of what looks like observations, notes about the session itself. I see fragments: "natural authority..." and something that might be "background..." before she notices my gaze and casually closes the journal.

"How's the exercise going?" I ask, trying to keep my voice light despite the sudden tightness in my chest.

Maya looks up, her expression serene. "Wonderfully. You have such a gift for this work. Almost as if..." She pauses, studying my face with those sharp, analytical eyes. "Almost as if you've been doing it your whole life."

I force a smile.

"That's kind of you to say," I reply, but my voice sounds strained even to my own ears.

Maya tilts her head slightly, still watching me with that unsettling intensity. "Have we met before, Samantha? There's something so familiar about you."

I almost stutter. "I don't think so. I'd remember."

"Hmm." She opens her journal again, pen poised. "Maybe it's just that you remind me of someone."

She means Erin, obviously.

Of course Maya would see it - everyone else has. It's meant to make the women feel more relaxed, but there's something in her expression that doesn't match the others' easy acceptance of our supposed similarity. Something more analytical. More suspicious.

When we saw her on the beach last night, was she following us, or was it coincidence that she was there? She soon disappeared when we looked in her direction.

My thoughts are halted as footsteps echo from the hall. Nicholas appears in the doorway, his expression unreadable but urgent. The energy in the room immediately shifts, and I feel a mixture of relief at the interruption and dread at what he might be about to tell me.

"My apologies," he says, his voice carrying across the space. "Samantha, I need to speak with you. Now."

The finality in his tone makes my stomach clench. Is Erin back? Or has he found something else - something about what I witnessed last night?

"Of course," I say, rising. "Ladies, please continue your discussions. We'll rejoin the group shortly for sharing."

As I follow Nicholas from the room, my legs feel unsteady beneath me. The confident woman who had been leading the session just moments ago seems to evaporate with each step down the hallway. Whatever Nicholas has discovered, whatever has stripped away his usual composure, I know it's going to change everything.

CHAPTER SEVENTEEN

In the hallway, Nicholas guides me a short distance from the door, his expression unreadable.

"You're leading the session," he observes. It's not approval. Not criticism either. Just a statement of fact. I'm surprised Layla didn't tell him, but at the same time, I'm not surprised at all.

"Someone had to," I say, a little more defensively than I mean to. "The participants were getting restless. Have you found her?"

He doesn't answer. "Walk with me," he says instead.

I remember Erin using the same words before we took to the beach yesterday. Nicholas's tone is more of a command than an invitation.

We move through the villa, and although his steps are unhurried, his demeanour grates on me. Every beat of calm from him feels less like composure and more like indifference.

"Aren't you worried?" I ask bluntly. "She's not answering her phone. No one's seen her all morning."

I hesitate, then add, "When did *you* last see her?"

The question hangs between us. I think of Erin on the beach last night, her white dress ghostly in the moonlight, taking something from that stranger.

Nicholas doesn't answer. Instead, he steps forward, opens the door to one of the rooms, and gestures for me to enter.

"Erin is perfectly capable of taking care of herself," he says. "She always has been."

Isn't that what I thought too? That this was just another of Erin's performances?

A faint shiver runs through me. Maybe we're both a little too quick to assume she's fine. A little too comfortable with her absence.

There's something disquieting about our shared calm. It's like standing in a room full of smoke and convincing yourself it's just steam.

Part of me thinks I should tell him everything I saw on the beach. But another part, perhaps the same part that never told Erin's university boyfriend that she was having a fling with the guy from the frisbee club, thinks this is something I should keep to myself – at least for now.

Some instinct warns me that getting involved in Erin's secrets never ends well for anyone.

He waits, holding the door.

I step past him into the room.

Inside, the master suite is starkly at odds with its setting, here in the laid back Caribbean. Where the rest of the villa leans into tropical opulence with soft furnishings, ocean breezes, and the faint scent of coconut and sea salt, Erin and Nicholas's room feels like a business bunker. The king-sized bed is pristine, the pillows smoothed and stacked with military precision. No sarong slung over a chair, no sandals kicked off at the door.

This isn't the room of someone who disappeared unexpectedly, it's the workspace of someone who finished their tasks and left everything in perfect order.

The confirmation sends a chill down my spine.

On the desk, a sleek laptop glows in sleep mode beside a rigidly ordered arrangement of colour-coded folders and printed schedules. Not a novel in sight. No evidence of relaxation, or pleasure. It looks less like a space for a woman to enjoy paradise and more like an operations room for orchestrating a war.

"She left a note for you."

The voice is so close behind me I flinch. I hadn't heard Nicholas move.

I turn sharply, pulse stuttering. He's standing just behind my shoulder, far too close. Calm. Watchful.

"For me?" I echo, trying to cover my unease.

A shadow crosses his face. "Well, it has your name on it. On the desk."

My eyes dart quickly. For a moment, I don't see the note. Then I spot it, beside the laptop. I take a step forward, the soles of my shoes too loud against the floor, and reach for it with fingers that feel stiff and uncertain.

The envelope is unsealed, flap tucked neatly inside. I draw out the note and unfold it carefully. The first thing I notice, before the words even register, is the handwriting. Precise, slanted, impossibly neat. So perfect a font could be created in its image.

A reflexive flicker of irritation stirs in me. Typical Erin. Always so composed, even in disappearance.

I catch myself.

She's missing.

This isn't how things were meant to be.

I shouldn't be thinking like this.

But even as I think it, doubt creeps in again. The pristine room. Nicholas's lack of concern. The careful arrangement of everything.

No one is worried, and I shouldn't be either.

The paper is smooth beneath my fingertips. For a second, I hesitate. It could say anything. An apology. A confession. A goodbye.

Bracing myself, I start to read.

Sam,

If you're reading this, I'm gone. I'm sorry for the abruptness, but it had to be this way. I need you to finish the retreat. You know the framework as well as I do, better, in some ways. The women will get what they came for.

Trust me when I say this is necessary. I'll explain everything when I can.

Remember when we used to joke about trading places? Now's your chance.

E

I read it twice, trying to make sense of the casual tone, the lack of explanation, the bizarre reference to trading places.

We *never* joked about that. Never.

We swapped clothes, sure, borrowed each other's jumpers and jeans, like all university flatmates do. And apparently, we swapped ideas too, if you can call her stealing mine *swapping*. But trading places? The lie sits there, bold and deliberate, as if she's rewriting our history even in her goodbye note.

140

"She planned this," I say, looking up at Nicholas. My voice sounds hollow to my own ears. "She knew she was leaving. And she didn't tell you?"

His expression remains maddeningly neutral. "Erin keeps her own counsel."

This man is infuriating. What does that even mean?

I can't control myself any longer.

"That's it? Your wife disappears without explanation in the middle of hosting eight paying clients, and your response is '*Erin keeps her own counsel*'?" Disbelief makes my voice sharper than intended. "Shouldn't we call the police?"

"And tell them what?" Nicholas counters. "That a grown woman chose to leave? That's not a crime, Samantha."

"But the retreat..."

"Will continue, apparently. With you in her place." He gestures to the note. "That's what she wants."

"And you're just... fine with that?"

Nicholas moves to the window, looking out at the perfect blue sky.

"Erin and I have an understanding. She does what she needs to do. I manage the consequences."

There's something in his voice. I'm not sure if it's weariness or resignation, but it catches me off guard. For the first time, I begin to question their marriage. What kind of relationship allows for this level of secretiveness, this casual disappearance?

And if he's not surprised... then maybe he knows more than he's saying.

Who did Erin meet last night?

Does Nicholas know?

141

Should I even ask?

Or should I protect her secrets, just like I always have?

I glance back down at the note, rereading the final lines. The calmness of her tone. The certainty.

Nicholas watches me. "I'll arrange payment for you, of course. For running the sessions."

I look up sharply. "Have you discussed this with Erin?"

He shrugs. "Did she mention it in the note?"

I shake my head, and something cold settles in my stomach. He's managing this like an HR issue, not a personal crisis.

He says nothing, as if it makes no difference either way.

And I realise: he didn't even bother to read Erin's note.

The only thing he's concerned about is keeping the retreat afloat. Erin ducks out, and his first instinct is payroll.

"Well," he says, as if that settles it, "you're stepping into her role. It's only fair."

My head spins at the implication. Erin earns tens of thousands from these retreats. Is he offering me a share of that just to step in and finish what she started?

"This doesn't make sense," I say. "Any of it. Why would Erin abandon her own retreat? Why would she ask me, specifically, to take over? Why didn't she tell you she was planning to leave? *Did* she tell you? Did you know?"

Nicholas turns back to me, his expression showing a flash of what might be anger, quickly suppressed.

"Those are excellent questions," he says. "Unfortunately, I don't have answers for you. What I do have are eight increasingly suspicious clients and a retreat that needs to be completed. So, the real question is: are you in, or out?"

I can't simply leave, abandoning these women who've paid small fortunes for transformation. But stepping fully into Erin's role feels like walking into a trap.

"I need to think about this," I tell him.

"You have until the end of the session currently taking place," Nicholas replies, his tone making it clear this isn't negotiable. "After that, either you're leading the retreat, or we're cancelling it and refunding eight very influential women. If you'll excuse me, I have some issues of my own to attend to."

He moves toward the door, then pauses.

"For what it's worth," he says without turning around, "I think you'll do better than she ever did. You actually believe in what you're teaching."

Then he's gone, leaving me alone with that loaded statement and a dozen new questions.

I sink into Erin's chair, trying to process what's happening. He's just left me here, in their room.

The seat beneath me still holds the faintest imprint of her presence, and yet she feels completely gone. I set the note down carefully on the desk and let my fingers drift toward the folders, the notebooks, the carefully arranged items that feel more like evidence than belongings.

Erin is gone.

Deliberately gone, not missing.

She expected, even planned, for me to take her place, to the extent of leaving detailed instructions. And Nicholas, rather than being worried or angry, seems merely inconvenienced.

But why? What does Erin gain by vanishing and leaving me in her place?

If she planned this, there might be more clues.

I start with the obvious places. The desk drawers. Pens lined up in perfect rows. Branded notepads. Retreat materials in labelled folders. But in the bottom drawer, beneath a stack of notes, something catches my eye: a sliver of paper tucked so close to the edge it almost disappears into the lining.

I slide it out with careful fingers.

Folded once.

No envelope.

Just a street address in Oranjestad, the island's capital, with today's date, and a time: 8:00pm.

My pulse quickens. Surely this can't be about the retreat.

Is this where Erin is?

Where she's meeting someone tonight?

I think of the stranger on the beach, the way they argued, the small object he handed over. Was this what they were discussing? An appointment? A deadline?

The clock on the wall shows 10:54am. Less than ten hours until whatever is supposed to happen at that address.

My mind races through possibilities, but the session I stepped out of ends in six minutes. I need to go back. Wrap things up. Smile. Reassure. Make everything look effortless.

But now I have a choice to make. Do I tell Nicholas about the address? Confront him with more questions he probably won't answer?

Or do I find out for myself what Erin is really up to?

I fold the slip of paper and slide it into my pocket alongside Erin's note, my heart thudding with the weight of both secrets.

Whatever game Erin is playing, I'm no longer content to be a passive piece on her board.

For now, I'll finish the session. Play the role she's cast for me.

I push open the door and step back into the hallway, the weight of both notes pressing silently against my side.

You have until the end of the session currently taking place.

After that, either you're leading the retreat, or we're cancelling it.

I take a deep breath I didn't realise I needed, and make my decision.

CHAPTER EIGHTEEN

I return to the main room where the participants are still engaged in their barrier identification exercise, their quiet conversations creating a low hum of therapeutic work. They look up when I enter, and I'm struck by the trust in their expressions. They've accepted me as a substitute for Erin with surprising ease.

"I'm so sorry about that interruption," I say, settling back into the circle with what I hope appears to be calm confidence. "Thank you for your patience. That was just some logistics we needed to sort out."

Several women smile reassuringly. "No problem at all," Julia says. "We've been having wonderful breakthroughs."

"I'm so glad to hear that." I check my watch. Four minutes until we're supposed to wrap. Nicholas's ultimatum echoes in my mind: *You have until the end of the session currently taking place.*

"Actually, let's make the most of our remaining time," I say. "Who wants to share their key insight from the exercise?"

Julia raises her hand first. "I realised my barrier isn't fear of failure, it's fear of being truly seen as successful. Like I don't deserve it."

"Beautiful recognition," I respond, the words flowing naturally despite my racing thoughts. "That's the paradox of authenticity. We fear being seen for who we really are because we've forgotten that person is worthy of love."

The women nod, several scribbling notes. I catch Maya watching me intently, her expression unreadable.

"Actually," I continue, making a split-second decision, "this energy is so powerful. Would anyone mind if we pushed through to lunch rather than taking a break? Sometimes the most valuable insights come when we stay in this flow state."

The women exchange glances, then nod eagerly.

"I'd love that," Sarah says. "I feel like I'm right on the edge of something important."

"Yes, let's keep going," Alessandra agrees, leaning forward. "I don't want to lose this momentum."

Even Judith, who'd seemed tired earlier, straightens with renewed energy. "This feels like exactly what I needed."

Only Maya remains silent.

"Wonderful," I say, warmth flooding through me at their enthusiasm. "Sarah, would you like to share what came up for you?"

Sarah takes a shaky breath. "I realised I've been sabotaging my own company because some part of me believes I don't deserve the success my father built. Like I'm betraying him by doing it differently."

"That's profound," I respond, leaning forward. "What if honouring his legacy means trusting the vision he saw in you when he left you the company?"

Her eyes fill with tears. "I never thought of it that way."

Alessandra shares next, her voice barely above a whisper. "I keep trying to make everyone else happy because I'm terrified they'll leave if they see who I really am. But I'm exhausting myself trying to be perfect for people who might not even like the real me."

"And what would happen," I ask gently, "if you trusted that the right people would love you not despite your imperfections, but because of your wholeness, including the messy, human parts?"

Each woman's vulnerability creates a deeper intimacy in the circle, and I find myself genuinely moved by their openness.

As we begin to wind down, I glance around the circle at their transformed faces. "What I want you to remember," I tell them, my voice taking on that particular rhythm I've heard Erin use countless times, "is that authenticity isn't about perfection. It's about presence. Being fully yourself in each moment, without apology."

My own words, but spoken in Erin's cadence. The realisation jolts me.

When did I start sounding exactly like her? The mystical phrasing, the pregnant pauses, even the way I'm holding my hands. Everything feels borrowed, performed.

"Excellent work this morning," I announce, standing gracefully and pushing away the unsettling thought. "Let's break for lunch now. We'll reconvene at one-thirty for our afternoon session on releasing limiting beliefs."

As the women gather their things, I'm satisfied with my decision to shorten the break. Less time for individual conversations means less opportunity for awkward questions about where Erin really is, or why I seem so familiar with concepts that are supposedly hers. In a group setting, the women support each other's transformations. One-on-one, they might start asking questions I'm not prepared to answer.

As the others move toward the terrace where lunch is being served, Maya approaches me. My strategic timing, it seems, hasn't deterred her at all.

"Quite a seamless transition," she observes. "From photographer to guru in less than a day."

"I'm just filling in," I say, keeping my tone light despite my racing pulse. "Erin will be back soon."

"Will she?" Maya tilts her head slightly, like a hawk studying prey. "Interesting that she'd leave in the middle of a retreat. Almost as if she knew someone could step in for her." She smooths her linen pants. "Someone who knows her material intimately. Almost as if they created it together."

"Erin had an emergency," I say, trying to sound believable. "I'm just trying to help."

"Of course you are." Her smile doesn't reach her eyes. "It's what friends do, isn't it? Step in when needed. Take over when necessary."

The words hang between us, loaded with implication. I open my mouth to respond, but nothing comes out.

Maya tilts her head, studying my reaction with obvious interest. "You know, I've been thinking about what you said yesterday. About capturing authentic moments." She taps her pen against her journal. "There's something so genuine about the way you handle the material. Almost like you've lived it yourself."

My pulse hammers in my throat. "I suppose all good facilitators draw from personal experience."

"Do they?" She takes a step closer. "Or do they draw from personal creation?"

The question lands square and hard. She knows. Somehow, impossibly, she knows.

"I should get to lunch," I manage, my voice barely steady.

"Of course." Maya's smile widens slightly. "We wouldn't want to keep the others waiting. They're so eager to continue learning from you."

Only then does she turn and walk towards the terrace, leaving me alone in the suddenly cavernous room.

I watch her go, noting the rigid set of her shoulders, the way she holds herself like she's perpetually braced for attack. No wonder she's so suspicious of everyone. She probably hasn't had a genuine human connection in years. All that analytical coldness, that need to dissect every interaction... Maya strikes me as the type of woman who's built walls so high she's forgotten there's supposed to be a door.

The thought is petty and cruel, completely at odds with everything this retreat teaches about compassion and authentic connection.

But it feels good.

I sink into the nearest chair, my legs suddenly unsteady. The morning crashes over me all at once: Erin's disappearance, Nicholas's ultimatum, the note

150

with my name on it, stepping into a role I never asked for but somehow knew exactly how to play. And Maya, with her pointed questions and calculating stare.

My hands are shaking. When did that start?

I take a deep breath, trying to think clearly. I just have to get through today. Lead the afternoon sessions, make it through dinner, act like everything is normal. Then tonight, I'll drive to that address in Oranjestad. Stay hidden, stay safe, just observe. Maybe I'll finally understand what Erin is really up to.

After that... well, I'll decide what to do with whatever I discover. Tell Nicholas? Go to the police? It depends on what I find.

But first, I have to survive the next eight hours without falling apart or letting slip that I know more than I'm saying.

Maya's questions are irritating, but she's not my biggest problem right now. She's fishing, but she doesn't actually know anything. I can handle one suspicious participant.

What I can't handle is eight wealthy women discovering that their guru has vanished and left an imposter in her place.

I stand up, smoothing my dress and checking my reflection in the window. Composed. Confident. Ready to continue the performance.

The lunch passes with a flurry of compliments on the morning session and gentle questions about Erin's return. I deflect with confident ease, surprised by how naturally the lies flow.

"Publishing emergencies," I explain with a knowing smile. "You know how demanding the industry can be."

The women nod sympathetically. Several mention they've enjoyed working with me, that I bring a different energy to the material. Warmer, they say. More accessible.

The praise should make me feel guilty about Erin's absence. Instead, it makes me feel vindicated.

Nicholas appears as we're finishing our grilled fish and tropical fruit salad. He moves through the dining area with his usual efficiency, checking that everything meets his exacting standards.

"How are we doing?" he asks, stopping beside my chair.

"Wonderfully," Julia answers. "Samantha has been incredible. We've had such breakthroughs this morning."

"I'm so glad to hear that." His smile is perfectly calibrated: warm but professional. "Erin will be delighted when she returns."

When, not if. The certainty in his voice strikes me as odd. How can he be so sure she'll come back when he doesn't even know where she's gone?

Unless he does know.

Or unless this is just another performance for the women.

Part of me wants to grab him by his perfectly pressed shirt and demand answers. *Your wife is missing*, I want to scream. *She left a cryptic note and vanished in the night, and you're standing here making small talk about lunch service like nothing's happened. What kind of husband are you?*

But I can't. Not here, not in front of eight women who've paid for a transformative experience. Not when I'm the only thing standing between them and complete disappointment.

So I smile and nod, swallowing my frustration like bitter medicine.

"She'll be so pleased to hear how engaged everyone is," I manage, my voice steady despite the anger churning in my chest.

Nicholas gives me a smile in return, as perfectly calibrated as mine, as hollow as the space where his concern for his missing wife should be. For a moment, we're co-conspirators in this performance, both protecting the retreat's facade for our own reasons.

The moment stretches uncomfortably before he moves on to check the dessert service, leaving me with the unsettling realisation that we're both very good at pretending everything is fine.

CHAPTER NINETEEN

The afternoon sessions pass more smoothly than I dared hope. I lead a workshop on '*Releasing Limiting Beliefs*' that builds naturally on the morning's work. The women are more engaged, more trusting, leaning into the process with an openness that both moves and energises me.

Sarah shares how she's spent years sabotaging her own success, afraid she'd surpass her late father's achievements. It comes from a place deep within that perhaps she would never have reached without this retreat. I'm rooting for her to feel like a true, unapologetic leader by the end of tomorrow.

Alessandra admits she's been so busy pleasing everyone else that she's forgotten what she actually wants. Now she is starting to remember – and is committing to make it happen.

Each revelation feels like a small miracle, a life genuinely shifting course.

By four o'clock, I'm riding high on their trust, their breakthroughs, their gratitude. I feel more competent, more valued, more myself than I have in months. Maybe years.

The final session focuses on '*Integration and Commitment*'. I guide them through a visioning exercise where they imagine themselves six months from now, living authentically, barriers removed. Their faces glow with possibility as they share their visions.

"The key," I tell them, settling back into the facilitator's rhythm, "is to remember that authentic transformation isn't about becoming someone new. It's about returning to who you were always meant to be."

My words. My philosophy. My framework.

And I'm delivering it with a clarity and warmth that feels completely natural.

As we prepare to close the circle, Maya speaks up for the first time in hours.

"That's an interesting perspective, Samantha," she says, her voice deceptively casual. "About becoming who we were always meant to be. Tell me, do you ever wish you were her?"

The circle falls silent, the other women looking confused by the apparent non sequitur, but I understand exactly what Maya's asking.

"Her?" I manage.

"Erin," Maya says without missing a beat, as if she'd been waiting for exactly that response. "Do you ever look at her life, the success, the recognition, this beautiful retreat, and wish you could trade places?"

The other women shift uncomfortably, sensing undercurrents they don't understand. Julia clears her throat softly.

"I think we should probably wrap up," I say, forcing my voice to remain steady. "It's been such a full day."

"Of course," Maya agrees, but her smile is sharp. "Sometimes the most important questions are the ones we can't answer."

155

Over dinner, conversation flows; compliments for the day's work, excitement about tomorrow's sessions, and gentle speculation about when Erin might return.

I check my watch: 7:05pm. The address in my pocket seems to pulse with urgency. Whatever is happening at 8pm, I need to leave soon if I'm going to make it to Oranjestad in time.

But how do I extract myself without raising suspicions?

My hands shake slightly as I cut into my filet mignon. Maya's question from this afternoon circles in my mind like a vulture. *Do you ever wish you were her?* The casual cruelty of it, delivered in front of the other women like a therapy exercise rather than the psychological dissection it actually was.

"I've been thinking," Julia asks across the table, "about what you said earlier. About returning to who we were meant to be. It made me realise I've been wearing masks for so long, I'm not sure who's underneath anymore."

"That's the courage of authenticity," I respond automatically. "Trusting that whoever you find beneath the mask is worthy of love."

The words feel hollow now, performative. How can I preach authenticity while living a lie? While wearing Erin's clothes, teaching her clients, inhabiting her life?

The thought bubbles up, but I push it away. This isn't deception, it's reclamation. I'm not stealing Erin's life; I'm taking back what was always mine.

"You know," Alessandra adds, "you have such a natural gift for this work. Have you ever considered doing it full-time?"

156

The question hangs in the warm evening air. Several women turn expectant faces toward me, waiting for my answer. The irony is so bitter I can taste it. Have I considered it? I created it. I developed every exercise they've experienced today, every insight they've had, every breakthrough they've celebrated.

I could have been doing this.

I should have been doing this.

This. Was. My. Life.

"Not really," I say, looking away.

I check my watch again, as discreetly as possible: 7:32pm. My stomach clenches. I need to leave *now*. But the women are still lingering over dessert, savouring both the key lime tart and the day's emotional revelations.

"This has been such a profound day," Judith says, dabbing at her eyes with her napkin. "I feel like I've been carrying this weight for decades, and now..."

She trails off, overcome. The other women murmur supportively, reaching across the table to squeeze her hand. It's beautiful, genuine: exactly the kind of breakthrough the framework was designed to create.

And I'm about to abandon them all for a clandestine meeting I know nothing about.

7:34pm.

"You know what?" I say, perhaps a beat too quickly. "I think this is the perfect moment to close our day together. Sometimes when we've gone this deep, we need space to integrate."

Sarah nods eagerly. "Yes, I can feel myself wanting to just... sit with all of this."

"Exactly," I stand, hoping it doesn't look as abrupt as it feels. "Let's honour the work we've done today by giving it room to breathe."

The women begin to gather their things with the languid movements of people pleasantly exhausted by emotional labour. Too slowly. Far too slowly.

7:36pm.

"I think I'll take a walk on the beach," I announce, already calculating the drive time in my head. Twenty-two minutes to Oranjestad in good traffic. "Clear my head before tomorrow's sessions."

"Want company?" Julia offers.

My pulse spikes. "That's sweet, but I could use some solitude to process everything." The words tumble out faster than I intend. "Sometimes the facilitator needs integration time, too."

She nods understandingly, but I catch her glancing at Maya.

7:38pm.

"You've been amazing today," Julia says as they finally begin to disperse. "Truly amazing."

I smile and nod, making appropriate noises about tomorrow's program, but inside I'm screaming. Move. Please, just move.

7:39pm.

Finally, finally, the last woman disappears into the villa, and I'm alone on the terrace with my hammering heart and the rapidly darkening sky. My heart pounds as I head for the entrance, keys to one of the rental cars already clutched in my sweaty palm. Nicholas said we could use them for errands, after all.

I pray this qualifies as an errand.

I could just call a taxi, but something stops me. A taxi would mean records, a driver who might remember where he picked me up, what time, where he dropped me off. If something goes wrong tonight, if whatever I witness requires police involvement, I don't want my movements traced back to the villa. Don't want to explain to eight retreat participants why their substitute guru was sneaking around Oranjestad in the middle of the night.

Better to take the rental car and hope Nicholas doesn't notice I've gone.

He doesn't care that Erin is missing. If I vanish too, maybe he'll just ask Layla to stand in.

My hands shake as I unlock the door to the small SUV. I sit and adjust the seat and mirrors, quickly but carefully. The engine starts with a quiet purr that sounds deafening in the evening stillness. I head out of the drive with exaggerated care, as if driving normally might somehow expose me.

It's only when I reach the main road that I allow myself to breathe.

And that's when the full magnitude of what I'm doing crashes over me.

I'm driving alone through a foreign country, in the dark, to spy on someone who might be dangerous. I don't know who Erin was meeting on the beach. I don't know what she gave him. I don't know what I'm walking into.

What if it's not just a business meeting? What if Erin is in actual danger? What if *I* am?

My foot hovers over the brake pedal for a split second. I could turn around. Go back to the villa. Tell Nicholas everything: about the man on the beach, about the note with the address and time, about my growing certainty that Erin's disappearance is part of some larger mystery.

But even as the thought surfaces, I know I won't do it. I can't.

Not when I'm this close to potentially understanding what Erin Blake is really capable of.

Whatever I'm about to discover, whatever I'm about to witness, there's no going back.

I press harder on the accelerator; the speedometer climbs as the road straightens. The setting sun paints the sky in shades of orange and pink that would be beautiful if I weren't so terrified.

In the distance, Oranjestad's lights twinkle against the darkening sky, a sprawl of civilisation that could hide any number of secrets.

My heart thuds as I drive toward the unknown, toward answers that might destroy everything I thought I understood about the woman who stole my life.

The clock on the dashboard reads 7:42pm.

Eighteen minutes until I discover the truth.

Or until the truth destroys me.

CHAPTER TWENTY

The unfamiliar weight of the steering wheel feels wrong in my hands as I navigate the darkening streets of Aruba. Everything is backwards here, not just the driving, but the entire situation I've stumbled into. The GPS glows blue in the dashboard, its mechanical voice my only companion as I drive toward whatever truth Erin has been hiding.

"In 800 metres, turn left," it announces in crisp, infuriatingly calm British tones.

Left. In Britain, *left* would be the passenger side. Here, left means crossing into oncoming traffic, and my palms are already slick with sweat against the steering wheel. Every instinct screams that I'm doing this wrong.

Just like everything else lately.

The road curves away from the coast, palm trees giving way to small businesses and residential areas. Porch lights flicker on as the sun disappears behind low hills, and I catch glimpses of families through windows: mothers clearing dinner dishes, children watching television, fathers reading newspapers. Normal lives. Safe lives. Lives where people don't drive alone through foreign countries to spy on missing friends who may or may not be sociopaths.

"Turn left in 200 metres," the voice continues in those same crisp, patronising tones, as if it knows exactly how lost and out of place I am and finds it amusing.

I check my mirrors obsessively, looking for headlights that might be following too closely, cars that might have been behind me since the villa. A blue sedan has been in my rear-view for the past kilometre, but that could be coincidence. Couldn't it?

"Turn left now," the GPS commands with what sounds like barely concealed impatience, as if it's tired of dealing with someone too stupid to follow simple directions.

The intersection approaches faster than expected. I signal, wrong direction first, then correct myself, and turn across traffic. A horn blares behind me, and my heart hammers against my ribs. The blue sedan continues straight, and I exhale shakily.

"Paranoid," I mutter to myself. "You're being paranoid."

But paranoia feels reasonable when my entire reality has been systematically dismantled over the past week.

The GPS guides me through narrow streets lined with modest houses painted in tropical pastels. Bougainvillea spills over garden walls in brilliant fuchsia cascades, and the air through my cracked window carries the scent of frying plantains and distant ocean salt. It's beautiful, peaceful: everything my mental state is not.

"In 600 metres, turn right onto Wilhelminastraat," it announces, pronouncing the Dutch street name with flawless precision that makes my own fumbling attempts at the local language feel even more pathetic.

At least turning right should be easier.

Except when I reach the intersection, there's no Wilhelminastraat. Just a narrow alley that looks barely wide enough for a bicycle, let alone a car.

"Turn right now."

"There is no right!" I snap at the screen. "That's not a street, that's a footpath!"

The GPS doesn't respond. How could it?

I drive past the intersection, scanning for street signs in the gathering darkness.

Nothing.

A local man walking his dog glances at me curiously as I slow to peer at a faded sign, and I quickly accelerate. The last thing I need is to look like a lost tourist.

Which is exactly what I am really.

"Recalculating," the GPS announces with what sounds like mechanical smugness. "Make a U-turn when possible."

"Where? Where am I supposed to make a U-turn?" The street is lined with parked cars and there's steady traffic in both directions. "This isn't London. I can't just swing around wherever I want."

My voice rises with each word, echoing in the small car. When did I start talking to machines like they were people? When did my life become so isolated that a GPS is my primary conversational partner?

"Make a U-turn when possible," it repeats, unhelpfully. I could swear it sounds more impatient with me this time.

I drive for another three blocks before finding a gap wide enough to turn around, my hands shaking now

163

from more than just unfamiliar driving patterns. Every minute that passes is another minute closer to eight o'clock, another minute that Erin might be waiting, or might decide I'm not coming and disappear again.

If she's even planning to show up at all.

The thought has been circling my mind like a vulture since I left the villa. What if this is another manipulation? What if the address in her desk drawer was meant for me to find, designed to send me on some wild chase across the island while she does something else entirely?

"Turn left onto Wilhelminastraat."

This time I see it. There's a proper street sign, partially hidden behind a flowering tree. I signal carefully and make the turn, joining a flow of traffic that actually seems to know where it's going.

My phone shows 7:51. Nine minutes to reach an address I've never seen, in a part of the island I don't know, while driving on the wrong side of the road in a country where I don't speak the language.

"In 1.2 kilometres, turn left onto Emanstraat," my GPS nemesis continues with what I can only describe as infuriating confidence, as if it has never once doubted its ability to navigate this maze while I'm falling apart at every turn.

Listen to yourself.

I'm assigning personality traits to a satellite navigation system when the real danger is almost certainly waiting for me at this address. The GPS isn't my enemy. Whatever I'm about to walk into definitely is.

Sorry, I think silently toward the glowing screen. *Truce? I might need you to get me out of here alive.*

The thought makes me want to pull over, sit on the side of the road and have a proper what-the-hell-am-I-doing moment. This is insane.

But I know I won't stop. Because despite everything Erin has done to me, the theft, the lies, the years of silence, I need to know she's safe. I need to know what's really happening.

The traffic thickens as I approach what must be Oranjestad's business district. Office buildings rise against the darkening sky, their windows mostly dark but for scattered lights where someone is working late or security systems glow. It looks like any business district after hours: vaguely ominous, full of empty spaces and shadows.

"Turn left onto Weststraat," the GPS announces, and without the filter of my projected anxiety, it just sounds like what it is: a machine trying to help me reach a destination I'm no longer sure I want to find.

My hands tighten on the steering wheel as I make the turn. 7:58. Two minutes. Whatever is waiting for me at that address, I'm almost there.

I signal and turn, scanning the street numbers as they increase. The address from Erin's drawer should be somewhere in the next few blocks. I drive slowly down Weststraat, peering at buildings in the gathering darkness. The glass facades reflect the streetlights and the occasional passing car. I scan the numbers frantically. 86, 88, 90, climbing toward the address I need.

94, 96, 98...

There. 100 Weststraat.

"You have arrived at your destination."

I park across the street, hands trembling as I turn off the engine. The sudden silence is deafening after the GPS's constant chatter and the hum of the air conditioning. Through the windscreen, I study the building I've driven across an island to find.

It's a modest office building, four storeys of glass and concrete that could house accountants or lawyers or any other perfectly legitimate business. At 8pm, it's completely dark except for a single light in a ground-floor window. The lobby is visible through the doors, but I can't see anyone inside.

I check my phone: 8:02.

I'm late. Not by much, not late enough that if Erin was here, she would have already left.

Maybe she's inside, waiting.

Maybe the light in that window marks exactly where I need to be.

Or maybe this is all another wild goose chase, and I'm sitting alone in a car in a foreign country, having abandoned eight retreat participants to chase shadows.

The street is quiet. A few other cars parked along the curb, their windows dark. Office workers gone home for the evening. No pedestrians. No sign of Erin's distinctive silhouette or flowing hair.

I settle back in the driver's seat to wait, adjusting the rear-view mirror so I can watch the street behind me. My hands won't stop shaking, and my mouth is dry despite the bottle of water I brought from the villa. Every few seconds, I glance across, looking for movement, for lights, for any sign that someone is inside.

Nothing.

A motorcycle roars past, making me jump. My heart pounds so loudly I'm sure someone outside the car must be able to hear it. I take deep breaths, trying to calm myself, but the silence between my heartbeats is somehow worse than the pounding.

What am I doing here?

The question loops through my mind as minutes tick by: 8:05. 8:07. 8:10. No sign of Erin. No movement in the building. No indication that anyone has any intention of meeting here tonight.

I'm watching the building so intently that I almost miss the movement in my rear-view mirror. A figure walking down the sidewalk behind me, moving purposefully toward my car. My stomach clenches as I adjust for a better view.

It's hard to make out details in the gathering darkness, but the person appears to be wearing dark clothing, hands shoved deep in pockets. Walking with the kind of deliberate pace that suggests a destination in mind rather than a casual stroll.

Coming straight toward my car.

I grip the steering wheel tighter, ready to start the engine and drive away if necessary. The figure draws closer... twenty metres, fifteen, ten... and I can see it's a man, medium height, broad shoulders. The same build as the stranger I saw with Erin on the beach last night.

My breath catches in my throat. Is this who Erin was supposed to meet? Is this her mysterious contact?

167

The man approaches the rear of my car, and I lose sight of him in the mirror. I hold my breath, waiting for him to appear on one side or the other, but seconds pass and nothing happens.

Where did he go?

I twist in my seat, trying to see behind me without being obvious about it, but the rear window shows only an empty sidewalk and the glow of streetlights. It's as if he simply vanished.

My heart thuds harder. Did he recognise the car? Does he know I'm here? Is he circling around to approach from a different angle?

I fumble for the ignition, ready to start the engine and escape, when another movement catches my eye in the passenger-side mirror. Someone walking along the sidewalk toward the front of the car.

But this figure is smaller, moving with a different rhythm.

I catch a glimpse of flowing fabric, long hair.

Erin?

I lean forward, straining to see better, my pulse racing with anticipation and dread. If it's really her, if she's actually here, then I'll finally have answers. I'll know what she's been hiding, what she's planning, why she abandoned her own retreat.

The figure moves closer, and I can see more details now. Definitely a woman, wearing what looks like a loose dress or tunic. But something about the silhouette seems wrong. Too short, maybe. Or the wrong build.

Not Erin.

As she passes under a streetlight, I catch a clear view of her face. Middle-aged, kind features, definitely local. She's not heading for the office building or looking around nervously, like someone attending a clandestine meeting. She's just walking home from work or visiting friends or doing any of the hundred normal things people do on Thursday evenings.

I sink back in my seat, disappointment and relief warring in my chest. Not Erin. Not the mysterious man from the beach. Just an ordinary woman living her ordinary life.

8:15.

If anyone was planning to meet here at eight o'clock, they're fifteen minutes late. Either something has gone wrong, or I've misunderstood something fundamental about what I was supposed to find here.

I'm studying the office building again, wondering if I should get out of the car and try the lobby doors, when something taps against the passenger window.

I shriek and whip around, my heart exploding into my throat.

CHAPTER TWENTY-ONE

A face peers through the glass, illuminated by the streetlight's glow. Dark eyes, weathered skin, greying hair gliding over her shoulders. The same woman I saw walking down the sidewalk, now standing directly beside my car with her hand still raised from knocking on the window.

She looks concerned rather than threatening, her expression gentle and questioning. But my entire body is flooded with adrenaline, every muscle tensed for flight.

She taps again, more softly this time, and gestures toward the window. Then she points across the street toward the office building and nods encouragingly, as if she's been waiting for me.

Waiting for me?

My mouth dries up as I realise she knows exactly who I am and why I'm here. But how?

She beckons toward the building again, then mimes rolling down a window. After a moment's hesitation, I press the button, lowering the glass just a few inches.

"You're very late," she says in accented English, her voice warm but concerned. "I was beginning to think you weren't coming."

"Late for what?" I waver.

"The collection," she says simply, as if this should be obvious. "Come. I'll unlock the door for you."

She turns and walks toward the office building, clearly expecting me to follow. I sit frozen, clutching my phone so tightly my hand aches. This woman, slight, middle-aged, harmless-looking, somehow knows I'm supposed to be here. But for what? And who is she working for?

The rational part of my brain catalogues her appearance: she's barely five feet tall, probably in her sixties, wearing a simple dress and sensible shoes. She couldn't physically overpower me if she tried. But the fearful part of my brain whispers that the real danger might not be her. It might be whoever she works for.

I take a deep breath and get out of the car, my phone still clutched in my hand like a lifeline. If something goes wrong, I can call for help. Not that I know who I'd call or what I'd tell them.

I watch as she unlocks the front door and holds it open, looking back at me expectantly. The lobby beyond is well-lit but empty, just a reception desk and some chairs. Nothing obviously threatening.

But then, nothing about this week has been obviously anything.

"Thank you for waiting," I say as I approach the door, trying to sound grateful rather than terrified.

"Of course," she replies with a warm smile. "Though next time, perhaps don't sit in your car so long. I've been watching for twenty minutes."

She's been watching me. The thought sends a fresh wave of anxiety through my chest, but I follow her into the lobby anyway. The door closes behind us with a soft click that sounds unnaturally loud in the silence.

"This way," she says, leading me toward the reception desk. She moves around behind it with confidence, settling into the chair as if this is completely routine.

Which, apparently, it is.

"You're here about box 117," she says, looking at me expectantly.

What?

I stare at her, my mouth opening and closing like a fish out of water.

Box 117?

I have no idea what she's talking about. I came here expecting to find Erin, or someone who could tell me where she is, not some mysterious box collection service.

"I..." I start, then stop, completely lost.

The woman studies me, her expression shifting from expectant to slightly concerned. Then she nods, as if my confusion confirms something.

"Identification?" she asks gently.

I hesitate, my mind racing. I don't know what name the box is under. Is it Erin's? Mine? Some alias I've never heard of? My wallet is back at the villa, but even if I had it, I'm not sure what she's expecting to see.

"I'm sorry, I don't have ID with me," I say, trying to sound apologetic rather than suspicious. "My friend sent me to pick something up. Erin Blake?"

At the mention of Erin's name, the woman's expression shifts slightly: not surprise, but recognition. As if she was waiting for me to say exactly that.

"One moment," she says.

She disappears through a door behind the reception desk, leaving me alone in the eerily quiet lobby. The

172

fluorescent lights hum overhead, and somewhere in the building, I can hear the distant sound of air conditioning cycling on.

What is this place? Some kind of private postal service? A storage facility? And how does Erin know about it?

The woman returns a minute later carrying a brown box and an envelope. She sets both items on the counter between us.

"This was left for collection today," she says, her voice matter-of-fact. "The instructions said it could be released to either Erin Blake or Samantha Foster."

My name.

I actually take a step backward, as if the counter has suddenly caught fire.

Erin specifically included my name in the collection instructions. But the question that makes my stomach lurch is: was I the backup plan, or was I always meant to be here?

If I hadn't shown up tonight, would Erin have had to come herself? Or was I supposed to pretend to be her? Was I meant to use our supposed resemblance, our matching clothes, our shared history to convince this woman I was Erin Blake collecting her own package?

The thought makes me feel sick. How long has this been arranged? And how long has Erin been planning to use me?

"Thank you," I manage, accepting the package with hands that aren't quite steady. It's heavier than I expected for its size, just slightly larger than a sheet of A4 paper.

"There's also this," the woman adds, sliding the envelope across the counter. "Left with the same instructions."

I take the envelope, noticing it's sealed and completely unmarked. No names, no addresses, nothing to indicate what it contains or who it's from.

"Thank you again," I say, backing toward the door. I need to get out of here, need to examine these items somewhere safe and private. Or public. Maybe public is better.

"Have a good evening," the woman calls after me, her tone pleasant and professional, as if mysterious evening package collections are perfectly normal parts of her job.

Maybe they are.

Outside, the night air feels thick and oppressive after the air-conditioned lobby. I hurry back to the car, my eyes scanning the empty street for any sign of movement, any indication that I'm being watched. The woman said she'd been observing me for twenty minutes. Who else might be out there?

I drive several blocks before finding a quiet stretch with a bench positioned away from the streetlights. Only then do I allow myself to examine what I've collected.

The envelope opens easily, revealing a single sheet of paper with a message written in Erin's neat handwriting: "Our uni address. Street number, road, postcode. No spaces."

I look at it, completely baffled. What? Our university address? Why would Erin want me to think about that musty flat we shared years ago?

My hands shake slightly as I turn to the package. The brown paper wrapping is secured with tape, no external markings or labels. I peel it away carefully, half-expecting something dangerous to spring out.

Inside is a laptop.

A sleek silver MacBook, unremarkable except for the fact that someone went to elaborate lengths to get it into my hands. There are no obvious identifying marks, no stickers or dents that might tell me who it belongs to or where it came from. It looks practically new. I pop it open.

Attached to the screen is a yellow sticky note with a single word written in Erin's precise handwriting: "Watch."

My eyes fixate on the note, my throat closing with anxiety. Watch what? And why did she go to such elaborate lengths to get this laptop to me?

I click, and immediately a password prompt appears. Of course. Nothing with Erin is ever straightforward.

I glance back at the paper from the envelope. "Our uni address. Street number, road, postcode. No spaces."

Oh.

The password.

Of course she'd use our old flat. 47 Brookside Road - that cramped little place with the leaky radiator and the kitchen that smelled perpetually of damp. I used to think it was romantic, the way we'd stay up until dawn sharing dreams and planning our brilliant futures. How naive I was, thinking we were partners in those late night brainstorming sessions.

Now I wonder if Erin was already cataloguing my ideas even then, filing them away for future use. Was she ever really my friend, or was I just a convenient source of inspiration she knew she could eventually discard?

The address burns itself into my memory as I type: 47BrooksideRoad. No spaces, just like Erin's instruction. Just like how she's eliminated all the spaces between truth and manipulation in my life.

I only pause for a beat before adding the postcode. It seems some things are etched on your brain forever.

I hit enter and the screen lights up immediately, showing a desktop with a single video file labelled with today's date.

Everything about this feels like I'm being led step by step through some elaborate maze that Erin has constructed. But I've come this far. I've driven across the island, collected a mysterious package from a strange woman, and now I'm sitting alone in a foreign park with this laptop.

My finger hovers over the trackpad, then clicks on the video file. Whatever Erin wants me to see, whatever truth or lie she's constructed, I'm about to discover exactly how deep this rabbit hole goes.

CHAPTER TWENTY-TWO

The video begins with a view of a beige wall, then resolves into a shaky image of Erin sitting on what appears to be the bed in her suite, her face filling the frame as she adjusts the camera.

"If you're watching this, Sam, then you're still as smart as you always were. Good." Erin's voice is calm, methodical, so at odds with her unexplained disappearance that a chill runs through me despite the warm Aruban night air.

I'm sitting on a bench in a park near the harbour, the laptop balanced on my knees, transfixed by the sight of the woman who's upended my life twice now.

"I don't have much time," she continues, glancing over her shoulder at something out of frame. "By now, you must know I've gone. I can't explain everything right now, but I had to get away."

The sound of waves lapping against the nearby seawall provides an incongruously peaceful backdrop to her ominous words. In the distance, I can hear music from a beachfront bar, the carefree laughter of tourists enjoying their Caribbean holiday, a stark contrast to my growing sense of dread.

"I know this is going to sound unforgivable," Erin says, her voice taking on a pleading quality. "But I've had to borrow something from you." She takes a deep breath. "I've booked a flight in your name, and I've... Sam, I've taken your passport."

My breath catches.

"I know how this looks," she continues quickly. "But it was the only way. I don't want to be followed. I need..." She pauses, as if thinking of what to say next, and then shakes her head. "I'm not sure you would understand. But I need to go. And I need to go now."

The laptop suddenly feels burning hot against my legs.

Erin used my name to leave the country.

Without my knowledge or consent.

My mind races through the implications.

I left my passport back at the villa. Of course I did, like any sensible person staying somewhere for a week. I even mentioned to that woman at the office building just now that I didn't have ID with me.

The rational part of my brain tries to reassure me. Erin wouldn't *actually* steal my passport. That would be a serious crime, not just manipulation or betrayal. That would be identity theft.

But the growing pit in my stomach tells a different story.

Why would she say it if it weren't true?

My mind fills with memories of all those little intrusions: my broken phone replaced overnight, my clothes mysteriously reorganised, that feeling of boundaries being constantly crossed. The thought hits me with sickening clarity. All those times she's been so helpful, so considerate, arranging my things while I've showered or slept.

She has had open access to everything I own.

I let her replace my clothes, my luggage... everything. All I had left was my passport and a few bank cards with no credit.

"I'll explain everything when I can. I promise," she says, though her eyes dart away from the camera. "But right now, I need you to understand that I had no choice. I tried, but... this is the only way."

"Here's what I need you to do," Erin says, her voice dropping lower. "Stay at the villa. Continue the retreat exactly as I would. Make the women feel they're getting their money's worth. I know you can do it."

She looks away again, tension visible in the tight line of her jaw. "There's something on this laptop I need you to see," Erin continues. "Something I should have given you years ago. Files, documents, proof of... well, you'll understand when you see it."

The video cuts abruptly, jumping forward to show Erin in the same position but with different lighting, as if time has passed.

"Sorry," she says, looking more dishevelled than before. "Had to make sure I wasn't interrupted. Listen carefully, Sam. Everything you need is on this computer." Her voice grows urgent.

"I know this sounds crazy," Erin continues on screen, running a hand through her hair. "But I need you to trust me. Just like in the old days, remember? You and me against the world?"

The old days.

When she was systematically cataloguing my ideas, my vulnerabilities, my weaknesses.

When she was building her empire on my foundations.

179

And now she's done it again, hasn't she?

Holy shit.

If she has my passport, I'm stuck here.

Completely trapped.

And suddenly, with horrifying clarity, I understand what this week has really been about.

All those comments from the retreat participants about how we look alike. How we could be sisters. How we have the same energy, the same approach. I'd found it strange at the time - we don't actually look that similar. But Erin kept dressing us in matching outfits, positioning us side by side, encouraging the comparisons.

She was testing whether people would see us as interchangeable.

It wasn't mentorship. It was an audition.

She was seeing if she could pass herself off as me.

But if that was the plan all along, if she's been working toward this moment... how long *has* she been planning it?

My thoughts race as Erin on the screen keeps talking, her voice suddenly sounding distant and hollow.

I can't leave Aruba without identification.

A couple walk past, arms linked, speaking in soft Dutch. A taxi idles near a hotel entrance, its driver scrolling through his phone. Normal sights. Innocent activities.

My hands shake as it hits home: I'm alone in a foreign country, with no passport, running a therapeutic retreat for eight wealthy women who have no idea their guru has vanished and isn't going to stroll back in tomorrow.

Screen Erin leans closer to the camera, her eyes intense.

"I can't tell you everything, not like this. But I promise you, Sam, when this is over, you'll understand why I had to do it this way. Just... trust me. One more time."

The video ends abruptly, freezing on Erin's desperate face before the screen goes black.

For several long moments, I sit motionless on the bench, my thoughts churning like the dark water of the harbour. The sounds of Oranjestad's nightlife, music, laughter, clinking glasses, wash over me but feel muted, as if I'm experiencing them through thick glass.

A man walks past, speaking quietly into his phone in a language I don't recognise. Is he just a tourist, or something more sinister? A woman sitting alone at a nearby café keeps glancing in my direction. Casual people-watching, or surveillance?

I force myself to breathe deeply, to think logically rather than let paranoia consume me. But the questions keep multiplying.

I close the laptop with trembling fingers. The weight of it feels different now, full of secrets and lies.

Do I go back to the villa and play the role she's asked of me? Continue the charade, smile at Nicholas over breakfast, lead workshops on authenticity while living the biggest lie of my life?

Or do I finally stop being Erin Blake's victim?

The thought surprises me with its clarity. For six years, I've defined myself by what she took from me. I've obsessed over what I could have had, what I could have been.

Even now, part of me wants to follow her instructions, to trust that she knows best.

But she's used my identity without permission.

Enough.

I stand up, tucking the laptop under my arm with newfound determination. The harbour lights reflect off the dark water, and somewhere out there, Erin Blake is starting a new life with my stolen identity while I clean up the mess she's left behind.

I'm going to see what she left for me.

Right now, I can't think of anything I want more than to know where she is and get her back here. With my passport.

And some answers.

CHAPTER TWENTY-THREE

I retrace the GPS route back through the streets of the island, Erin's words echoing: *I've taken your passport, booked a flight in your name.*

The casual assumption that I'll clean up her mess while she disappears into my identity, like slipping on a coat. I force myself to maintain the speed limit, even as rage builds in my chest.

The villa's entrance appears ahead. No other cars. No movement in the windows. The driveway sits empty. The evening staff have finished clearing dinner service and gone home to their families. I envy their simple, peaceful lives.

When I kill the engine, Caribbean night sounds settle around me: distant beach bar music, waves against shore, wind through expensive landscaping.

My heart pounds too fast. The laptop feels heavier when I lift it, as if knowledge has physical weight. Whatever else Erin has left for me, it's going to change everything. Again.

What I do know is that I underestimated her.

Just as *she* assumed I hadn't changed since university, I thought the same of her.

I thought I knew her.

Now I'm not sure what I know at all.

I don't want conversation with any of the attendees tonight, so I slip round to the side of the villa. Voices drift from the courtyard as I approach the French doors to our session area. I duck into wall shadows, feeling like the world's worst spy. Clandestine meetings and sneaking through darkness aren't exactly my forte.

Thinking on my feet, I follow the building's edge toward the side entrance I've seen staff use.

Please be open.

It is.

I clutch the laptop and pause, listening before I slip inside. Footsteps upstairs? Air conditioning hum? Each step feels like a betrayal, as if I'm violating sacred space. It's ridiculous, of course. I'm a guest here. Yet everything about this evening feels illicit and wrong.

There's a narrow passageway past the small staff rest room into the back of the kitchen. Soft light emanates as I approach, warm gold against cool blue accent lighting.

I freeze halfway along.

Someone's there.

I stand motionless, watching.

I wanted to avoid conversation with the women, but I wanted to avoid someone else even more.

And here he is: Nicholas.

I can't work out what he's doing at first. He seems so out of place in the vast staff kitchen. But with no one around to man it, he is doing what English men do: he's making tea.

It's so desperately domestic that I can only stare.

Even though I'm tucked away in the corridor, I jolt in shock as he speaks without turning to look at me.

"What are you doing sneaking around?"

His voice is calm, conversational, as if we're discussing the weather. The fact that he sensed me without seeing me sets my nerves on edge.

Still, he doesn't face me; he doesn't even pause in his tea preparation. Just continues his ritual while addressing me with characteristic directness.

My mouth goes dry, but I reply, "What are you doing making tea?"

My voice sounds steadier than I feel, which is good. I can't let him know how rattled I am.

It's a deflection, but it's all I can manage with my heart trying to climb out of my throat.

He finally turns to face me, and as I step into the light, his eyes immediately fix on the laptop pressed against my chest like a shield.

"You got it then."

It's not a question, it's a statement delivered with the same calm certainty he brings to everything else.

He knew about the laptop.

He speaks as if he's been waiting for this exact moment, this exact conversation, this exact revelation.

"You *knew*?" I keep my voice level, but inside I'm calculating. If he knew about the laptop, what else does he know? What else has he been planning?

Nicholas reaches for a second cup and pours tea into it with the same methodical care.

"I knew she would leave you something." He doesn't look at me as he speaks. "I didn't know what, exactly."

"Do you know what she did?" I step closer. "She stole my passport, Nicholas. She's using my identity to leave the country while I'm trapped here. That's not

185

leaving me something, that's identity theft. That's a serious crime."

His hand stills for just a moment - so briefly I might have imagined it - before continuing to stir the tea.

"She did what?"

I watch his face carefully for micro-expressions.

The surprise looks genuine, but Erin seemed genuine too when she was systematically destroying my life.

"Don't pretend you don't know."

"I know she's been acting strangely for weeks, secretive about meetings, evasive about her plans." He sets down the spoon and finally meets my eyes. Direct contact. Either he's telling the truth or he's very, very good at lying. "But stealing your passport? That's..." He runs a hand through his hair. "That's madness."

"I'm calling the police," I say, pulling out my phone. "This has gone too far."

My thumb hovers over the emergency number, but suddenly my hand freezes. My hands are still shaking from the adrenaline, making it hard to hold the phone steady.

The thought hits me before I even press the first digit.

I don't have a visa.

I'm here as a tourist, leading therapeutic sessions for money.

Working illegally in a foreign country.

If I call the police about my stolen passport, I'll have to explain what I've been doing here. I'll have to admit I've been working without proper authorisation, taking payment for services I'm not licenced to provide.

"What is it?" Nicholas asks, watching my face. He's studying my reaction as carefully as I'm studying his.

I lower the phone, my hand shaking. "I can't," I whisper.

"Can't what?"

"Call the police. I don't have a visa, Nicholas. I've been working here illegally..." My voice trails off as the full scope of my trap becomes clear.

Nicholas's expression doesn't change, but I catch something that might be sympathy in his eyes. "I see."

"Did you know?" I demand. "Did Erin plan this too? Make sure I'd be too compromised to seek help? Back when you were telling me it was just a friend helping a friend. No need for a visa, Sam. Everything will be just fine. Come to paradise and let me steal your identity."

"I don't know *what* she planned to do," he says quietly. "But you're right - reporting this now would create problems for you as well as her."

His admission is too convenient. Like he's leading me to the conclusion he wants me to reach.

Don't worry, Nicholas, I'm already there.

The phone feels heavy in my hand. My last lifeline, and I can't use it without potentially destroying myself.

"This is what she wanted, isn't it?" I say bitterly. "To make me complicit. To make sure I couldn't expose her without exposing myself."

187

"Maybe," Nicholas acknowledges. "Or maybe she just didn't think it through. Erin's always been impulsive when she's emotional."

He pushes one cup across the marble surface toward me. I don't touch it.

Never accept food or drink from someone you can't trust.

"Upstairs, there are eight women who paid twenty thousand pounds each for a transformation experience. Women that you could help. This is what you wanted, isn't it?"

And there it is. He's trying to manipulate me through guilt and obligation, just like Erin always did. But something clicks in my mind - a strategic realisation.

Eight wealthy, well-connected women. Women who trust me now, who see me as their guide and confidant. Women who could be valuable allies if I play this right. Women that I could help, but maybe, just maybe, women that could help me.

"What I wanted?" I let myself sound defeated. Let him think his argument is working. "Are you out of your mind? Have you not heard anything I just said? I am trapped here. Trapped! And it's all because of your wife."

I can't bring myself to refer to her as my friend, because when has she ever really been that? "Those women aren't my problem. I honestly don't give a f-"

But even as I perform outrage, my mind is racing with possibilities. Julia works in tech - she'd have contacts, resources. Sarah owns a manufacturing company - she understands business law, international

188

regulations. Maya, with her finance background, would know about moving money, about systems and loopholes.

Maya. Is she the one I can trust the least, or the most?

If I can't go to the authorities, maybe I don't need to. Maybe I can build my own network of help.

"They're not my responsibility," I say, trying to fill my voice with conviction.

"Aren't they?" Nicholas takes a sip of his tea, watching me over the rim. "You've been leading their sessions. You've guided them this far. Are you really going to abandon them now?"

"I didn't choose this role. It was forced on me," I protest.

"But you chose to stay. You chose to continue the sessions instead of walking away." His voice is quiet, but there's steel underneath. "Those women trust you now. They've opened up to you, made themselves vulnerable based on that trust."

Perfect. He's practically writing my cover story for me.

I let a long moment pass, as if I'm wrestling with my conscience. Really, I'm calculating how to use tomorrow's sessions to gather information, while building alliances with women who have the resources to help me.

"You don't understand," I say, my voice rising. Just enough to seem genuinely distressed. "I can't leave. Even if I wanted to walk away, I can't. She took my passport. I'm trapped here."

"For now," Nicholas acknowledges. "But Erin will be back."

"Will she?" I laugh bitterly, and this time it isn't part of the act. "How can you be so sure? What if something happens to her? What if she decides never to come back? What if this whole thing was designed to trap me here permanently?"

"Because I know her." There's something in his voice - not love, but a kind of weary familiarity. "She's reckless, impulsive, makes terrible decisions when she's emotional. But she's not cruel. Not deliberately."

He doesn't sound like a man in love with his wife. He sounds... tired. Resentful, almost.

"Not cruel?" I stare at him in disbelief. "She stole my life's work six years ago. Now she's stealing my identity. How is that not cruel?"

Nicholas is quiet for a long moment, studying his tea.

"I think," he says finally, "that Erin has been trying to find a way to give you what she took. And I think she's been making increasingly desperate choices because she doesn't know how."

"So she thought stealing my passport would help?"

"I don't know what she thought." He looks up at me directly. Again with the eye contact. Either genuine honesty or masterful manipulation. "But I know those women upstairs don't deserve to pay the price for her mistakes."

The kitchen falls silent except for the soft hum of expensive appliances and my own elevated heartbeat. I let the silence stretch, as if I'm genuinely wrestling with the decision.

"One day," I say finally, as if the words are being dragged out of me. "Tomorrow's sessions, and then I'm calling the authorities, whether Erin's back or not. And if that means having to face the consequences of working here without a visa..." I turn my eyes away, as if ashamed.

Nicholas nods. "Fair enough."

"Nicholas?" I add, as if the thought just occurred to me. "If you're playing me, if this is all just another layer of manipulation..."

"Yes," he finishes calmly. "I know."

The certainty in his voice is either completely genuine, or he's the best actor I've ever met.

Either way, I have a plan now. Tonight: examine the laptop, understand what Erin left for me. Tomorrow: use the retreat sessions to gather intelligence and build alliances with eight powerful women.

I feel like I'm the one making strategic choices instead of just reacting to other people's manipulation.

I clutch the laptop and head for the stairs, my mind already racing with plans. Every step feels different now - not the movements of a victim, but of someone taking control.

At last.

CHAPTER TWENTY-FOUR

My hands are still trembling slightly as I climb the stairs to my room, the laptop clutched against my chest. Every shadow feels threatening, every sound makes me freeze and listen.

The hallway is warmly lit by expensive sconces at staggered distances. I tread lightly so my feet make no sound as I approach the door to my room, but something feels wrong. I can't put my finger on what.

Paranoia, I tell myself.

Again.

After everything that's happened tonight, of course I'm jumpy.

I slide my keycard through the reader and push open the door. The bedside lamp is on, casting a rosy glow across the pristine white bedding.

Wait.

I didn't leave a light on.

I didn't come back up here after the sessions.

This isn't right.

"Hello, Samantha," a voice says.

It's Erin, I think. *She hasn't taken my passport. She hasn't abandoned me. It was a joke. A game. She's here.*

But of course, she is not.

Instead, sitting in the armchair beside the window, looking perfectly composed despite being uninvited, is Maya.

The laptop nearly slips from my hands. Every muscle in my body goes rigid, fight-or-flight flooding my system with adrenaline.

Maya has broken into my room.

She's been sitting here waiting for me to return.

"What the hell are you doing in my room?" The words come out as a snarl, all pretence of politeness stripped away by raw panic. I pull my phone out of my pocket.

Maya doesn't flinch at my tone. She's dressed in dark clothing, jeans and a black top, as if she's a shadow herself. Her hands rest calmly in her lap, but her eyes are alert, calculating.

"Before you call security," she says in a calm voice, "there are some things we need to discuss."

"Get out." I don't move from the doorway, keeping my escape route clear. "Get out of my room right now or I'm calling security."

"With that phone?" Maya's voice is steady, reasonable. "The one Nicholas gave you? The one that's probably being monitored?"

The observation stops me cold. I hadn't even considered that possibility, but of course she's right. The phone, like everything else, came from Erin and Nicholas.

I have nothing that's my own, not anymore.

I thought I'd lost everything when I was in the motel. I was wrong.

I gave away the very last of my belongings when I accepted the clothes, the phone, the suitcase, this borrowed life from Erin.

My duffle bag was trash, but it was mine.

Now I really do have nothing.

That won't stop me calling for help if I need it, though.

"You broke into my room," I say, my voice shaking with anger and fear. "You've been sitting here in the dark waiting for me. That's not normal behaviour, Maya. That's intrusion. It's stalking."

I'm stumbling for words, trying to sound confident and combative when I feel anything but. I don't know what you'd call what Maya has done, but it's wrong.

"These locks are just for show. Any competent person can bypass them." Her tone is matter-of-fact, as if breaking and entering is perfectly reasonable. "Especially when keycards are so easy to get hold of."

"Why?" The word comes out strangled. "What do you want?" I'm still standing in the doorway while Maya is sitting in my chair. I feel like *I'm* the intruder here. I want to put the laptop down, but I can't. There's no way I'm letting go of it with this near-stranger in my room.

Maya leans forward slightly, her expression serious. "Come in, Sam. Please."

I look up and down the corridor behind me, and clumsily wrangling both the phone and the laptop, I step into my room.

"I wanted to talk to you in private," she says simply. "I want to know why you didn't tell anyone what you saw on the beach."

Instinctively, I move towards her, ducking down, closer. There's no one else here to hear us, but something about the clandestine subject of discussion makes me lower my voice.

"The beach?" I repeat.

"Three this morning. You saw Erin meet someone down there, didn't you?" Maya's eyes never leave my face. "I saw you watching from your balcony. You were there for the whole thing."

The world tilts beneath my feet. She saw me watching? How long has she been observing me?

"I saw it too," Maya continues. "My room is on the other side of the courtyard." She gestures toward the opposite side of the villa through my window. "You saw him give her your passport, didn't you?"

I shake my head slowly. "From where I was standing, I couldn't see what he gave her. It was too dark, too far away." My voice is barely a whisper. "You think it was my passport?"

"What else could it have been? Small, rectangular, valuable enough for Erin to meet someone secretly at three in the morning?" Maya's tone is analytical. "And now your passport is conveniently missing."

Inconveniently, if you're me.

The logic is sound, but hearing someone else confirm my worst fears makes it feel more real, more terrifying.

"How did you know?" I whisper. "About the passport?"

Maya's expression shifts slightly, almost apologetic. "I didn't. Not for sure. I was trying to figure out what could have been worth a secret meeting at three in the morning. And then Erin goes missing..." She pauses. "A passport made sense. But I was just testing the theory until you confirmed it just now. Shit, I didn't know how far Erin was prepared to go. And to do that to her friend."

Her tone is almost sympathetic, but my stomach drops. I've been played again, led into revealing information I meant to keep to myself.

"I was waiting to see what you'd do." Maya says. "Whether you'd tell Nicholas, whether you'd confront anyone, whether you'd try to get help. Very interesting that you chose to keep it secret."

"You've been watching me like some kind of experiment." Rage builds in my chest, hot and clean, but I still keep my voice under control. "While I've been falling apart, thinking I was going crazy, you've been sitting back and taking notes."

"I've been gathering evidence." Maya stands up, moving closer to the window. "Something's very wrong with this whole setup, and I needed to understand what before I made any moves."

"Evidence of what?"

Maya turns back to face me, her expression grim. "That Erin Blake has been systematically destroying you. Not just this week - for years."

The certainty in her voice makes my skin crawl. "What do you mean?"

"Sit down, Sam. Please." For the first time, Maya's voice softens slightly. "I know you don't trust me right now, and you shouldn't. But I have information you need, and you have something *I* need."

I sink into the room's only other chair. There's a low table between us, but I still can't bring myself to release my grip on the laptop. I keep it on my knees as I shift uncomfortably.

"What could you possibly need from me?"

Maya's smile is thin, calculating. "Let's just say Erin Blake has a pattern of destroying people who trust her. And sometimes those people find ways to fight back."

"You're talking about revenge."

"I'm talking about justice." Maya's voice hardens. "She's done this before, Sam. What she's doing to you, she's done to others. The question is whether you want to be another victim, or whether you want to help stop her."

The pain in her voice is raw, real. This isn't just about helping me - Maya has her own score to settle.

"Erin and I have history," Maya continues. "Fortunately, she is too caught up in herself to dive too deeply into her clients' pasts."

"You came to a retreat before," I remember. "Someone mentioned that on my first night. Before you all arrived."

"Oh yes," Maya says wryly. "But our history goes beyond that."

She pauses, studying me carefully. "I didn't know you were going to be here, Sam. That was... unexpected. What I did know, what I'd discovered during my research into Erin's business practices, was that she didn't actually create the Authentic Self Framework."

I go very still. "What do you mean?"

How does she know?

And what does it even matter now?

"I mean, the entire foundation of her empire is built on stolen intellectual property. I just didn't know who

197

the original creator was until you showed up." Maya's voice is matter-of-fact, analytical. "The way you handled the sessions, the natural authority when you explained the concepts - it was obvious you weren't just a trained facilitator. You were teaching your own work."

I close my eyes briefly. After everything that's happened, being seen feels almost as violating as being invisible. Am I that obvious?

"But instead of exposing her," Maya continues, "instead of demanding credit, you just... played along. I couldn't understand it. Why would someone let their life's work be stolen and say nothing?"

Why indeed?

Because I was living on borrowed time in a motel room? Because Daniel left me with nothing but debt and shame? Because when Erin found me, I was so broken I would have agreed to anything that looked like salvation?

Is that what she thinks?

Because I was grateful? Pathetically, desperately grateful that someone wanted me, even if it meant swallowing my pride and pretending the past didn't matter?

Because I convinced myself it was enough just to be using my framework again, even if I couldn't claim credit for it? Even if I had to watch her get the recognition that should have been mine?

That's what it must look like to Maya, to Nicholas, and above all to Erin.

That's what it must look like.

"I have my reasons," I say finally, my voice steady despite the chaos in my chest.

Maya's eyes narrow slightly, studying my face with new intensity.

"I'm sure you do," she says quietly, and there's something in her tone that suggests she understands more than she's letting on.

Is it possible that she can see through what no one else can?

Maya holds my gaze for a few seconds longer before continuing.

"I've been documenting everything, Sam. Her patterns, her methods, the way she identifies and exploits vulnerable people. And now I have proof of identity theft, illegal confinement, and fraud."

"What do you want from me?"

"I want to bring her down completely." Maya's voice is deadly calm. "Not just expose her, but destroy her the way she destroyed us. And to do that, I need your cooperation."

"You want to use me as bait."

Maya's pause is telling. "I want to give you back your life. Your framework, your recognition, your future. But yes, it requires taking significant risks."

I look down at the laptop in my arms, then back at Maya's calculated expression. She's not offering unconditional help - she's proposing an alliance of mutual benefit. Two women Erin has destroyed, working together to destroy her in return.

"What's your plan?"

"First, tell me all about the laptop. What's on it?" Maya gestures toward the device. "My evidence so far is strong, but, maybe you have something else we can use? I don't have paperwork to prove she stole from me. I've been trying to find other ways to... well, you know."

"What do you have?" I ask, still defensive. I'm not giving up the computer just yet. I don't even know what Erin has left me.

"Illegal business practices." Maya's smile is sharp. "I have a stack of financial documentation that doesn't quite add up. It's not quite enough. But now that I know about the passport theft, we can have her on federal crimes. And... maybe there's more?"

The scope of Maya's investigation is staggering. She hasn't just been a suspicious participant this week, she's been conducting a full-scale investigation.

I feel my grip loosen slightly. "Why should I trust you?"

"Because you don't have any other choice." Maya's bluntness is almost refreshing after days of manipulation. "And because I have resources you need - money, connections, legal knowledge. Things that can actually get you home and get your life back."

She's right, and we both know it. I'm trapped on this island with no passport, no money, no legal recourse. Maya represents my best chance of escape and justice.

But trusting another person who's been watching me, manipulating information, playing a long game... it feels like stepping into another trap.

"If we do this," I say slowly, "if we work together, I need complete honesty. No more watching from the shadows, no more withholding information."

200

Maya nods. "Agreed. And in return, I need you to follow my lead when it comes to legal strategy. I know how to build cases that will stand up in court."

It's not friendship she's offering. It's a business arrangement between two people who've been wronged by the same person. Cold, calculated, and probably my only chance at survival.

We need to see what we are dealing with. As I set the laptop down and open it, Maya pulls her chair closer. The screen illuminates both our faces in the lamplight, and I realise this is the moment everything changes. Whatever secrets Erin has left for me, whatever twisted narrative she's constructed, I won't be facing it alone.

But more than that, I won't be facing it as a victim anymore.

For the first time since that Instagram like that started this nightmare, I have an ally who sees through Erin's manipulation. Someone who understands that beneath my apparent compliance, I might have been planning something all along.

The cursor blinks on the password screen, waiting.

"Ready?" I ask.

Maya's smile is razor sharp. "Let's destroy her."

CHAPTER TWENTY-FIVE

The password screen disappears, and Maya leans in as I navigate to the folder that Erin has simply named *SAM*. The laptop casts a blue glow across our faces in the dimly lit room, and I can smell Maya's faint perfume mixed with the tropical humidity that clings to everything here. My hands are steadier now, curiosity replacing panic. Whatever Erin has left for me, I need to understand it.

The folder opens to reveal dozens of files, organised with Erin's characteristic precision. Video files, documents, spreadsheets, images. Everything labelled and dated with obsessive detail.

"Jesus," Maya breathes, scanning the file names. "She's documented everything."

I click on the first document: "Original Framework Development - S. Foster 2018." The blood drains from my face so quickly I feel dizzy. My heart stops as I recognise my own work, time-stamped and saved in its original form. The initial concept sketches I'd drawn on napkins in our university flat, now professionally scanned and preserved. It really goes back that far.

I was careless, but she was careful.

She kept everything, and now she is giving it to me.

"This is incredible," Maya whispers, leaning over my shoulder. I can feel the heat radiating from her body, her breath warm against my ear. "This is your original work, with metadata proving you created it. Sam, do you understand what this means legally?"

I scroll through page after page of documentation. My fingers move mechanically across the trackpad, each click revealing another piece of my stolen soul. Email drafts I'd never sent, research notes I'd forgotten existed, even photographs of my handwritten brainstorming sessions. Every iteration, every development phase, meticulously preserved.

"She kept *everything*," I murmur, giving voice to my thoughts as I click through the files. The thoroughness is staggering. It's like finding out someone has been dissecting your life under a microscope, preserving every thought like specimens in formaldehyde.

Maya points to another folder. Her manicured nail taps against the screen with a sharp clicking sound. "Look at this. *'Business Financial Records.'*"

I open the folder and Maya gasps audibly. She clearly understands what the files mean more than I do.

"Sam," she says. "Open that one."

The spreadsheet opens to reveal six years of financial success. Numbers blur together on the screen as my eyes water with rage I'm trying to suppress. Revenue, profit margins, client fees, speaking engagements, book deals. 3.2 million pounds in total revenue.

"My God," Maya's voice is hushed. The reverence in her tone makes me want to slam the laptop shut. "Sam, this is a complete audit trail. Every transaction, every contract, every payment traced back to your stolen framework."

I grip the edge of the desk.

"She's documented every penny she's made from your work. It's all here."

It doesn't stop there. I keep clicking. There's another folder labelled '*Legal Documentation.*' Inside are copyright transfers, trademark assignments, business incorporation papers. All seemingly prepared by expensive lawyers, all ready to be executed.

"She's transferring ownership back to you," Maya says, her excitement building. She's practically vibrating with energy beside me, while I feel like I'm slowly turning to stone. "The entire business. The copyrights, the trademarks, everything. This isn't just evidence, it's complete restitution."

I open another folder. The clicking and scrolling sounds fill the silence between us like tiny hammers. I watch Maya's face glow with vindication as I click through file after file.

"This is everything we need to destroy her, Sam. Not just for what she did to you, but for her entire pattern of predatory behaviour. If she's admitting to this..."

But something feels wrong as I continue scrolling. My stomach churns with a sick feeling that has nothing to do with the rich dinner we ate hours ago. Too neat. Too convenient.

"There's a video," I say, spotting a file labelled "For Sam - Please Watch First."

It's too late to watch it first. Even so, we need to watch it.

I click play, and Erin's face fills the screen. The sudden appearance of her features makes me flinch backward, as if she might reach through and grab me.

"Sam," she begins, "if you're watching this, then you've found everything. And you probably still hate me right now."

Maya falls silent beside me as we watch Erin's performance unfold. I can hear her breathing, shallow and controlled, while my own breath comes in short, angry bursts.

"I know what I did was wrong. I've known it for six years. Every success, every interview... part of me has been thinking about you. About what I stole."

My hands clench in my lap, nails digging crescents into my palms.

Erin takes a shaky breath. "I've been planning this for months. Finding a way to give everything back. The framework was always yours, Sam. I just... I saw how brilliant it was, and I wanted it so badly."

My chest tightens as she continues. "I convinced myself I was just borrowing it, that I'd include you eventually. But then it took off, and there was money, and recognition, and I didn't know how to go back."

Her eyes fill with tears. On screen, her vulnerability looks practised, performed, and it makes my skin crawl. "Everything is yours. The business, the copyrights, the profits from the last six years. All you have to do is sign the documents, and it's like the last six years never happened."

Like the last six years never happened.

The phrase echoes in my head like a bell tolling, and something cold and vicious unfurls in my chest.

"We can both start fresh," Erin continues. "This is yours now."

The video ends, leaving us in silence.

205

I reach forward, clicking, sure there must be more. But there isn't.

This is yours now.

That's the end of it.

Maya immediately starts talking, her words tumbling over each other. "This is unbelievable. A full confession, complete financial records, legal documentation. Sam, she's voluntarily returning everything. Do you know how unprecedented this is in intellectual property cases?"

I stare at the frozen image of Erin's hopeful face.

And suddenly it hits me: she never said sorry. Not once. Just restitution without remorse, like I'm a business transaction rather than a person she destroyed. '*I know what I did was wrong*' isn't the same as '*I'm sorry I hurt you.*' She's treating this like a corporate restructuring, not a betrayal between friends.

Maya continues, oblivious. "Combined with the pattern of evidence from other victims, this could take down her entire operation. We could recover damages not just for you, but for everyone she's stolen from."

I close the laptop slowly.

"Sam?" Maya's excitement falters. "This is good news. This is everything we wanted."

"Is it?"

"What do you mean?"

I stand up, moving to the window. The perfect paradise continues below, waves lapping against manicured shores. "She said it's like the last six years never happened."

"Right. Full restitution. That's exactly what..."

"No." I turn back to Maya. "That's what she wants. She gets to give me my life back like it's a present. Like she's doing me a favour."

Maya's confusion is obvious. "Sam, she's returning stolen property and admitting guilt. That's not a favour, that's justice."

Something cold spreads through my chest. "Is it? Or is it the final manipulation?"

"I don't understand."

"She gets to be the repentant friend who makes amends," I say, my voice getting steadier. "The successful businesswoman who does the right thing in the end. She gets to sleep peacefully knowing she fixed her mistake."

"But you're getting everything back..."

"Six years, Maya." The words come out sharper than I intend. "Six years of watching her build an empire on my work. Six years of seeing my concepts quoted in magazines as her brilliant insights."

Maya's excitement is fading. "Sam..."

"Do you know what those six years did to me?" I'm pacing now, energy building. "Six years of self-doubt. Of wondering if I was ever actually talented or if I just imagined it. Six years of being the woman who 'never follows through,' who has brilliant ideas that go nowhere."

"But now you can reclaim..."

"What? My stolen life? You can't reclaim six years of being the wrong person, Maya. You can't undo watching someone else live your dreams while you forget why you ever thought you were capable of anything."

Maya sinks into her chair, studying my face with growing concern.

"Maybe if I'd been successful," I continue, "if I'd had the career I was supposed to have, my husband wouldn't have left. Maybe I wouldn't have ended up in that motel room wondering if I was worth anything at all."

"Sam, you can't blame yourself for..."

"I don't blame myself." My voice is cold now, certain. "I blame her. She didn't just steal my framework, she stole my future. My confidence. My entire life trajectory."

The silence stretches between us.

"And now she wants to give it back to me like it's a gift," I say quietly. "Like I should be grateful for the chance to have what was always mine."

Maya's face has gone pale. "What are you saying?"

"I'm saying I don't want it back."

"You don't want..."

"I don't want her charity. I don't want her guilty conscience making her feel better." I look at Maya directly. "I want her destroyed. Like you said."

Maya stares at me. "Sam, that's not justice. That's revenge."

"Yes," I say, and the admission feels like coming home. "It is."

The words hang between us in the humid air. Maya stares at me, and I can see her recalibrating everything she thought she knew about me. Neither of us speaks for a long moment.

Outside, the evening continues its peaceful rhythm - waves against the shore, distant laughter from other resorts, the soft rustle of palm fronds. As if nothing has changed. As if I haven't just admitted I want to destroy someone's life.

Maya runs a hand through her hair and sinks back into her chair. "I want to bring her down just as much as you do," she says finally.

"Do you?" I study her face in the dim light. "Because she brought me out here, dressed me up, tried to make me into some kind of replica of her. Put me in her clothes, in her role, to the point that everyone kept saying we looked alike, that we were so similar..." I pause, the full scope of it hitting me. "I don't know how she made that happen to where she could make herself enough like me to use my fucking passport, but..."

"Well," Maya says quietly, "you *do* look kind of alike. Your hair's a couple of shades darker, but the bone structure, the height..."

"Jesus," I breathe. "She's done a Mr Ripley on me."

Maya's mouth quirks upward despite everything. "At least she didn't take you out in a boat."

The dark humour should appal me, but instead it's oddly comforting. Like finding someone who speaks the same twisted language.

When you've had your identity stolen and you're stranded in paradise, apparently gallows humour is how you cope.

The laughter dies quickly, replaced by cold determination. Erin thinks she's played us perfectly, but she's given us weapons she doesn't know about. I close the laptop, my mind already shifting to strategy.

209

But as the initial rush of vindication fades, questions start creeping in. Why now? Why this elaborate setup with the laptop, the documentation, the legal papers? Erin's never done anything without calculating every angle.

I replay the video in my mind: her practiced vulnerability, the way she positioned herself as the repentant friend making amends. Too neat. Too convenient. And that phrase: *'like the last six years never happened.'* Not an apology, but a transaction.

Maya's still buzzing with excitement about the evidence, but something cold settles in my stomach.

"She's not giving me this from the goodness of her heart, Maya." I know there's more to it. I get the feeling that this isn't a gift horse, it's a Trojan horse wrapped in pretty paper. "So, what is Erin really running from?" I ask, knowing that neither of us has the answer.

Maya sighs. "That's what I can't figure out. Someone doesn't just abandon a multimillion-pound business and flee the country without a serious reason."

"Maybe she's in some kind of legal trouble? Financial problems we don't know about?"

"Maybe." Maya doesn't sound convinced. "But why give you the framework first? Why not just disappear?"

"Unless..." I pause, thinking. "What if she wants out? What if she's tired of Nicholas, tired of the business, and this is her escape plan?"

"But why involve you?"

"Because she needs someone to take the fall? Or..." I trail off, another thought occurring to me. "What if she actually means it? What if she really does want to make amends, but only because she's planning to disappear forever anyway?"

Maya turns back to me. "Like a deathbed confession."

"Exactly. Clear your conscience before you vanish."

"But vanish from what? Her marriage? Her business? The spotlight?" Maya shakes her head. "None of it makes complete sense."

My eyes linger on the closed laptop, trying to piece together Erin's psychology.

"Whatever she's running from, she's been planning this for months. The framework documentation, the legal papers, finding me, bringing me here..." I say.

"Which means whatever spooked her happened recently. Something that made her accelerate the timeline." Maya agrees.

"Or someone."

We sit in silence, both lost in speculation.

"We need more information," Maya says finally.

"Agreed. But how do we get it when we're stuck here, and she's gone?"

I think for a moment, then smile. "We have something she might not have considered."

"Which is?"

"Eight very wealthy, very well-connected women upstairs who think I'm their trusted guide. Women who've paid significant money to be here and won't appreciate being abandoned."

211

Maya's eyes light up with understanding. "You want to use the retreat participants."

"I want to turn them into allies. They all have connections, influence, money."

"And they trust you now."

"They trust the person they think I am. Erin's protégé, her chosen successor." I stand up, energy building. "What if we tell them the truth? Not all of it, but enough. That Erin has abandoned them, that there are serious questions about her business practices?"

Maya grins. "Rich people hate being scammed."

"Rich people have lawyers, investigators, connections we could never afford." I move to the window, looking out at the perfect paradise. "Instead of hiding what's happening, we use their resources to find out what Erin's really running from."

"And when we find her?"

I turn back to Maya, and she must see something in my expression because her grin widens.

"Then we make sure she can't run again. Whatever she's trying to escape, we drag her back to face it."

Maya nods slowly. "I like it. But we'll need to be careful about how we reveal things. Too much too fast and they'll think we're crazy."

"So we start tomorrow. During the sessions. Plant seeds of doubt. Let them discover inconsistencies themselves."

"What about Nicholas?"

I consider this. "Nicholas is a victim too, in his way. But he's also the person most likely to know what Erin's really afraid of. We might need to get him talking."

Maya extends her hand to me. "Partners?"

I shake it, feeling the firmness of her grip. "Partners. But Maya? Whatever we discover about why Erin ran, it doesn't change what she did to us. It doesn't make her theft any less real."

"Agreed. No matter what sob story emerges, she still destroyed our lives."

"Good." I look out at the tropical night, where somewhere out there, Erin Blake thinks she's escaped the consequences of her actions. "Because whatever she's running from, she's about to discover that some things follow you, no matter how far you go."

Maya nods. "Especially when you've given your enemies the perfect hunting ground."

We stand there in the darkness, two women bound by shared purpose and a plan that will either give us the answers we need or destroy us in the pursuit.

Tomorrow, the real match begins.

CHAPTER TWENTY-SIX

The next morning arrives with merciless Caribbean sunshine streaming through my windows, though I've barely slept. I've spent the hours since Maya left my room staring at the ceiling, rehearsing what I'm going to say to seven women who have no idea their world is about to shift as dramatically as mine has.

Now I stand before the group, my hands trembling. The sun blazes through the floor-to-ceiling windows, but the sweat beading along my hairline has nothing to do with the temperature and everything to do with the terror clawing at my chest.

The women sit in their now-familiar circle, sipping infused water. They trust me. From the moment Erin introduced me as her dear friend and collaborator, she made sure they would. Yesterday, when I stepped in to lead their sessions, that trust held. They responded to my guidance because Erin had already positioned me as someone worthy of their respect.

Notably absent is Layla, who should be here managing logistics, ensuring everything runs smoothly. I haven't seen her since yesterday morning when she desperately asked me to step in for Erin. Has she fled too? Or is she somewhere in the villa, frantically trying to manage a crisis she doesn't understand? I add it to my growing list of concerns, but now isn't the time to worry about it.

"Good morning, everyone." My voice cracks slightly, and I clear my throat. The humid air sticks to my skin like guilt.

"Good morning, Sam," they chorus back, their warmth making my chest tighten with shame.

Maya catches my eye from across the circle, her expression carefully neutral but her slight nod reminding me of our plan.

Find a way to tell them the truth.

Get them on our side.

But standing here, I feel like I'm about to shatter something precious.

"Before we begin today's session," I start, then stop. Should I just continue the lie? Tell them that Erin's publishing issues are taking longer than expected to resolve? This is their last day on the retreat. Their last chance to see the woman they paid twenty thousand each to change their lives.

She transformed mine too, though I paid a very different price.

Julia tilts her head with concern. "Sam? Is everything alright?"

Nothing is alright.

I'm trapped on a foreign island with no passport, surrounded by lies, leading therapeutic sessions based on my own stolen work while the thief has left me with a laptop full of evidence, legal documents, and warnings about her husband that I still don't know whether to believe.

"I need to address Erin's continued absence," I say, my voice unsteady.

The shift in energy is immediate. Sarah shuffles uncomfortably, Alessandra's posture noticeably tenses. Even in paradise, these successful women can sense when something's seriously wrong.

215

"Her publishing emergency?" Judith asks.

My mouth goes dry. Publishing emergency. I wish I had never gone along with the lie. These women deserve honesty. After all, that is why they are here.

I glance at Maya, who gives me the subtlest encouraging nod.

"That's... that's not entirely what happened," I admit.

"What do you mean?" Sarah's CEO instincts are sharpening her voice.

"The truth is," I say, and then have to take a breath. "I don't know where Erin is."

A tropical bird calls from somewhere in the garden, its cry sounding almost mocking.

"You don't know?" Julia says. "But surely there's been communication, updates about when she'll return?"

"No. Not about this." The admission feels like stepping off a cliff. "No communication. No updates. No indication of when, or if, she's coming back."

Maya leans forward. "Sam, maybe you should tell them everything."

The other women snap to look at their fellow attendee.

"Not about this?" Julia repeats. "So, what is this *everything* that you need to tell us?"

Everything. The word echoes in the stifling heat. Everything would mean admitting I'm not who they think I am. Everything would mean revealing that their beloved guru built her empire on theft. Everything seems like too much.

"I tried calling her last night," Sarah says, her frown deepening. "Her phone went straight to voicemail. And when I searched for information about this publishing crisis, I couldn't find anything current."

My heart lurches. "You tried to call her?"

"I wanted to thank her for the incredible work you did with us yesterday. And ask whether she would be back today." Julia's expression hardens. "There's nothing on her social media since her first day. Probably because our photographer is now apparently our facilitator."

"There's something else," Alessandra adds, her voice tight with growing suspicion. "I've been following Erin's work for years. I specifically chose this retreat because I wanted to learn her revolutionary Authentic Self Framework."

Revolutionary. The word lands like a punch to the gut.

"Her framework," I repeat, my voice hollow.

"Yes," Alessandra continues, oblivious to my distress. "The groundbreaking system she developed for authentic transformation. That's why I paid twenty thousand pounds to be here. No offence, Sam, but you aren't Erin Blake."

As the group murmur in agreement, something inside me snaps.

Twenty thousand pounds.

To learn my framework.

To experience the concepts I created when I was broke and broken, convinced I was worthless.

My revolutionary system that helped me understand why people feel so disconnected from who they really are.

But they don't want to hear it from *me*. They want her.

The tropical air feels suffocating.

"Sam?" Maya's voice cuts through my spiral. "You're safe here. Tell them."

Safe. These women have with their transformations, despite me not being Erin.

Did I really wish I was her?

"The framework you've been experiencing," I say, my voice growing stronger despite the tremor in my hands. "The exercises that have been helping you, the concepts that have been transforming your lives..."

I pause, looking at each of their faces. The humid air presses against me like a weight.

"They didn't come from Erin Blake."

The silence that follows is electric. Julia sets down her water glass with a sharp clink that echoes in the sudden quiet.

"What do you mean?" Sarah asks carefully.

Maya leans forward, her support evident but subtle. "Sam, tell them what you told me."

The permission in her voice gives me courage. These women deserve the truth. They've been working with the real framework, guided by its actual creator.

"I developed the Authentic Self Framework six years ago," I say, each word feeling like reclaiming a piece of my soul. "Every exercise you've worked through, every breakthrough you've experienced, came from my research, my insights, my understanding of authentic transformation."

I watch their faces process this information, see the mental recalibrations happening.

"*You* created it?" Julia's voice is sharp with disbelief. "Then why is Erin Blake touted as its creator?"

"Because she stole it." The words come out clean and final. "Six years ago, when we were best friends, I shared my work with her. Everything I'd developed. And then she took it, built an empire around it, and erased me completely."

The only sound is the relentless hum of air conditioning and the distant crash of waves. A paradise soundscape accompanying the destruction of carefully maintained lies.

"That's why yesterday felt so natural," Maya says, her voice filled with understanding. "You weren't following someone else's methods. You were teaching your own work."

"My God," Sarah breathes, her business instincts grasping the implications immediately. "So when you were leading our sessions..."

"I was sharing concepts I developed during the darkest period of my life," I finish. "I created the framework to help people remember that who they really are is enough. And to support them in reclaiming their true, authentic self."

Alessandra's eyes fill with tears. "And she just... took it?"

"Built a multimillion-pound business on it while I watched from the sidelines, convinced I was worthless."

Through the open doors, the scent of tropical flowers feels cloying rather than beautiful.

"So you became a photographer instead?" Judith asks.

I feel the blood rush to my cheeks.

"No," I admit quietly. "I was never really a photographer. It was a hobby. Erin asked me to come along to help her out."

I've done that in more ways than I can count.

Being honest with these women about the origins of the framework is one thing. Sharing my tales of woe and shoddy motel room angst is a step too far. I spare them the backstory.

"Where is she now?" Julia asks, her voice hardening with protective anger.

"I don't know," I admit. "But I think she's running. And she's left me here to clean up whatever mess she's made."

"Running from what?" Sarah asks.

I shake my head. I don't have an answer.

But it seems I don't need one. These women, successful, powerful, accustomed to taking control when things go wrong, are processing what it means to have been deceived.

"This is completely unacceptable," Sarah says. "We paid significant money under false pretences."

"More than that," Julia adds, her fingers moving across her phone. "We're talking about intellectual property theft, fraud, abandonment of fiduciary duty."

"She stole your work. We were..." Judith struggles to say the word. When she does, it comes out as a heavy, breathless sound. "*Scammed.*"

"I can have investigators on this within hours," Sarah continues. "Corporate fraud is something my company deals with internationally."

They are mobilising.

I didn't even have to ask for their help. They know what's happened is wrong.

"What do you need from us?" Judith asks with the authority of someone used to solving complex problems.

I look around the circle at these remarkable women, each offering her expertise and resources. For the first time in six years, I don't feel alone in this fight.

"I need help finding out what Erin's really running from," I say. "I need to find her. And then I need help making sure she faces the consequences."

"Consider it done," Sarah says.

Julia's fingers fly across her phone.

"So, how do we start?" she asks.

I take a breath, feeling stronger than I have since this nightmare began. The oppressive heat doesn't feel quite so suffocating anymore.

"We start by..."

"What the hell do you think you're doing?"

The voice cuts through our planning like a scissor blade slicing through silk. Every head snaps toward the doorway where Nicholas stands, his usually controlled facade completely shattered.

His eyes lock onto mine with an intensity that makes the tropical air feel suddenly arctic. The careful, distant Nicholas is gone, replaced by someone watching his entire world crumble in real time.

The sound of waves continues beyond the windows, but paradise has just become a battlefield.

CHAPTER TWENTY-SEVEN

The silence stretches for several heartbeats as Nicholas stands in the doorway, his expression carefully neutral but his posture rigid with barely contained tension. He surveys the scene with the same analytical calm he brings to everything else, though I catch the slight tightening around his eyes as he takes in the circle of mobilised women.

"Nicholas," I say, keeping my voice steady despite my racing heart. "We were just..."

"I heard *exactly* what you were doing." He steps into the room, with his characteristic controlled movements. "Which is precisely why we need to pause before anyone says something they might regret."

The threat is delivered so smoothly, wrapped in such reasonable language, that it takes a moment for the implications to sink in.

Sarah rises from her cushion with the fluid authority of someone used to boardroom confrontations. "Excuse me, but who are you to tell us what we can and cannot discuss?"

"I'm trying to protect everyone here," Nicholas says, his eyes darting between me and the circle of women. "Including you. Sam is having some kind of breakdown. She's not thinking clearly."

The accusation hangs in the humid air. Through the windows, I can see palm fronds swaying peacefully in the breeze, a mockery of the tension crackling through the room.

"A breakdown?" Julia says. "'She just led us through one of the most insightful sessions we've had all week."

"She's not qualified to lead anything," Nicholas continues, desperation bleeding into his tone. "She has no training in therapy or coaching. What she's telling you..."

"Is the truth," Maya interrupts, standing to join Sarah. "About the framework *she* created."

Nicholas's face goes pale.

"You don't understand what you're dealing with. Sam has always been jealous of Erin's success. She's been bitter for years about their friendship ending."

"Their friendship ending?" Alessandra's voice carries disbelief. "Is that what you call intellectual property theft?"

"That's not..." Nicholas starts, then stops, running a hand through his hair. "Look, all I know is that Erin built a legitimate business helping people transform their lives."

"Using Sam's work," Sarah says flatly.

"You don't know that." But even as he says it, Nicholas's certainty wavers. *He* knows it. He knows what Erin did.

I catch the flicker of doubt in his eyes, quickly suppressed.

I stand up slowly, feeling the strength of seven powerful women behind me.

"Nicholas. Where is your wife?"

"She'll be back," he says immediately. "Once this publishing crisis is resolved."

"What publishing crisis?" Julia asks, pointedly. "There doesn't seem to be any mention on the internet."

Nicholas's jaw tightens. "It's confidential."

"Bullshit," Sarah says bluntly. "I've worked in international business for fifteen years. I know what genuine crises look like, and I know what cover-ups look like." She leans towards Nicholas, unashamedly direct. "This is a cover-up."

The ceiling fan churns overhead, stirring the humid air but bringing no relief from the heat building in the room.

"Erin left," I say quietly, watching Nicholas's reaction. "She planned it. She's not coming back."

The women don't need to know about my passport.

They don't need to know the depth of my problems.

Nicholas is on the defensive, almost literally backed up against the wall.

"That's not accurate." The words come out with careful precision, but I hear the strain underneath. "She has no logical reason to leave. We have a successful partnership. A thriving business. Everything we've worked for."

The admission reveals more than he realises. Maya and I exchange a glance. We both heard it. *We* have a successful business. Not *she* has. We.

"What exactly is your role in the business, Nicholas?" Judith asks with professional curiosity.

"I handle operations, financial management, legal compliance." His defensive tone suggests he's had to justify his position before.

"And how much of the actual business revenue do you generate?" Sarah asks.

Nicholas's composure slips slightly. "Business partnerships aren't about individual metrics. We're a team."

"A team," Julia repeats slowly. "Built on stolen intellectual property."

"That's an unfounded accusation," Nicholas replies, but his voice lacks its earlier conviction.

I step forward, feeling braver with each word. "She left evidence. Files, documents, proof of where the framework really came from. All documented on that laptop she wanted me to find."

"She's been planning this for months," I continue, studying his increasingly strained expression. "Getting everything in order. Making sure the truth would finally come out. The question is: did she tell you why?"

Nicholas shakes his head. "Erin always puts the business first. She wouldn't do this. It doesn't make any sense."

"Have you considered," Maya suggests quietly, "that she couldn't live with what she'd done anymore?"

Nicholas turns to her. "You don't know Erin. She's dedicated her career to helping people. Everything she's built has been focused on authentic transformation."

"Built on Sam's stolen work," Sarah interrupts. "We've established that."

"And now she's fled," Alessandra adds, "leaving you to manage the fallout."

"She hasn't fled." For the first time, Nicholas's control cracks slightly. "She's coming back. She has to come back. Without her, without the business infrastructure we've built..."

He stops abruptly, realising he's revealed too much.

"Without the business, what?" Julia presses. "You lose your lifestyle? Your income? Your identity as the successful entrepreneur's husband?"

The accuracy of her assessment is written across Nicholas's carefully composed features.

"You don't *care* where she is," I realise, the truth hitting me. "You don't care what she has *done*. You care about what her absence means for your financial security."

"That's not... that's not true," he protests, but his eyes won't meet mine.

"Have you even tried to find her?" Sarah asks with businesslike directness. "Contact authorities? Hire investigators? Take any actual steps to locate your missing wife?"

Nicholas's silence speaks volumes.

"You've been focused on damage control instead of finding your missing wife," Maya observes. "Because you're more concerned about business implications than her wellbeing."

"She's not missing," Nicholas says, his voice tightening. "She'll be back."

The words echo in the suddenly quiet room.

"What makes you so sure?" I ask quietly, because I can see that he honestly believes it.

Nicholas stares at me, his face cycling through careful control, growing desperation, and something that might be shame.

"She wouldn't leave me. She wouldn't leave this," he says finally. "She wouldn't let me down."

The admission settles over us like the oppressive heat. Here is a man whose wife has vanished, possibly forever, and his primary concern is protecting the lifestyle her stolen work has funded.

"If this becomes public... the allegations, the business practices, the foundation being questioned... it won't just affect Erin. Every client testimonial, every business partnership, every professional relationship." He gestures weakly toward the windows, toward the paradise outside. "All of this disappears."

"Good," I say simply.

The finality in my voice seems to break something in Nicholas. For a moment, he looks like what he really is: a man whose comfortable life has been built on someone else's stolen dreams, finally forced to confront the price of his wilful blindness.

Outside, the Caribbean continues its eternal rhythm, indifferent to human guilt and consequences. But inside this perfect villa, the reckoning has finally begun.

CHAPTER TWENTY-EIGHT

Nicholas remains frozen near the windows, his usual composed facade cracking as he watches these eight women morph from retreat participants into a formidable tactical unit. His mouth opens as if to speak, then closes again when no one looks his way.

"Ladies," he finally manages, his voice carrying a forced authority, "I really think we should consider the implications before..."

"Before what?" Sarah interrupts without looking up from her phone. "Before we investigate fraud? Before we track down someone who's stolen intellectual property and abandoned paying clients?"

Nicholas's face goes pale, but he doesn't retreat. He can't afford to.

"Right," Sarah announces, turning to the group as if Nicholas no longer exists. "First priority: we track Erin's movements. Julia, you mentioned you could trace digital footprints?"

"Already on it." Julia's fingers dance across her phone screen. "I'm reaching out to contacts at payment processing companies. If she's used any cards, we'll know within the hour."

I watch this mobilisation with something approaching awe. Twenty-four hours ago, I was a desperate woman standing in for a missing person. Now I have a team of millionaire investigators working on my behalf.

"Judith, you said you have publishing connections?" Alessandra asks. "Can you verify whether there actually is any crisis with Erin's book?"

"Done. I'm texting my editor at Penguin Random House right now." Judith's thumbs move with surprising speed. "If there's a genuine publishing emergency involving Erin Blake, someone in my network will know about it. The best lies are based on truth, so maybe there was some kind of issue."

Maya catches my eye and smiles. This is exactly what we'd hoped would happen.

"What about flight manifests?" Sarah asks. "Immigration records?"

"Petra, didn't you mention you have contacts in immigration law?" Julia prompts.

"I can handle that," Petra says, pulling out her tablet. "If Erin left Aruba legally, there'll be a record."

The energy in the room is intoxicating. For the first time since discovering my passport was missing, I feel like I'm not completely powerless.

"Sam," Sarah turns to me, "we'll need any additional details you can provide. Account numbers, personal information, anything that might help us track her."

"I don't know her details," I say with a frown. "Why would I?"

"Not hers," Sarah says. "Yours."

The request stops me cold. Account numbers. Bank details.

When did I last check my bank cards?

The thought hits me like ice water. In the chaos of the past few days... the villa, the clothes, rental car, everything being provided for me... I haven't even thought about my own cards.

But - again - why would I? It's not like I have any money in my accounts.

"Julia," I say slowly, "when you're tracking card usage... would you be able to see attempted transactions that were declined?"

"Of course. Why?"

I sink back onto my cushion, mind racing through the implications. "She had access to my things. My passport was in my bag, but so was my wallet. I haven't checked because..." I trail off, embarrassed.

"Because why?" Sarah prompts gently.

"Because there's no money in the accounts." The admission burns. "The cards are maxed out. I've been living on credit for months, and even that's gone. I wouldn't check them because there's nothing to check."

The sympathy on their faces makes my cheeks flame, but Julia leans forward with renewed interest.

"That's actually perfect for tracking. If she's been trying to use cards with no available credit, every attempted transaction will be logged. We'll have a complete picture of where she's been and what she's tried to buy."

Hope flickers back to life in my chest. Maybe my financial disaster could finally work in my favour.

"I'll need your card numbers," Julia continues, pulling out a tablet. "And we should move fast. The longer we wait, the more the digital trail could be compromised."

I recite the numbers from memory. They're burned into my brain from months of declined transaction shame. Then Julia concentrates on her screen, connecting to systems I can't even comprehend.

"Interesting," she murmurs after a few minutes. "I'm seeing attempted transactions starting yesterday morning. Multiple declined attempts at ATMs in Oranjestad, then what looks like attempted purchases at... a pharmacy, a clothing store, the airport."

"The airport?" My heart leaps. "So, she did leave?"

"All I know is that she was at the airport. But..." Julia frowns at her screen. "The transactions all stopped after about six hours. Last attempted use was yesterday at 11am."

When Layla came to ask me to stand in for Erin, she was still on the island. I could have found her. I could have stopped her.

I didn't even try.

"Maybe she gave up when nothing worked?" Alessandra suggests.

"Maybe," Julia says, but her expression is troubled. "Or maybe she found another way to get money. She must have had some cash with her."

Judith looks up from her phone. "I've heard from my publishing contacts. There's no crisis with Erin Blake's book. In fact, her publisher hasn't heard from her in weeks. They're starting to worry about missed deadlines."

"Flight records," Petra announces, consulting her tablet. "I've got preliminary information from my immigration contact. No record of Erin Blake leaving Aruba on any commercial flight in the past 48 hours."

"And Samantha Foster?" I ask. "Erin took my passport. She would have booked in my name."

Petra checks again.

"Nothing," she says.

I don't know what this means.

I watch these women work with a mixture of gratitude and growing unease. They're more thorough, more connected, more capable than any official investigation could be. So why do I feel like we're missing something fundamental?

"There's another possibility," Maya says quietly. "What if she never left at all?"

The suggestion hangs in the humid air like a physical presence.

Nicholas takes a step forward, his composure finally cracking. "She's not even called me. If she was still here, if she was..." He stops, the implications hitting him. His voice becomes smaller. "She would have called me."

I almost feel sorry for him.

The women immediately chat between themselves about Maya's suggestion, speculating, voices overlapping as they plan a systematic search of the villa. But even as they formulate an action plan, something nags at me. A detail that doesn't fit. Another absence that suddenly feels glaring.

"Wait," I say, stopping their logistics discussion. "Before we tear apart the villa looking for Erin..."

I look around the circle of concerned, intelligent faces. Women who've been here for four days, who've attended every session, every meal, every planned activity.

"Where the hell is Layla?"

The question drops into the room like a stone into still water, sending ripples of realisation across eight faces.

"I haven't seen her since..." Julia starts, then stops, her expression shifting.

"Since Erin went missing," Sarah finishes grimly.

Layla. Erin's efficient assistant. The woman who was managing every detail of this retreat until the moment Erin disappeared.

"The last time I saw her," I say, "was when she asked me to stand in for Erin. She came to my room, then sent me over the session plans. After that... nothing."

"She should be here," Petra says, looking around as if Layla might materialise from the shadows. "Managing this crisis, handling logistics, communicating with Erin's business partners."

"Instead, she's just... gone," Maya observes.

The silence that follows differs from our earlier contemplative pauses. This silence carries weight, implications, the sudden understanding that we've been so focused on finding Erin that we've overlooked the person who could know exactly where she is.

Through the open doors, the Caribbean continues its eternal rhythm, waves against sand, palm fronds rustling in the breeze. But inside our air-conditioned bubble, the tropical paradise suddenly feels less like sanctuary and more like a carefully constructed stage.

And we're just beginning to realise that some of the most important players have been performing in the shadows all along.

CHAPTER TWENTY-NINE

Eight wealthy women, one desperate husband, and I all stare at each other as the implications sink in. Layla, efficient Layla who managed every detail of this retreat with military precision, has simply vanished.

And none of us missed her.

The woman who should be here coordinating damage control, fielding calls from Erin's business partners, reassuring clients everything is under control.

Gone.

Instead, there's just silence where her competence should be.

Maya leans backwards, fingers drumming against her knee with increasing agitation. Alessandra worries at the hem of her linen tunic. Even Nicholas has gone pale, though whether from the realisation about Layla or the mounting evidence of his wife's deception, I can't tell.

Sarah breaks first, her designer sandals clicking against the marble as she begins pacing.

"Right. We need to split up and search every inch of this villa systematically. She has to be somewhere." Her mind is already working, assigning territories like a military operation. "Alessandra, you take the staff quarters. Petra, the business offices. Julia, you handle the..."

"She could have left already," Petra interrupts, her frown deepening. "She's had so much time."

"Then we check with the front desk," Sarah shoots back without missing a beat, her voice gaining that boardroom intensity. "See if anyone spotted her leaving. Get security footage if we have to. Track down a taxi driver who might have…"

"We could just call her."

Judith's voice cuts through Sarah's escalating battle plan like a scalpel through silk. Quiet, matter of fact, devastatingly practical.

Everyone freezes. Sarah's mouth closes mid-sentence, her pacing interrupted.

Judith sits calmly in her chair, phone already in hand, watching us with the patient expression of someone who's spent decades in publishing meetings, watching brilliant people overcomplicate simple solutions.

"If Layla's been managing this crisis… and by crisis, I mean whatever this absolute shitshow is that Erin's orchestrating… she'll have her mobile with her." She gestures with her phone toward our circle of increasingly frazzled faces. "I have her number from the retreat coordination emails."

The suggestion is so blindingly obvious that I feel heat flood my cheeks. We were about to plan an elaborate villa-wide manhunt when the answer was sitting right there in Judith's contacts list.

"Christ," Sarah mutters, deflating as she abandons her search formation. The transformation from general to ordinary person happens in seconds. "You're absolutely right."

Nicholas shifts nervously by the windows, his hands clasped behind his back, expression caught between desperate hope and mounting dread as Judith's finger hovers over the screen.

"Put her on speaker," Sarah adds, settling back into her chair with the slightly sheepish look of someone who's just been out-manoeuvrer by simple common sense.

The phone rings once, twice, then Layla's familiar voice fills the room.

"Judith? Is everything alright?"

"We're all here, Layla," Sarah says, taking control. "All the retreat participants. We've been wondering where you've been."

A pause. When Layla speaks again, her voice carries that carefully modulated tone of someone choosing their words.

"I'm so sorry for my absence. I've been assisting Erin with the publishing emergency. It's been quite intense, requiring round-the-clock damage control."

The women exchange glances. Julia clears her throat.

"Layla, we've checked with publishing contacts. There is no emergency with Erin's book. She hasn't even spoken with her publisher. We called them."

Silence stretches across the phone line. I can almost hear Layla's mind racing.

"I... there may have been some miscommunication about the nature of the crisis," she says finally. "It's quite complex, involving multiple stakeholders..."

"Cut the bullshit," Maya interrupts bluntly. "We know Erin's disappeared. We know she's abandoned her retreat and her clients. The question is: where are you?"

Another pause, longer this time.

"I'm handling the situation as best I can," Layla says, but her voice lacks conviction. "Erin will be back with you this afternoon. Everything will return to normal."

"Normal?" Alessandra laughs harshly. "You mean after she stole Sam's intellectual property and built her entire business on fraud?"

I hear what sounds like a sharp intake of breath through the phone.

"That's... that's not..." Layla starts.

"We know everything," Sarah says with businesslike directness. "The framework was Sam's creation. Erin stole it six years ago. And now she's fled, leaving everyone to clean up her mess."

"She hasn't fled," Layla says quickly. Too quickly. "She's just... she's working through some personal challenges. She'll be back. She always comes back."

Nicholas steps forward, hope creeping into his voice. "Layla, is she alright? Can I speak to her? I've been worried sick..."

"She's..." Layla hesitates. "She's not taking calls right now. But she's safe. She's..."

"She's what?" Julia presses.

The silence that follows carries a different weight. Through the phone, I can hear background noise: the faint sound of waves, what might be a door closing.

"Layla," I say quietly, "tell us the truth. Please."

When she speaks again, her voice is barely above a whisper.

"She's right here with me."

The admission drops into the room like a bomb. Nicholas actually reaches his hand out to the wall to steady himself. The women lean forward instinctively, as if proximity to the phone might help them understand better.

"Right there with you," Maya repeats slowly. "She's been there all along."

"Yes," Layla says, her voice regaining some of its professional polish. There's a pause, a slight hesitance, like she's reading from a script. "She's been working through some personal matters, but she'll be back with you shortly."

Layla speaks as if the past two days have been perfectly ordinary. As if we didn't all watch Erin vanish into thin air without a word.

"Put her on the phone," Sarah demands.

"Of course. One moment."

The handover is too easy. No hesitation. No protest. Just seamless professionalism, as if we're booking a dinner reservation.

Then Erin's voice fills the speaker, warm, steady, unmistakably composed.

"Hello, everyone. I'm so sorry for any confusion."

We freeze. That voice. Smooth, confident, perfectly pitched. No panic. No guilt. She sounds exactly like she always does: like she's in control.

"Confusion?" Julia's voice is sharp. "Erin, you disappeared. You abandoned your retreat, your clients..."

"I can understand how it might have seemed that way," Erin says. "But I had urgent personal matters to

239

deal with. Layla has been managing everything in my absence."

I stare at the phone, fists tightening at my sides. She's doing it again, rearranging reality in real time. Calm. Soothing. Ruthlessly composed.

Nicholas leans in closer, bewildered. "Personal matters? You didn't say anything to me. You just... left."

"I know, darling. And I'm sorry for worrying you. But it's all sorted now. I'm already on my way back. I'll be there very soon."

Nicholas's mouth parts slightly. "You're coming back now?"

"I am. I'll see you all shortly."

It's clinical, almost cold, the way she separates personal from professional, as if we're nothing more than names on a client list.

"Tell us where you are," I say. "We'll come to you."

"That's not necessary," Erin replies, her voice brisk, confident. "Stay where you are. I'll be there within the hour."

"Erin, wait..." Nicholas starts.

But she has hung up.

Not an abrupt end. Not a panicked exit.

A dismissal. Clean and final.

We sit frozen, staring at the phone. Through the windows, the late morning sun burns relentlessly, but inside, a chill settles in the room.

Erin Blake is coming back.

CHAPTER THIRTY

The silence after the line goes dead feels like holding my breath underwater. Eight faces stare at the phone as if Erin might somehow materialise through the speaker. The tropical air presses against my skin like a wet blanket.

"Within the hour," I repeat, my voice barely above a whisper.

"Well," Sarah says, attempting her boardroom confidence, but I catch the slight tremor underneath. "At least we'll have answers."

Answers. The word should be comforting, but my chest tightens with each heartbeat. A few minutes ago, I was surrounded by allies. Now, as reality sets in, I can see doubt creeping across their faces like shadows.

Through the open doors, I can hear the eternal rhythm of waves against sand, but the paradise soundtrack now feels mocking.

"She's been gone for two days," I say, trying to recapture the certainty I felt earlier. "Two days without explanation, leaving paying clients stranded... She abandoned you."

"But she's coming back," Julia interrupts gently. "That suggests she hadn't really abandoned anything."

The logic is reasonable, rational, exactly the kind of thinking that successful businesswomen excel at. It's also completely missing the point, but I can't articulate why without sounding paranoid.

"You don't understand," I begin, then stop. How do I explain six years of psychological manipulation to women who've known me for four days?

"Help us understand," Sarah says, but her voice has lost its earlier fire. She's back in negotiation mode, seeking middle ground rather than choosing sides.

Outside, I hear the distant sound of a car door closing. Footsteps on gravel. The measured pace of someone who's completely in control.

"Maybe," Alessandra says quietly, "we should hear what she has to say before making any judgments."

The words feel like a betrayal, but I can see the logic from their perspective. They've paid twenty thousand pounds to meet Erin Blake, not to get caught up in some byzantine personal drama between old friends.

Nicholas moves toward the doorway, his entire posture changing. The defeated man who'd watched his world crumble is gone, replaced by someone anticipating salvation.

"I should..." he starts, then stops as we hear the front door open.

"Hello? Nicholas? Where is everyone?"

The voice carries easily through the villa's open layout. Confident, untroubled, exactly what you'd expect from someone returning from a brief business trip rather than someone who's been missing for two days.

"In here," Nicholas calls, his voice carrying relief and desperate hope.

Her footsteps approach. Measured, unhurried. The sound of someone who owns every space she enters.

And then Erin Blake appears in the doorway.

She looks perfect. Not like someone who's been hiding or running or dealing with a crisis. Her hair is styled, her makeup flawless, her white linen dress crisp and unwrinkled. She carries herself with the same serene confidence she's always possessed, as if the last forty-eight hours were a minor inconvenience rather than a complete abandonment of responsibility.

Her gaze sweeps the room, taking in the circle of women, Nicholas, and finally settling on me with something that might be amusement.

"Well," she says, moving into the room with fluid grace. "This looks very serious."

She doesn't apologise. Doesn't explain her absence. Doesn't acknowledge the chaos she's caused. Instead, she positions herself at the centre of the circle as if nothing has changed, as if she's simply returning from a coffee break.

"Erin," Nicholas breathes, and the relief in his voice is painful to hear.

"Hello, darling," she says, but her attention remains focused on the group. "I hope Sam has been taking good care of everyone in my absence."

The phrasing is deliberate. Taking care. Not leading, not facilitating, not teaching. Taking care, like a babysitter minding children.

"We've had some very interesting conversations," Maya says, her voice carrying an edge I haven't heard before.

Erin's smile doesn't falter, but something shifts in her eyes. "I'm sure you have. Sam's always been full of fascinating theories."

Theories. Another dismissal, subtle but devastating.

"She told us about the framework," Julia says. "About how she developed it originally."

"Did she?" Erin settles into the chair I'd been occupying, claiming the facilitator's position with effortless authority. "How interesting. And what exactly did she tell you?"

The question is asked with genuine curiosity, as if she's inquiring about an entertaining story rather than addressing accusations of theft.

"She said you stole her intellectual property," Sarah states bluntly.

Erin's laugh is light, musical, completely devoid of defensiveness.

She looks around the circle, her expression warm and understanding, like a patient teacher dealing with a confused student.

"What Sam is referring to happened during our university days." She settles back in her chair as though she's about to tell a bedtime story to children. "We were in our tiny flat, drinking wine from a box, the cheapest we could find, eating store-brand crisps because that's all we could afford." Her voice takes on a faux warmth, the kind perfected through thousands of coaching sessions.

"Sam had been going through one of her... episodes." She pauses deliberately, scanning the circle of faces. "Another boy had disappointed her, and you know how that goes when you're twenty-one..."

A few knowing smiles appear around the circle. Petra nods with sympathetic understanding, and Julia's expression softens with recognition.

"She was having an existential crisis about authenticity," Erin continues, emboldened by their response.

I feel heat rise to my cheeks, but Erin continues seamlessly.

"She suggested something vaguely similar to what became the Authentic Self Framework. Very rough, very theoretical. The kind of late night philosophising students do when they're drunk and feeling sorry for themselves."

Her tone remains affectionate, almost protective, which somehow makes it worse. Because even though I want to deny it, I know she's not entirely wrong.

"But suggesting an idea and building a business are completely different things, aren't they?" She looks directly at Julia, then Sarah. "Creation without execution is just... dreaming."

I want to scream that none of this is true. But the ugly reality sits in my chest like a stone: she's right about the wine, the crisps, my heartbreak over some boy whose name I can't even remember now. She's right that I was drunk and *philosophising* instead of planning.

"I have evidence. Documentation. Proof of what really happened. You *gave* it to me. You were leaving... you... you..."

"Evidence?" Erin's eyebrows rise with polite interest. "How fascinating. I'd love to see it."

"You left that laptop..."

The smile that spreads across Erin's face is genuinely puzzled. "What laptop, Sam? I have no idea what you're talking about."

The denial is so smooth, so convincing, that I doubt myself momentarily. But Maya was there. She saw the files.

"The laptop with all the financial records and legal documents," I press. "The evidence of everything you've done."

Erin turns to the group with an expression of gentle concern. "I'm not sure what Sam's been showing you, but I can assure you I haven't given her any laptop. Perhaps she found something online? The internet can be quite convincing these days."

"She didn't show us a laptop," Judith says. I can't read her tone, but I know she doesn't sound as friendly and supportive as she did earlier.

The implication hangs in the air. That I've fabricated evidence. That I'm delusional.

"Maya saw it too," I say desperately.

Erin's gaze shifts to Maya, and her expression changes subtly. Recognition. Not pleasant recognition.

"Maya Lawson," she says slowly. "I knew I recognised your name. It took me a while to put the little pieces together, though."

The use of Maya's full name sends a chill through the room. The women look between them, sensing undercurrents they don't understand.

"You two know each other?" Sarah asks.

"Oh yes," Erin says, her voice taking on a different quality. "Maya and I have history. Don't we, Maya?"

246

Maya's face has gone pale, but her voice remains steady. "We do."

"Maya attended one of my early workshops," Erin continues, addressing the group but keeping her eyes on Maya.

Instead of throwing what she knows about Erin out for everyone to see, Maya tilts her head and looks at our leader.

Erin's smile is patient, understanding. "She's convinced herself that I somehow wronged her, and now she's found someone else who shares her delusions."

The psychology is masterful. Erin's positioning Maya and me as co-conspirators, mentally unstable women who've found each other and reinforced each other's paranoid fantasies.

"Sam's framework changed my life. Even before this retreat," Julia says quietly, but there's uncertainty in her voice now.

"I'm so glad you've found value in the work," Erin replies warmly. "The Authentic Self Framework has helped thousands of people. It's been my life's work."

My life's work.

The casual ownership, as if *my* contribution never existed.

"But Sam created it," Alessandra says, though she sounds less certain than before.

Erin's expression becomes gentle, almost pitying. "Sam likes to think she contributed to the early development, and in a way, she did. But talking about ideas and actually building a framework, a business, a methodology that works... those are very different things. The name was hers, and I admit I should have asked before I borrowed it, but everything else was mine. The work was all mine."

She turns to look at me directly, her voice taking on a note of sincere compassion.

"You've always been such a dreamer, and I loved that for you," she says. "But you were always dreaming up businesses, never following through."

The words land like punches. Around the circle, I can see the women processing this new narrative. The successful businesswoman explaining reality to the delusional friend who can't distinguish between inspiration and creation.

"The laptop..." I try again weakly.

"There is no laptop, Sam," Erin says gently. "At least, not from me. The mind can play tricks when we're under stress."

She stands, moving to the centre of the circle with the same graceful authority she's always possessed.

"What I suggest," she says, addressing the group, "is that we use our remaining time together productively. You've all made remarkable progress, and I'd hate for this... confusion... to derail your transformative work."

Confusion. Not theft, not fraud, not abandonment.

"Sam's been leading our sessions," Judith says. "She's been excellent."

"I'm sure she has," Erin agrees. "She's learned so much over the years of watching me. She's absorbed so many concepts. But there's a difference between understanding ideas and having the experience to guide others safely through transformation."

The implication is clear: I'm a gifted amateur, she's the professional.

"I think," Petra says slowly, "we need some time to process all of this."

Agreement murmurs around the circle. The unity that felt so powerful an hour ago has completely dissolved. These women don't know who to trust, what to believe, or how to reconcile two completely different versions of reality.

Erin has achieved exactly what she set out to do: she's made truth negotiable.

"Of course," she says graciously. "Why don't we break for lunch? Give everyone a chance to reflect. We can reconvene this afternoon and decide how to proceed."

She moves toward the doorway, pausing beside Nicholas.

"Darling, could I speak with you privately?"

Nicholas nods eagerly, following her like a grateful puppy.

As they leave, the remaining women look at each other with expressions of complete bewilderment. The confident investigators of an hour ago have become confused participants in a drama they don't understand.

Maya meets my eyes across the circle. Her face is pale but determined.

"We need to get that laptop," she mouths silently.

My chest tightens. If Erin's this confident, this casual about dismissing it...

The laptop is already gone.

CHAPTER THIRTY-ONE

The walk to my room feels like a funeral march. Maya trails beside me, her jaw set with barely contained fury. Neither of us speaks until we reach my door.

"She can't just..." Maya starts, then stops as I slide the keycard through the reader.

The room looks exactly as I left it this morning. Bed made neatly, surfaces gleaming, everything in its perfect place. Except for one crucial absence.

As expected, the laptop is gone.

I move through the motions of checking under the bed, in the wardrobe, the bathroom. Maya joins the search, her movements growing increasingly agitated.

"Shit," she breathes. "She took it. She actually took it."

I sink onto the bed, letting my shoulders slump in apparent defeat. "It's gone. All of it."

Maya stops searching and looks at me with something like pity. "Sam, I'm so sorry. I know how much that evidence meant to you."

"Six years," I whisper, voice carefully pitched between anger and despair. "And the one chance I had to prove it..." I let the sentence hang unfinished.

Maya sits beside me. "Listen, I still have documentation. Financial records, evidence from other victims. We can still expose her."

"With what?" The bitterness in my voice is only half-performed. "She just convinced eight intelligent women that I'm delusional. That the laptop never existed. Your word against hers won't be enough."

250

Maya's voice is heavy with frustration. "What I have is good, but it's not a smoking gun."

I stand and move to the corner where the room safe sits, its digital display blinking quietly.

Maya watches me with confusion. "What are you doing?"

The safe opens with a soft beep. Inside sits the Leica Q2. Erin's already taken everything I'm supposed to value, but she left me this one gift.

"It's the group's last afternoon," I say, lifting the camera out carefully. "I came here to do a job, and I'm not leaving without finishing it."

Maya frowns. "Sam, taking pictures isn't going to fix this. We need to focus on exposing her properly."

"I will help you," I say, meeting her eyes. "But trust me. I need to do this my way."

Something in my tone must convince her because she nods slowly. "Okay. But whatever you're planning..."

"Trust me," I repeat, checking the camera's settings with performed efficiency.

We make our way back downstairs. I can hear Erin's voice flowing from the main room, warm and confident, already beginning the afternoon session as if nothing has happened.

"Remember, transformation isn't about becoming someone new," she's saying. "It's about realising who you were always meant to be, and embracing that inner self."

My words. My philosophy. Being delivered with the polished perfection she's spent six years refining.

Maya takes a seat at the edge of the circle while I position myself at the back of the room, camera raised.

Erin doesn't notice me immediately. She's too focused on reclaiming her audience, rebuilding the connection with these women.

"The authentic self isn't hidden," she continues. "It's simply waiting for us to stop performing and start being."

I raise the camera and take my first photograph. The soft click echoes in the quiet room.

Erin's flow stutters for just a moment, but she recovers smoothly. "Today, I want to explore what it means to live authentically in a world that rewards performance."

Another click. Several women glance toward the sound.

"Sam?" Julia asks. "Are you documenting this session, too?"

"Just finishing my work," I reply evenly.

Erin's eyes find mine across the room. For a split second, confusion flickers across her face, but then her professional smile returns.

"Of course," she says. "Documentation is so important."

She continues her session, but I notice her gaze drifting toward me more frequently. Each photograph I take seems to disrupt her rhythm slightly.

"The framework teaches us that authenticity requires courage," she says, her voice gaining intensity as she tries to regain control. "The courage to face uncomfortable truths about ourselves."

Click.

"The courage to admit when we've been living someone else's version of our story."

Click.

Her delivery is becoming more stilted now, her attention divided between her audience and the woman at the back of the room with the camera she gave me.

"Sometimes we have to let go of old narratives," Erin continues, but there's a new edge in her voice. "Even narratives we've... inherited from others."

Click.

Her eyes lock onto mine as she says this, and I see the exact moment realisation dawns. Not about what's on the camera - she can't know that yet. But about the camera itself. About what it represents.

Documentation. Evidence. Proof.

The colour drains from her face as understanding builds.

But I'm not done. I raise the camera one more time, making sure she sees me frame the shot carefully.

Click.

Erin stops speaking entirely, her gaze fixed on the camera in my hands. The camera she gave me. The camera she never thought to consider when she was destroying my evidence.

The room falls silent as she stares at me, and I see the moment she puts it together. Not what's on it - not yet. But what it could contain.

And for the first time since she walked back into this villa, Erin Blake looks afraid.

Perfect. The high intensity psychological tennis match is about to begin, and I have first serve.

CHAPTER THIRTY-TWO

The silence in the room stretches like a held breath. Erin stares at the camera in my hands, her face cycling through confusion, realisation, and growing dread.

"Perhaps," she says carefully, "we should take a short break now."

"Oh no," I say, my voice cutting through the humid air like a blade. "I think everyone should hear this."

I hold up the camera, letting it catch the light streaming through the windows. The weight of it feels different now, not just expensive equipment, but evidence. Justice. The very weapon Erin handed me herself.

"This is a Leica Q2, Erin. You made such a big deal about giving me the best equipment," I continue, my voice gaining strength. "Professional grade. Top of the line. Nothing but the finest for capturing your authentic moments."

"Sam," Erin says, her voice taking on that soothing tone she uses with difficult clients. "Whatever you think..."

"Do you know what's funny about that, Erin?" I interrupt, taking a step closer to the circle. "You didn't actually need a photographer at all."

The observation hangs in the air.

"When I stepped in to lead yesterday's sessions, there was no replacement photographer," I explain, my smile sharp. "No one rushing to document the profound transformations. No concern about missing those authentic moments you claimed were so important."

Erin's composed mask is starting to crack around the edges.

"It was all just a ruse, wasn't it?" I laugh, but there's no humour in it. "Getting me here. Giving me purpose. Making me feel useful." I gesture with the camera. "It would be like asking someone to sing at your wedding just because they did drunken karaoke when you were eighteen."

I pause, letting that sink in before delivering the real blow.

"Because that's all I ever was with photography, wasn't it? Remember those terrible photos I took at uni? That ancient Canon I bought second-hand that was probably older than we were?" The memory brings a bitter smile to my lips. "I thought I was so artistic, wandering around campus taking blurry shots of pigeons and badly framed portraits of you looking bored."

"You used to laugh at them," I continue, my voice gaining momentum. "Those wonky horizon lines, the overexposed skies, the way I could never quite get the focus right. 'Sam's abstract period,' you called it, because everything was so out of focus it looked intentional."

Erin's face flickers with what might be recognition or perhaps regret.

"I remember that photo I took of you by the Thames, where I cut off half your head and somehow managed to get a perfect shot of a crisp packet in the foreground instead." The laughter that escapes me is sharp, self-deprecating. "You said it looked like evidence from a crime scene."

"That's not..." Erin starts.

"But you know what?" I cut her off, my voice rising. "I wanted to prove to you that I could do it. Despite being a complete washup, despite having nothing, despite being so pathetic you found me in a motel room counting coins..." The admission burns, but I push through it. "I wanted to show you that I do have skills. I do have talent."

The vulnerability in my confession seems to surprise everyone, including myself. But it's the truth that makes what comes next so much more devastating.

"So I spent two solid days learning what this camera could do." I trace the sleek surface with one finger. "Every button, every function, every capability. Forty-seven-point-three megapixel full-frame sensor," I recite, my voice gaining strength with each technical specification. "Capable of capturing the finest details in both photo and video mode."

"I researched white balance settings, exposure compensation, focus peaking. I learned about ISO performance and dynamic range. I practised with the manual controls until I could adjust them in my sleep." My smile grows wider as I watch understanding dawn in Erin's eyes. "You asked me to capture everything, remember? Every session, every *breakthrough*, every *authentic moment*."

"Sam," Erin says. "You're clearly upset about the laptop, but..."

"The laptop?" I laugh, and the sound is sharp enough to make several women flinch. "Oh, Erin. The laptop was never the real evidence. You gave it to me, and I know that anything you gave me, you could take away just as easily."

I tap the camera's display screen, and the soft blue glow seems to illuminate the growing horror on Erin's face.

"Every file. Every document. Every piece of proof you thought you destroyed when you took that laptop from my room." I pause, savouring the moment. "All right here. Preserved in crystal clarity."

The colour drains from Erin's face so completely she looks like she might faint.

The women around the circle look between us with growing confusion, sensing the undercurrents but not understanding them.

"That's... that's impossible," she whispers.

"Is it?" I scroll through the camera's menu with ease, each beep and click echoing in the suddenly quiet room. "You gave me the tools, after all. Professional equipment. Professional training. And a photographer's first instinct is to preserve important images. *I always had such a good eye.*"

The irony is delicious. Erin, in her arrogance, in her need to control every detail, handed me the very weapon that would destroy her. Like a villain in a fairy tale, undone by her own machinations. It's like taking the poisoned apple and making a pie for the evil Queen.

"You see, when you gave me this camera and told me to document everything, I took that instruction

257

very seriously." I advance another step toward her, watching her instinctively back away. "I documented the laptop contents before you could steal them back. I documented the legal papers transferring your business to me. I documented your financial records showing exactly how much you've made from my stolen work."

Erin takes another step backward, her usual poise completely shattered.

"You're bluffing," she says, but her voice is thin, desperate. "You couldn't have... there's no way..."

But I know that she is already sure.

"Would you like me to show them?" I ask conversationally, my thumb hovering over the playback button. "I have video of you confessing that the framework was originally my concept. Audio of you admitting you '*borrowed*' my work without permission. Time-stamped proof of every lie you've built your empire on."

"No." The word comes out sharp, panicked. Erin's hands are actually trembling now. "You can't... there's no way you could have..."

She trails off, staring at the camera as if it's a loaded weapon pointed at her heart.

Around the circle, the women are leaning forward now, understanding beginning to dawn on their faces. Julia's expression has shifted from confusion to sharp interest. Sarah's eyes narrow as she processes the implications.

I watch Erin stare at the camera, and I can practically see her mind racing.

"You're wondering how, aren't you?" I say softly. "How the woman you trapped on this island managed to turn your own evidence against you?"

Erin's silence is answer enough.

For a long moment, she just stares at me. Then, slowly, something changes in her expression. The terror fades, replaced by something else.

Not fear. Not defeat.

Pity.

CHAPTER THIRTY-THREE

Victory tastes like adrenaline and tropical air. I grip the camera tighter, letting its weight anchor me in this moment of complete triumph. For the first time in six years, I have Erin Blake exactly where I want her. Exposed. Terrified. Trapped by her own arrogance.

Eight successful women lean forward in their chairs, sensing they're witnessing something far more complex than a simple confrontation between old friends. The tropical air feels thick, oppressive, but I'm breathing it like oxygen.

The pity in her expression should worry me, but I'm too high on vindication to care. Let her pity me. In five minutes, she'll be facing fraud charges while I walk away with everything she's stolen.

Then Erin begins to clap.

Slow, deliberate applause that echoes through the perfect villa like gunshots. Her expression shifts from pity to something far more dangerous: admiration mixed with condescension, like a teacher proud of a student who's finally grasped a simple concept.

Around the circle, the women shift and murmur between themselves. Julia's expression has shifted from interest to concern. Sarah's instincts are clearly screaming that something's wrong with this picture. She looks from Erin to me and back again, as though we are playing psychological tennis. They blur into the background now. I don't care about them. I don't care what they hear. This is the showdown I have wanted for six years. This is about Erin and me and nothing else.

"Oh, Sam," Erin says, her voice warm with what sounds almost like genuine affection. "You clever, clever girl."

The tone makes my skin crawl. This isn't defeat. This is... something else entirely. It's not the expression of someone who's lost. That's someone who's about to return serve.

"How proud you must be," Erin continues, still clapping that maddening rhythm. "Standing there with your little camera, thinking you've finally outmanoeuvred me." Her smile is radiant, delighted. "How satisfying it must feel to believe you've won."

"I *have* won," I say, but even as the words leave my mouth, they sound hollow. Uncertain.

"Have you?" Erin tilts her head, studying me with that same analytical gaze she uses on difficult clients. "Tell me, Sam, what exactly do you think you've accomplished here?"

"I've exposed you," I reply, raising the camera. "I have proof of everything you've stolen."

"Proof." She lets the word hang in the air, savouring it. "Yes, you do have proof. Beautifully documented evidence of my... shall we call them confessions?" Her laugh is light, musical. "And what were you planning to do with this proof?"

"Destroy you." The words come out more forcefully than I intend, but I need to regain control of this conversation. "Show the world what you really are."

"And then what?" Erin's voice takes on that gentle, therapeutic tone. "Walk away from all this and return to your... what was it? That charming motel room? Your thriving career prospects? Your robust financial situation?"

Heat floods my cheeks.

"You admitted to using my ideas," I say, my voice gaining strength as I find my footing again. "I have it all documented. I can sue you for everything."

Erin shakes her head slowly, her expression almost pitying. "Oh, Sam. You've known about this for six years. You've known since I told you I was going to make the Authentic Self Framework into a reality, into a business - not just an idea you scribbled on a tear-stained tissue."

The casual cruelty of the dismissal makes several women shift uncomfortably.

"You sat there for six years," Erin continues, her voice taking on a lecture-like quality, "watching me build workshops, develop methodologies, create training programs, establish a client base, write books, build systems. And you did... what? Nothing."

My mouth opens, but no sound comes out.

"In legal terms, Sam, that's called acquiescence. Abandonment. Laches, if you want the technical term." Her smile is sharp, professional. "You watched someone build an empire for six years, did nothing to stop it, said nothing to claim it. You can't just decide you want it back now because you're feeling bitter."

Nicholas shifts by the window, his expression unreadable.

"But I created the concept," I whisper.

"Ideas aren't copyrightable, darling. Only specific expressions. And even if they were..." She shrugs elegantly. "Your delay in asserting any rights would bar any claim. No court in the world would give you ownership of a business you watched someone else build while you did absolutely nothing."

Erin stretches her arms above her head like a yoga pose, then shakes her hands out in front of her as if relieving tension.

"You think I care about money?" I snap. "This isn't about..."

"Oh, but it is, isn't it?" Erin interrupts, her voice gaining strength. "It's always been about what I have and what you don't. What I've built and what you've... well, what you haven't. And you nearly had it all," she sighs. "I had this beautiful plan. Make the women comfortable with you during the retreat. Let you discover your talent for leading sessions. Position you as my natural successor." Her eyes never leave my face. "Then I would gracefully step away from it all. Transfer the business, the recognition, the wealth. The life you've always believed you deserved."

Nicholas, who's been silent throughout all of this, makes a small sound, whether protest or recognition, I can't tell.

The room spins slightly.

"Why?" The word comes out as barely a whisper.

"Because I wanted *yours*." The admission is delivered with casual simplicity, as if she's discussing the weather. "Your simple, uncomplicated existence. Your freedom from constant performance. Your authentic life."

She pauses in her pacing, her expression becoming almost wistful. "Do you know what it's like to be 'on' every moment of every day? To have thousands of people watching your every move, waiting for you to slip up? Three million Instagram followers who expect you to be perfect in every image. To have built something so successful that it's become a prison? I can't eat pizza. I can't sit around in my sweatpants and not wash my hair for three days. I can't even wear the same outfit twice, for God's sake. My pancakes have to be perfectly round. My latte perfectly positioned next to my laptop. It's fucking hell, Sam."

I take a moment to process the reactions of the women that circle us. It's quite the revelation that Erin Blake, wellness guru extraordinaire, might as human as they are.

"I envied you, Sam. I envied your quiet marriage, your ordinary job, your peaceful little life. No pressure. No expectations. Just... authenticity." Her voice gains passion. "I thought if I could step into your world, I'd finally have what I've been searching for. Peace. Simplicity. The chance to just exist without constantly achieving."

"So you decided to steal my identity," I say, my voice rising. "Take my passport, trap me here while you escaped into my life."

"I was liberating us both," Erin corrects with that infuriating calm. "You would get the empire you always deserved, and I would get the simple life I've always wanted. A perfect exchange."

"Except you had to steal my passport to do it."

This wasn't a transaction, it was fraud.

Her expression doesn't change. "Procurement was surprisingly easy. Getting your wallet required minimal effort. The passport took slightly more coordination, but nothing that couldn't be arranged for the right price. Most moral objections tend to evaporate when the compensation is sufficient."

The casual admission of theft, delivered with such matter-of-fact ease, makes several women gasp audibly.

"But, as you can tell, the execution didn't proceed as smoothly as anticipated."

Something in her tone makes my stomach clench. "What do you mean?"

Erin's smile takes on a sharp edge. "I mean, Sam, that when I actually tried to live your life, I discovered just how spectacularly awful it is."

The words hit like a physical blow. Around the circle, the women go completely still.

"Your credit cards," Erin continues conversationally, "are not just maxed out, they're aggressively declined. I couldn't buy a coffee, let alone book accommodation or transportation. Your bank accounts contain... what was it? Two pounds and forty-three pence? I can't withdraw that from a cashpoint, Sam. They don't spit the pennies out like a slot machine."

Shame burns through me like acid. Every detail of my financial collapse laid bare in front of eight successful women who've never known true desperation.

"I spent three hours trying to use your identity to secure basic necessities," Erin says, her voice gaining momentum. "A hotel room, a meal, transportation off this island. Nothing. Your credit rating is so catastrophic that automated systems reject transactions before human review."

"Stop," I whisper, but she's just getting started.

"Do you know what it's like to realise that the life you've envied, the simple existence you've fantasised about escaping into, is actually a complete disaster?" Her voice rises with what sounds almost like genuine distress.

Nicholas moves closer to the circle, his face pale. "Erin..."

"I found myself trapped," she continues, ignoring him completely, "unable to move forward into your worthless life or backward into my own without raising suspicions. Stuck in this paradise with someone else's maxed-out credit cards and a passport that couldn't get me anywhere I wanted to go."

The admission hangs in the humid air like a toxic cloud. The successful women around the circle stare between us, watching this psychological excavation with expressions ranging from horror to fascination.

"So you came back," I manage, my voice barely audible.

"I had to reclaim my own life," Erin says with something approaching relief. "Return to the empire I'd built, the success I'd created, the world where my identity actually has value." Her smile returns, sharp and predatory. "Which meant dealing with you."

"By taking back the laptop."

"By managing the narrative," she corrects. "Making sure you understood your place in all this."

The truth crashes over me like a cold wave. "You never intended to give me anything permanently. This was always temporary."

"I intended to give you everything," Erin insists, her voice taking on that therapeutic warmth again. "But only if your life was worth stepping into. When I discovered it wasn't..." She shrugs elegantly. "Well, plans had to change."

"Why didn't you just offer me the business?"

"I offered a partnership. If you had accepted, I would have stepped down, away from the limelight. Let you lead."

"But you ARE the Authentic Self Framework." The words come out before I realise I'm saying them.

I'm struck by the revelation. Erin didn't just steal my idea—she became it. She built workshops, trained facilitators, created systems, helped thousands of people. She made something real from my scribbled thoughts.

The truth sits in my chest like a stone I don't want to swallow. All those nights in the motel room, fantasising about reclaiming my empire, imagining myself as the successful guru... but what would I have actually done with those napkin sketches? Filed them away with all my other brilliant ideas that never went anywhere? Left them rotting in a drawer next to my abandoned app concepts and half-finished business plans?

The realisation should terrify me, but instead it feels like... relief? I don't actually want her empire. I never did. I just wanted her to pay for being better at my own idea than I ever would have been. For having the follow-through I've never possessed. For turning my drunken philosophy into something that actually helps people.

No. I spent six years hating her for this. Six years building my rage, my righteousness, my sense of being wronged. If I don't want what she stole, then what was it all for? What does that make me?

Erin smiles as though she is waiting to receive her applause.

But I'm not done yet.

"Go ahead," I say. "You think that means you've won? I came here to destroy you. All these women have seen you for who you are. I hope your husband has too."

"You can't see it, can you? I'm not here because I was desperate. I'm here because I had nothing..."

"That's the same thing, Sam," Erin interrupts with that infuriating calm.

"No, I had nothing to lose."

Erin's smile falters slightly as she processes what I've just said. Having nothing to lose versus being desperate - she's smart enough to understand the distinction, and dangerous enough to recognise the threat.

"What do you mean?" she asks, and for the first time, there's uncertainty in her voice.

"I mean," I say, stepping closer, "that Instagram like that started all this? The one that brought us back together after six years?"

Her face goes white.

"It wasn't an accident."

Ace. Game point to me.

CHAPTER THIRTY-FOUR

I'm not done. Not even close. My hands shake as I grip the camera, but not with defeat. With rage. Pure, clean fury at being manipulated, used, discarded like a broken toy.

Erin Blake has made one crucial error.

She thinks she knows everything about how this started.

She has no idea.

Silence suffocates the room. Even the sound of waves from outside seems to fade.

"I am here because I had nothing left to lose. I am here because I wanted to be. Here's what you never realised - you weren't just wrong about my life being worth stealing." My voice drops to something almost conversational, intimate even. "You were wrong about how this all started."

I pause. I'm shaking with the emotion that is ripping through my body now.

"That moment that brought us back together after six years of silence?"

Erin freezes, grabbing the chair.

"That accidental Instagram like that made you reach out to your poor, desperate old friend?"

I watch understanding dawn in her eyes.

"Here's the thing about accidents," I continue, my smile growing wider with each word. "They're only accidents if they're unplanned."

Eight successful women stare at me with expressions ranging from shock to fascination.

Nicholas stands frozen by the window, his face cycling through confusion and dawning horror. And Erin... Erin looks like she's watching her entire world crumble in real time.

"I didn't accidentally click on your stupid Instagram post," I say, each word precise and deliberate. "I did it on purpose."

"I wanted back in your life, Erin. I had nothing, and you... you had everything I should have had."

Erin stares at me as if I've grown a second head. "You... planned this?"

"Every. Single. Step." I'm pacing now, energy building with each revelation. "The desperate woman in the motel room? The grateful friend accepting charity? The broken photographer just happy to help? All of it. Performance."

My voice is rising now, years of suppressed rage finally breaking free.

"Because I knew exactly what you'd do when you saw that like notification. I knew you so well, Erin. You'd see your old friend's desperate engagement with your perfect life and your saviour complex would kick in immediately."

My voice gains momentum, years of planning finally spilling out. "You'd want to swoop in, throw out the rescue rope, play the magnanimous success story helping her poor, broken friend. I knew you'd invite me to stay. I was counting on it."

I gesture around the villa. "Aruba was unexpected. I'll give you that. But it was perfect, wasn't it? Bringing me into your inner sanctum, your business, making me complicit in your fraud. It gave me everything I needed to tear you apart from the inside."

I have to stop to take a breath. I'm so fired up, I can feel the burn sear through me.

"Did you really think I'd just... forget? Move on? Accept that my life's work belonged to you?"

"Sam..." Nicholas starts from the corner, but I whirl on him.

"And you!" I whirl on Nicholas. "Her loyal husband, so dependent on the business you can't even afford your own lifestyle without my stolen framework! Well, she wasn't just leaving, was she? She was leaving you behind, too."

The colour drains from Nicholas's face so completely he looks like he might faint. He grips the back of a chair, knuckles white.

"Nicholas," Erin starts, but he cuts her off.

"I gave up everything for this business. My career, my independence, my..." His voice cracks. "And you were planning to abandon me?"

The silence that follows is deafening. Nicholas stands there, trembling with what might be rage or despair, looking between Erin and me like a trapped animal.

"Where would I go?" he says finally, his voice hollow. "What would I do? I don't even have my own bank account anymore."

The admission hangs in the air like a confession of complete defeat.

But I don't care.

He can have his moment with her later. This is mine.

I turn back to Erin, who's staring at me with something approaching horror.

"You thought you were so clever, didn't you? Give me just enough evidence to feel vindicated, hand over the wheel, then disappear into my simple little life while I picked up the pieces of your empire." I advance another step. "But you made one crucial miscalculation."

The room hangs on my every word. I'm breathless with the reveal.

"You discovered my life wasn't worth stealing. When you tried to use my identity and couldn't even buy a coffee because my cards are maxed out, my accounts empty." My voice gains strength.

"And all that nonsense about us looking alike?" I let out a harsh laugh. "Nobody ever said that. Nobody in their right mind would think we look alike. You've been planting that idea in everyone's heads so they'd accept me as an adequate replacement. Dressing me up as your dolly, trying to mould me into Erin-lite."

I can see the women processing this, remembering the comments about our supposed resemblance. Comments that some of them actually made themselves.

"But really, Erin, did you really think you could use my passport?" I ask. "Step into my broke, broken life and somehow make it work for you?"

Erin's mouth opens and closes like a fish gasping for air.

"I couldn't make it work and I've had time to acclimatise to it. You know, like when you buy a new fish from the shop?" My voice takes on an almost conversational tone, as if I'm explaining something perfectly reasonable. "You can't just dump it straight into the tank. The shock would kill it. You have to let it adjust slowly, get used to the new water conditions."

I gesture around the perfect villa, at all of Erin's stolen success. "I've been swimming in poverty for months, Erin. My life is toxic - maxed-out credit cards, no job prospects, an ex-husband who won't even return my calls. It's like living in polluted water."

My smile turns savage. "But you? You've been living in pristine conditions your whole career. Crystal-clear success, filtered through my stolen work. When you tried to jump into my life..." I let out a bitter laugh. "The shock nearly killed you, didn't it?"

She looks at me intently, as if processing everything I've revealed. Then something shifts in her expression. Not shock. Not defeat. Recognition.

And then, to my complete surprise, a smile begins to spread across her face.

It starts small, almost wondering, then grows into something radiant.

"Oh, Sam," she says, shaking her head with what looks almost like admiration.

The smile becomes a chuckle, then full laughter that echoes through the villa. The sound is genuinely delighted, as if I've just told her the most amusing joke she's ever heard.

"Did you really think you were the only one playing a long game?"

My stomach drops. She's not just returning my serve - she's smashing it at me with interest.

"I knew you'd be back. I knew your pride wouldn't let you stay away forever." Her smile is radiant, triumphant. "I've been waiting for you to make your move."

What's happening? I thought I'd won the point, but now...?

"The *desperate woman in the motel room* was no act, and we both know it."

The words hit like a physical blow, deflating some of my righteous anger.

"So you planned the Instagram like," Erin says, dismissing my big reveal as though it were nothing. "But everything else? Your desperation? Your gratitude? Your pathetic relief when I offered you a way out? All real."

She pauses, her voice dropping to something almost pitying.

"If you'd had a life worth living, I'd be somewhere far from here right now, living it. Instead, your broken, bankrupt identity was impossible to salvage. It didn't go as I planned, exactly, but, darling Sam," Erin says, her voice full of affectionate condescension, "if you think you were the one that started this, you're about to learn something that's going to blow your pretty little mind."

CHAPTER THIRTY-THREE

The laughter dies in Erin's throat, but her smile remains. She studies me with something that might be admiration.

"Oh, Sam, she says again, shaking her head. You really thought you had me, didn't you? That you'd finally outsmarted me after all these years?"

Erin begins pacing, energy building, completely forgetting the eight women watching this psychological warfare unfold.

"Here's what you still don't understand, darling. Your destitution wasn't an act because I created it. I just... pushed it too far." Her voice takes on the quality of someone sharing a cherished memory.

And there's her backhand down the line. Perfect placement. I can't even reach it. The words don't register at first. They're too impossible, too monstrous.

"Your marriage, for instance." She waves a hand dismissively. "Daniel was going to leave you anyway, Sam. He just needed a little... encouragement."

"I met him on a dating app. Bumble, I think? He wasn't hard to seduce." She pauses, tilting her head as if considering. "Of course I didn't want him - your type has never been my type - but I wanted him to leave you."

The room spins. I can't speak, can't breathe, can't process what she's saying.

"And your apartment," she continues conversationally, "I'm so sorry about that mortgage extension being denied. Funny how banks get nervous when they receive anonymous tips about borrowers' financial instability."

"Your job was trickier," she muses, completely absorbed in her own cleverness. "HR departments are usually more lenient about mental health absences. But a sizable donation to their wellness program, along with some concerns about an employee's erratic behaviour..." She shrugs elegantly. "Well, you know how that ended."

I try to speak, but no sound comes out. Around the circle, the women sit frozen in horror, watching this confession unfold.

"Why?" Nicholas's voice cuts through the silence, raw and disbelieving. "Erin, why would you do this?"

Erin turns to him with genuine surprise, as if the answer should be obvious.

But she doesn't answer him. She spins her attention back to me.

"I was saving you from mediocrity, Sam." She addresses me directly, her voice warm with what she clearly believes is love. "I watched you for six years, settling for that boring marriage, that dead-end job, that small life. You were brilliant, Sam. You created the framework!" She waves her arms in genuine frustration. "But there you were wasting your potential on a life that was far too small for someone like you."

"Daniel never believed in you. I could see it in how he talked about your ideas, how he dismissed your dreams. You needed to be free of him to become who

276

you really were. And that job? They were never going to promote you. I could see they didn't value you."

Her voice gains passion, conviction. "I had to strip away everything that was holding you back. The comfortable mediocrity that was killing your genius. You needed to hit rock bottom to find your strength. You needed to want success badly enough to fight for it."

She gestures around the villa, at the retreat, at me standing there in shock.

"And look! It worked! Look how brilliantly you've been leading the retreat. Look how powerful you are when you're not settling. I gave you the gift of desperation because I knew you were capable of greatness."

"No." Nicholas's voice is barely a whisper. "No, why... why would you do that? What's wrong with your life? You have everything. Success, money, recognition..."

He still doesn't understand. Even now, he can't see past the surface.

Erin's expression shifts, becoming almost vulnerable. "*I was successful but miserable*, Nicholas. *Classic burnt-out executive*. Constantly performing, always 'on,' never allowed to just... be."

The words echo something familiar, and I see recognition dawn on Nicholas's face. The same description he'd given me about himself when Erin found him. He must have repeated the story of how they met so many times that she knows it word for word. And now she is weaponising it.

"I couldn't tell you I was feeling these things," Erin continues, turning the spotlight on him, "because I didn't want you to think I was weak. Like you were when we met."

Nicholas flinches as if she'd slapped him.

"The Authentic Self Framework made me see that this isn't what I want," Erin continues, her voice gaining strength. "I don't want to be switched on twenty-four hours a day. I don't want to perform authenticity - I want to live it."

She turns back to me, eyes bright with what she clearly sees as revelation.

"I thought I would give it all back to you. But I knew you wouldn't just accept it if I offered. There's too much bitterness, too much resentment. You'd have thrown it back in my face out of pride."

Her voice drops to something almost tender.

"So I had to create the circumstances where you'd have no choice but to reach for it yourself. Where you'd be desperate enough to fight for what was always yours."

She pauses, her expression becoming almost wistful.

"Do you want to know the truth, Sam? For years, I wished I were you."

The admission catches me completely off guard.

"I watched you from afar - the simple marriage, the quiet job, the uncomplicated life. No pressure, no performance, no constant scrutiny. Just... authenticity. I envied that so much."

Her voice grows quieter. "I thought if I could just... step into your life, I'd finally have what I'd been searching for. Peace. Simplicity. A chance to just exist without constantly achieving."

She lets out a bitter laugh. "But when I actually tried to use your identity... your cards, your accounts... I realised how truly desperate your situation was. I couldn't even buy a coffee, let alone get off this island. That's when I knew I'd gone too far."

Something crystallises in my mind as she speaks, a realisation so clear it cuts through my shock.

"You wished you were me," I say slowly, my voice gaining strength. "And I... I wished I were you."

Erin nods, as if this proves her point. "See? We each had what the other wanted. I just... facilitated the exchange."

"No." The word comes out harder than I intend. "You're wrong. I didn't want your life because it was simple. I wanted it because you built an empire on my idea while I did nothing."

I look around, at everything she's created.

"You know what the real difference between us is, Erin? It's not talent. It's not brilliance. It's that you were prepared to do the work, and I just wanted the reward."

Her confident expression falters slightly.

"I had the idea, but you executed it. You built the business, developed the methodology, took the risks. While I..." I pause, the truth bitter in my mouth. "While I sat in pubs complaining about how unfair life was."

"That doesn't excuse what you did," I continue, my voice steady now. "Stealing my work, destroying my life. But I understand now why you succeeded, and I

279

didn't. You were willing to do whatever it took. Even if it meant becoming a monster."

Erin's face cycles through confusion, hurt, and something that might be recognition.

"I wanted your success without earning it," I say quietly. "And you wanted my simple life without understanding how empty it really was."

The silence that follows is deafening. Around the circle, eight women sit transfixed by this psychological dissection, this mutual revelation of two lives built on false assumptions about the other.

"*You have to wish you were her,*" I murmur, almost to myself. That old line from my framework. "We both got exactly what we asked for. And we both learned to be careful what we wish for."

The silence stretches between us, heavy with the weight of everything we've both admitted. Everything we've both destroyed. Everything we've both learned about ourselves in the space of a single, devastating conversation.

Then, as if waking from a dream, I become aware of the room around us again. Game suspended. We've been so focused on destroying each other, we forgot we have an audience.

Eight successful women sit frozen in their circle, faces cycling through shock, horror, and something that might be fascination. They came here for personal transformation and instead witnessed the complete psychological dissection of two women who've been systematically destroying each other for years. Nicholas stands pressed against the wall like he's trying to disappear into it entirely, his face pale with the realisation that his entire life has been built on lies within lies within lies.

We've just confessed to fraud, identity theft, systematic life destruction, and mutual obsession in front of eight witnesses who paid twenty thousand pounds each to learn about authentic living. The irony would be funny if it weren't so absolutely, utterly devastating.

CHAPTER THIRTY-FOUR

Eight faces stare at us with expressions ranging from horror to fascination to something that might be professional interest in watching a complete psychological breakdown unfold in real time.

And then Maya stands up.

"Well," she says, her voice cutting through the stillness with surprising calm, "I think that about covers everything."

She's holding her phone, and something about the way she's holding it - deliberately, purposefully - makes my stomach drop.

"Maya?" Sarah asks uncertainly. "What are you doing?"

Maya turns the phone around so we can see the screen. A live video feed showing our circle, showing Erin and me standing in the centre like gladiators who've just finished destroying each other.

"Recording," she says simply. "Actually, live-streaming. To about fifteen thousand viewers and counting."

Erin's face flickers as though she is trying to hide her emotions and failing.

"The beauty of social media," Maya continues conversationally, "is how quickly things can go viral. Especially when they involve famous wellness gurus confessing to fraud, identity theft, and systematic life destruction."

"You've been filming this whole time?" Erin's voice is barely a whisper.

"Since you sat back down in that chair thinking you were so clever," Maya replies. "Since you started manipulating these women all over again."

She looks around the circle of stunned faces. "Ladies, meet the real Erin Blake. Not the polished guru you paid twenty thousand pounds to learn from, but the woman who just confessed to destroying someone's life for sport."

"Maya," I start, not sure if I'm going to thank her or beg her to stop, but she cuts me off.

"Oh, I'm not done yet." Her smile is sharp as glass. "Because you see, Erin, you didn't just steal from Sam. You stole from me, too."

The confession hangs in the air. Around the circle, the women lean forward, sensing another layer to this psychological excavation.

"Maya *Lawson*," Erin says slowly, recognition finally dawning. "It was *your* company? Three years ago."

"Very good," Maya says with mock approval. "Though you deleted any mention of me from *your* website, didn't you? It was my process. My methodology for helping trauma survivors reclaim their sense of self."

"I came to you as a potential partner," Maya continues, her voice gaining strength. "Shared my research, my techniques, my client case studies. Everything I'd developed working with abuse survivors."

She turns to address the livestream directly. "Within six months, Erin had incorporated my trauma recovery techniques into her 'revolutionary' framework. No credit, no compensation, no acknowledgment. Just theft."

"That's not..." Erin starts, but Maya cuts her off with a laugh.

"Oh, but it is. And now fifteen thousand people know it. Along with everything else you've just confessed to."

She looks at her phone screen. "Sixteen thousand. Almost seventeen thousand. Yes, there it is."

The authentic confession of Erin Blake spreading across the internet in real time. Maya just scored match point in a game Erin didn't even know she was part of.

"You destroyed my research credibility," Maya says, her voice steady but filled with years of suppressed rage. "Made it impossible for me to publish my work because you'd already popularised corrupted versions of my techniques. So I did what any good analyst does. I gathered evidence."

Nicholas, who's been silent through this entire revelation, finally speaks.

"How many people have you stolen from?" His voice isn't angry, just... tired. Resigned.

Erin turns to him. "Nicholas, I..."

"No," he says quietly. "I get it. I understand."

The unexpected gentleness in his voice catches everyone off guard.

"I know what it's like to be desperate," he continues, his eyes meeting Erin's across the wreckage of their life together. "To see something you want so badly, you convince yourself you deserve it.

284

To be so afraid of losing everything that you destroy it instead."

He looks around the villa, at the luxury that's about to disappear. "I've been living in terror ever since I found out about Sam, knowing this was all built on someone else's work. Knowing that someday it would all come crashing down."

His voice drops to something almost gentle. "I just didn't realise you were as trapped as I was."

The livestream viewer count hits twenty thousand. Comments are flooding in faster than the screen can display them. The Authentic Self Framework empire is crumbling in real time, broadcast to the world.

"Twenty-three thousand viewers," Maya announces cheerfully. "This is going to be everywhere by tomorrow. News outlets, social media, business journals. The complete destruction of Erin Blake's wellness empire, captured live."

She looks directly at Erin. "Congratulations. You're about to experience the most authentic transformation of your life. From millionaire guru to unemployed fraud."

Erin sinks into a chair, the weight of complete ruin settling over her like a shroud. Everything she's built, everything she's stolen, everything she's destroyed others to create - gone. Broadcast to the world in her own words.

"The irony," Maya says, addressing her phone camera, "is that this might be the first time Erin Blake has ever been completely authentic. And it's destroying everything she claimed to stand for."

She ends the livestream with a satisfied tap.

"Well," she says to the room, "I think that's a wrap."

The silence that follows Maya's announcement feels different from all the others. This isn't the charged quiet of confrontation or the stunned pause of revelation. This is the hollow emptiness that comes after complete destruction.

Twenty-three thousand people have just watched the Authentic Self Framework empire collapse in real time. By tomorrow, it'll be millions.

"Well," Julia says finally, her voice carefully controlled, "this has been... educational."

She stands, smoothing her linen dress with the composure of someone used to managing crises. "I think we can all agree that this retreat is officially over."

The other women rise, moving with the efficient purposefulness of executives abandoning a sinking ship. No one looks directly at Erin, who sits slumped in her chair like a broken doll.

"The cars will be here in an hour," Sarah announces, already on her phone. "I've arranged transport back to the airport for anyone who wants to leave immediately."

"What about refunds?" Petra asks, though her tone suggests she's more curious than concerned.

Sarah glances at Erin's devastated figure. "I think we can write this off as an expensive lesson in due diligence."

One by one, they file out of the room, leaving whispered conversations and the rustle of hastily packed luggage in their wake. Within twenty minutes, the villa that had been filled with transformation and possibility is eerily quiet.

Maya is the last to leave, pausing in the doorway with her phone still in hand.

"For what it's worth," she says, addressing the three of us left behind, "I didn't plan for it to end quite like this."

"Yes, you did," I say quietly. "And we both know it."

She considers this, then nods. "You're right. I did." She looks at Erin, who hasn't moved from her chair. "But I thought I'd feel better about it."

After she's gone, the three of us sit in the wreckage of everything we've built and destroyed. The villa feels enormous and empty, like a stage set after the audience has gone home.

"The business accounts will be frozen by morning," Nicholas says eventually, his voice matter-of-fact. "Legal investigations, media scrutiny, civil lawsuits. It'll take years to untangle."

Erin finally looks up. "I'm sorry," she says, and for the first time, it sounds genuine. "I'm sorry I dragged you into this. Both of you."

"We dragged ourselves in," I reply. "All of us."

Nicholas stands, moving to the window that overlooks the perfect Caribbean paradise we can no longer afford. "The ironic thing is, I feel... relieved. For the first time in years, I know exactly where I stand. Which is nowhere, but at least it's honest."

CHAPTER THIRTY-FIVE

One day later, we're on a plane back to London. Business class seats that were booked when Erin still had a business, when the Authentic Self Framework was still worth millions instead of being the punchline of every wellness industry scandal.

These seats cost more than most people's monthly salary, and we're sitting in them as three of the most unemployable people in the wellness industry. By the time we land, Erin and Nicholas will face frozen credit cards, investigations, the complete destruction of everything they've built. Their multimillion-pound lifestyle, their country estate, their financial security... all gone.

For me, it's different. I'm returning to roughly the same situation I left: broke, jobless, nowhere to go. But somehow, that doesn't feel as devastating as it should.

Maybe it's because I've already survived rock bottom once.

Maybe it's because Daniel was going to leave me anyway. Erin just accelerated the inevitable. He never believed in me, never supported my ideas, never saw me as anything more than the woman who 'never follows through.'

And if my job could get rid of me so easily after years of service, maybe I was already disposable there too.

The apartment? Well, that one still stings. Having an actual home would have been better than motel life.

But even that mortgage was built on borrowed time and borrowed money.

What Maya did... broadcasting our mutual destruction to twenty-three thousand viewers... should horrify me. Instead, I feel something closer to gratitude. She exposed the truth. All of it. The framework theft, Erin's systematic destruction of my life, my own calculated revenge. No more lies. No more performances. Just the raw, ugly reality of what we'd all become.

I had nothing left to lose, and now neither do they.

The flight attendant offers us champagne with the kind of smile that suggests she hasn't yet seen the viral videos of our public implosion. We all decline. It's almost like there's nothing to celebrate.

I'm sitting between them, which feels fitting somehow. The woman who stole my life on one side, her husband who enabled it on the other, and me in the middle, the architect of the idea that destroyed us all. Erin stares out the window, watching the Caribbean islands disappear beneath puffy white clouds. The paradise that was supposed to be her perfect backdrop has become the scene of her complete undoing.

Nicholas has been reading the same page of *Business Week* for the past hour, though I suspect he's not absorbing a single word. The magazine's cover story is about *'Authentic Leadership in the Digital Age.'* It seems like a cruel cosmic joke, considering our circumstances.

None of us have spoken since take-off. What is there to say? We've already confessed everything, destroyed everything, laid ourselves bare in front of the world. The silence feels heavy with unfinished business, but really, what else is there?

At least Erin processed the five thousand pounds she promised for the week yesterday. I got the notification while we were still packing to leave Aruba - a bank transfer that felt both pathetic and crucial. It's not nearly enough compensation for what she stole, but it might be enough to keep me out of another motel room while I figure out my next plan.

I never got the extra payment for running the sessions, though.

I almost laugh at the thought. After everything that's happened, I'm still worried about money. Some things never change.

The foldout table in front of me holds the remnants of a fancy airline meal of seared duck with micro herbs that tasted like expensive cardboard. The cloth napkin beside it is crisp white linen, the kind of detail that once would have impressed me. Now it just feels like evidence of how far we've all fallen.

Without really thinking about it, I pull a pen from my bag and start sketching on the napkin's edge. Old habits die hard, apparently. Even broke and disgraced, I'm still the woman who thinks with her hands, who processes ideas through doodles and diagrams.

Just idle doodling at first: circles and arrows, the kind of abstract shapes that help my mind wander. Then something more deliberate begins to emerge. A framework. Not the *Authentic Self* process this time, but something new. Something born from the wreckage of everything we've experienced.

It starts with three overlapping circles. Loss. Reckoning. Rebuilding. About what happens when you discover that everything you thought you knew about yourself was wrong. About finding who you really are when everything you thought you were gets stripped away and broadcast to millions of strangers.

This isn't about removing barriers to find your authentic self. This is about building something entirely new from nothing. About the strange freedom that comes with having no reputation left to protect, no image left to maintain.

I sketch quickly, ideas flowing faster than I can capture them. Exercises for people who've lost everything. Frameworks for rebuilding when you can't go back to who you were before. Concepts for transformation that doesn't require you to believe you were somehow always meant for greatness.

This is for people like me. People who fucked up spectacularly. People who made terrible choices and have to live with the consequences. People who might not deserve redemption but need to figure out how to keep existing anyway.

'After the Fall,' I write beneath the diagram. *'A Framework for Rebuilding from Nothing.'*

My framework. My concepts. My work.

And this time, I'm not sharing it with anyone.

The ideas keep coming: modules about accepting consequences, exercises for building something meaningful from rubble, techniques for moving forward without forgiveness or closure.

I feel Erin shift beside me, catch her glancing toward my work. Immediately, I fold the napkin and slide it into my bag, protecting it from view. The movement is sharp enough that she notices, and she looks away quickly.

Good. Let her wonder. Let her curiosity eat at her.

I want her to see.

I want her to know that I still have ideas. I'm still a dreamer.

But this is different.

It's darker than the *Authentic Self Framework*. More honest about the messiness of real transformation. Less concerned with helping people feel good about themselves and more focused on helping them survive when everything falls apart.

This time I'm going to follow it through.

My track record speaks for itself: brilliant ideas, enthusiastic starts, inevitable abandonment when the real work begins. Daniel was right about that much.

But maybe that's exactly why this will be different. I'm not starting from a place of hope or ambition or naive belief in my own potential. I'm starting from nothing, with nothing to lose, nowhere to fall.

Hitting absolute bottom is exactly what I needed to finally build something that lasts.

This time, I won't stuff these notes in a drawer somewhere and go back to applications for jobs I'll never get, references I can't give. I don't want a future that looks exactly like my past.

The plane hums steadily through the darkening sky, carrying us all back to whatever comes next. Beside me, Erin and Nicholas sit with their own ruins, their own uncertain futures. By tomorrow, their perfect life will be as gone as if it never existed.

Like the last six years never happened.

I should feel satisfied by their downfall. Instead, I just feel empty.

But I am ready to start over.

For the first time in years, putting in the work doesn't terrify me.

It feels like possibility.

I pull out my phone as the plane begins its descent into Heathrow. The screen lights up with dozens of notifications - mostly messages, and social media alerts about the viral video. But there's only one person I need to contact right now.

Maya, I type. *Thank you for all your help with the research. I couldn't have developed* After the Fall *without your collaboration. Time to launch?*

Her response comes back immediately: *You brilliant, beautiful mastermind. Yes. Time to show the world what authentic recovery looks like.*

I smile, tucking the phone away as London spreads out below us through the aircraft windows. The truth is, I've been planning *After the Fall* for over a year, ever since I first lost my job. When Daniel left, when the mortgage fell through, when I ended up in that godforsaken motel - I could have seen it all as failure. Instead, I saw it as research.

You can't teach people how to rebuild from nothing unless you've actually lived in nothing. You can't guide others through authentic rock bottom unless you've genuinely hit it yourself. My years in

293

marketing taught me that authenticity is everything. People can smell fake transformation from miles away.

But someone who's genuinely been through hell, documented every moment of the climb back up, and turned their suffering into a systematic framework for helping others? That's someone people will believe in. That's someone people will follow.

The whole world just watched me at my most broken and most powerful. They saw the real consequences of betrayal, manipulation, and systematic destruction. They also saw me survive it, analyse it, and prepare to transform it into something meaningful. The viral video is proof of concept: your worst moments can become your greatest qualifications.

Now they'll believe in me when I tell them they can do the same.

And for the first time in years, I believe it too.

I look over at Erin, slumped in her seat like a broken doll. I used to wish I were her. Now I wouldn't wish her life on anyone.

But I'm not building an empire; I'm building something real.